Claire Douglas has worked as a journalist for fifteen years, writing features for women's magazines and national newspapers, but she has dreamed of being a novelist since the age of seven. She finally got her wish after winning the Marie Claire Debut Novel Award with her first novel, *The Sisters*, which was one of the bestselling debut novels of 2015. She lives in Bath with her husband and two children.

Local Girl Missing

CLAIRE DOUGLAS

PENGUIN BOOKS

PENGUIN BOOKS

UK | USA | Canada | Ireland | Australia
India | New Zealand | South Africa

Penguin Books is part of the Penguin Random House group of companies
whose addresses can be found at global.penguinrandomhouse.com.

First published 2016
001

Set in 12.5/14.75 pt Garamond MT Std
Typeset by Jouve (UK), Milton Keynes
Printed in Great Britain by Clays Ltd, St Ives plc

A CIP catalogue record for this book is available from the British Library

ISBN: 978–1–405–92639–3

www.greenpenguin.co.uk

Penguin Random House is committed to a sustainable future for our business, our readers and our planet. This book is made from Forest Stewardship Council® certified paper.

To my husband, Ty

Thursday

I

Frankie

February 2016

It's a dreary afternoon, just after lunch, when I finally find out that you're dead.

My mobile vibrates with an unrecognised number and I pick it up, distracted by the mountain of paperwork I'm immersed in.

'Is this Francesca Howe?' A male voice burns a hole in my memory. His warm, country timbre doesn't belong in my office on the top floor of my parents' hotel, with its minimalist furniture and views of the Gherkin. It belongs in the past; to our hometown in Somerset where seagulls squawk at dawn, waves crash against the pier and the smell of fish and chips permeates the air.

'Daniel?' It comes out as a croak and I grip the edge of the desk with my free hand as if to anchor myself to this room, to the present, so that I don't go spinning head first into the past.

There can only be one reason why he's calling me now, after all these years.

It means there is news. About you.

'Long time,' he says, awkwardly.

How did he get my number? My legs are as weak as a new foal's as I stand up and stagger over to the rain-splattered window that overlooks the city. I can feel the air filling up my lungs, hear my ragged breathing.

'Is this about Sophie?'

'Yes. She's been found.'

My mouth fills with saliva. 'Is she . . . is she alive?'

A beat of silence. 'No. They've found something . . .'

His voice cracks and I try to picture what he looks like now, your big brother. Back then he was tall and skinny, permanently dressed in black with matching hair and a long pale face. Unhealthy looking, like a vampire in a teen film. I can tell he's struggling to retain his composure. I don't think I've ever seen him cry; not when you first went missing, not even when the police decided to give up the search after days of trawling the undergrowth and sending boats out to sea, or when the public lost interest after one of your navy blue Adidas trainers was found at the edge of the deserted pier and it was assumed you had fallen into the Bristol Channel and been swept away by the tide. When everyone apart from us began to forget all about you, Sophie Rose Collier, the sometimes shy, often funny, twenty-one-year-old girl from Oldcliffe-on-Sea who disappeared from a club late one night. The girl who cried at the old BT adverts on the TV, who fancied Jarvis Cocker, who couldn't open a packet of biscuits without scoffing them all.

Daniel clears his throat. 'Some remains have been found, washed up in Brean. Some of it . . .' He pauses. 'Well, it fits. It's her, Frankie, I know it.' It feels strange to hear him call me Frankie. You always called me Frankie too. I haven't been 'Frankie' for years.

I try not to imagine what part of you they've discovered amongst the debris on the shores of Brean Sands. I hate to think of you that way.

You are dead. It's a fact. You are no longer just missing, I can't delude myself into believing that you've lost your memory and are living it up somewhere, maybe Australia, or more likely Thailand. We always wanted to travel. Do you remember our plans to go backpacking around South-east Asia? You hated the cold winter months. We would spend hours dreaming about escaping the biting winds that whistled through the town, shaking the bare branches of the trees and throwing sand in our paths so that we could feel the grit of it between our teeth. Oldcliffe out of season was grey and depressing without the tourists to add the much-needed hustle and bustle.

I finger the collar of my shirt away from my throat. I can't breathe. Through my partially open door I can see Nell tapping away at her computer, her red hair piled on top of her head in an intricate bun.

I move back to my desk, slumping onto the swivel chair, the phone hot against my ear. 'I'm so sorry,' I say, almost to myself.

'It's OK, Frankie.' I can hear the whistle of wind in the background, the whoosh of tyres parting puddles, the indecipherable chatter of passers-by. 'It's not like we didn't expect it. Prepared ourselves for it.' What city or town is he calling me from? Where did your big brother end up? 'Her remains need to be formally identified. Things are difficult because of how long' – he takes a deep breath – 'because of how long she's been in the water. But they are hoping by the middle of next week.'

'Do the police . . .' I swallow down bile. 'Can they tell how she died?'

'Frankie, it's impossible to tell by now, and because there was no body there's never been an inquest. Everyone just assumed that she was drunk, that she fell into the sea, that she shouldn't have been on that pier. You know the score.' A note of anger creeps into his voice. 'But I don't believe it. I think someone knows more about that night, Frankie. I think someone knows what happened to my sister.'

My fingers itch to pull at my hair. Instead I move a paperweight around my desk, straighten a framed photograph of me astride a pony with my father standing proudly beside me, a territorial smile on his face. I was always Francesca to him. 'What makes you say that?'

'The night she disappeared, she was afraid. She said somebody was out to get her.'

Blood rushes to my ears. I grip the phone tighter. 'What? You never mentioned that before.'

'I told the police at the time but they dismissed it. She was jittery, paranoid. I assumed she'd taken a dodgy tab – you know how many drugs were flying about the place at the time. But Sophie would never have taken drugs. I know that. I've always known it deep down. She was a good girl. The best.' His voice catches.

He doesn't know about the time we both took speed at Ashton Court Festival, does he, Soph? You made me promise not to tell him as we sat there watching Dodgy, talking nineteen to the dozen and getting more and more paranoid with every passing minute.

I close my eyes, remembering that last night. You were standing in the corner of The Basement watching everyone jumping up and down to 'Born Slippy'. The date is etched in my memory: Saturday, 6 September 1997. I was on the other side of the dance floor chatting to the DJ but when I looked back through the fug of smoke that constantly hung in the air, you had disappeared, vanished in the throng. You hadn't looked scared, or particularly worried. If there had been a problem you would have confided in me. Wouldn't you?

I was your best friend. We told each other everything.

'Will you help me, Frankie?' Daniel says, his voice suddenly urgent. 'I need to find out what happened to her. Someone knows more than they're letting on. The pier –'

'The pier was rotten, dangerous, closed to the public . . .'

'I know. But that didn't stop us all going there, did it? I just can't believe she went by herself. There must have been someone with her that night . . .'

I can hear the desperation in his voice and my heart goes out to him. It's been difficult for me over the years not to constantly relive that night. But for your brother, it must have been unbearable at times. All those unanswered questions swirling around in his mind, keeping him awake at night, preventing him from moving on with his life.

'People don't want to talk to me about it. But you, Franks . . . you could get them talking.'

Of course he's going to do this for you. Always the protective big brother. I'd expect nothing less.

'I don't know. I've never been back, not since we moved to London . . .' The thought fills me with dread. Throughout my adolescent years I longed to escape the claustrophobic seaside town we grew up in, where, more often than not, three generations of the same family lived and you were thought of as odd if you had aspirations to leave.

The town where a dark secret of the past is never forgotten.

Or forgiven.

'Please, Frankie. For old times' sake. She was your best friend. You knew all the same people, ran with the same crowd. Don't you want to know what happened to her?'

'Of course I do,' I say. Could I really return after eighteen years? I'd vowed never to set foot in that town again. But what choice did I have? I suppress a resigned sigh. 'When do you want me to come back?'

I shoulder on my red wool coat and inform Nell in my most crisp, convincing voice that I'm not feeling well and need to go home. She stares at me in wide-eyed shock because I'm never ill. But I ignore her looks of concern and head out of the office, scurrying through the rain as fast as I can in my too-high heels and tight pencil skirt, to hail a cab. My head is still reeling as I sink into the back seat, the leather cold against my calves as we head to Islington.

The finality of your death suddenly hits me.

It's over.

And then I recall the phone conversation with Daniel and his calm insistence that I return to Oldcliffe to help him excavate the past and I suppress a shudder.

It's never going to be over.

I remember when I first saw you, Soph. It was September 1983 and we were seven. It was your first day at our primary school and you stood in front of the class with our teacher, Mrs Draper, and you looked so forlorn, so lost, with your lank hair and blue National Health glasses. Your not-quite-white socks fell down your skinny legs so that they pooled around your ankles. You had a grubby-looking plaster covering one of your knobbly knees and the hem of your green school skirt was coming down. When Mrs Draper asked for someone to volunteer to be your buddy, my hand shot straight up. You looked like you needed a friend.

The house seems unusually cavernous and tidy as I let myself in, as if I'm seeing it through new eyes, through your eyes. What would you think now? Would you look at my three-storey townhouse and say I've done well for myself? Or would you tease me in that way you always used to, with that sardonic smile on your face that was so like Daniel's, and tell me I'm still a daddy's girl?

I pause in front of the hallway mirror and a professional thirty-nine-year-old woman stares back at me. My hair is still dark and glossy with no hint of grey, thanks to my hairdresser, and I have a few fine lines around my green eyes. Would you think I look old? You probably would. Ageing is something you'll never have to worry about. You'll always be fixed in time as young and fresh-faced. Forever twenty-one.

I turn away from my reflection. I need to start packing. I run upstairs to my bedroom. Daniel has already organised a place for me to stay. A friend of his owns a holiday apartment and, as it's February and out of season, I can have it at a discounted rate. I'll drive down in the morning.

I need to be doing something constructive. I pull my Louis Vuitton holdall from the top of the wardrobe and leave it open on the bed. Questions speed through my mind like galloping racehorses. How many days should I pack for? How long is this going to take? Then a new thought hits me: how am I going to explain all this to Mike?

I'm in the basement kitchen frantically peeling and chopping when I hear Mike call out a hello. He fitted this kitchen for me last year as a favour, before we got together, although I knew him before that, when he helped renovate the new hotel. Solid and strapping, with sandy hair and a strong jaw, I'd been instantly attracted to him, despite us having nothing in common. Now the white glossiness of the units and the thick Corian worktops remind me of us: they all look so clean and new on the outside, but on the inside the hinges are loose and there is a crack in one of the cabinets.

The radio is turned up loud and I allow Rachmaninov to wash over me, to soothe my frayed nerves. A large glass of Merlot is also helping. I've already put two washes on, packed for tomorrow and made a start on the stew for dinner. Mike looks puzzled, not only to find me home – I'm usually in the office until late – but to find me cooking.

'Are you OK, Fran?'

Fran. Much more grown up than 'Frankie' or 'Franks'. It conjures up someone sophisticated, someone mature, someone far removed from the Frankie of my past.

'Are you crying?'

'It's just the onions,' I lie, wiping my hands on my apron and going over to him. I reach up and kiss his still-tanned cheek, enjoying the roughness of the bristles on his chin. He smells dusty, of bricks and concrete.

He pushes me gently away from him. 'I'm filthy, I need a shower.' He sidesteps me and leaves the room. A few minutes later I can hear the gush of the water overhead.

Over dinner I tell him about you.

'I've never heard you mention her before,' he says

through a mouthful of beef and carrots. It's true that I've never told anyone about you, Soph. Not Mike, my work colleagues, the few friends I allow myself, not even my ex-husband. We were – are – so intrinsically linked that to talk of you would be to acknowledge the old me. I needed to make a fresh start, to wipe the slate clean. It was the only way I could cope with what happened.

I take a large gulp of wine. 'She was my best friend growing up,' I say, as I place the glass on the table with an unsteady hand. I pick up my fork and prod at a potato so that it sinks further into the gravy. 'We were so close, joined at the hip as my mother used to say. But Sophie went missing nearly nineteen years ago. I found out today that her body – or rather, *remains* – have been recovered.' I put my fork down. I have no appetite.

'After all this time? What a shitter.' He shakes his head as if contemplating how much of 'a shitter' it really is, and I can't read what's going on behind those pale eyes. I think, I *hope*, he's going to ask me about you; how we met, how long we knew each other, what you were like, but he doesn't. He'll never know that when we were nine we made up a dance routine to Madonna's 'True Blue'; that you were the first person I told after I kissed Simon Parker behind the bike sheds when I was thirteen; that you poured your heart out to me about missing the dad you could barely remember; that once I made you laugh so much when you were sitting on my shoulders that you peed down my neck. Instead I swallow these little truths of our friendship down with my red wine while Mike resumes eating, methodically chewing the beef, around and around in his mouth like a cement mixer.

I have the sudden urge to throw my drink in his face, just to provoke a reaction. My friend Polly always says that Mike is so laid back he's horizontal. A cliché perhaps, but it's true. I don't think he's being cruel, he just lacks the emotional capacity to cope with me – or rather, with my issues.

I wonder if it's occurred to him yet that our relationship isn't working. I regret asking him to move in, but he caught me at a weak moment and I felt sorry for him, I suppose, living in that run-down house in Holloway with students half his age. And then, three weeks ago, just as I was about to sit down with him to talk, I received the call from Mum about Dad's stroke. I should have taken my dad's advice. He always warned me to be careful asking guys to move in, telling me that it's hard to get rid of them once you've invited them to share your home, your life, that you become intricately bound, financially and emotionally, like two threads tied in a knot. I haven't got the energy now to extricate myself from this relationship, to pick apart that knot. I get up from the table and scrape my food into the bin.

I tell Mike my plans as we get ready for bed.

'Sophie's brother, Daniel, is organising an apartment for me to stay in. A holiday let,' I say as I step out of my skirt and throw it over the back of the bedroom chair.

He's sitting up in bed, his muscly, almost hairless,

chest bare. I still fancy him, I still care about him, I just know our relationship isn't leading anywhere.

'At such short notice?' He raises a bushy eyebrow, watching me as I unbutton my shirt.

I shrug. 'It's out of season, and you know how I feel about hotels.' After spending most days working in one, the last place I want to stay is in a hotel or guest house. It needs to be self-catering and self-contained, away from others.

'Why now? You said she's been missing for eighteen years. Why wait until now to find out what happened?'

I feel the prickles of irritation crawling up my spine. How can he not see that your remains being found is a game-changer?

'Because now we know for definite that she's dead,' I snap.

He looks taken aback. 'I've never been to Oldcliffe-on-Sea,' he muses, picking at a non-existent spot on his upper arm. If he's hinting to accompany me I ignore it.

'You're not missing much.' I pull a silk camisole over my head. There is no way I want him to come with me. I need some breathing space.

'It must have been fun growing up by the seaside.'

I smile stiffly, trying not to shudder at the memory of growing up in that pastel-pink monstrosity overlooking the sea. Thank goodness Dad had the sense and money to sell up and buy a place in London before the property boom. I tug back the duvet and slide into bed next to him.

'So, how long will you be gone?' He pulls me close, nuzzling my neck.

'Not long,' I say, switching off the lamp. 'I'm hoping just a few days. I can't leave the hotels for too long, not now that Dad's . . .' I swallow. I still can't bring myself to say the words. My dad, always so strapping, so capable, now reduced to a shadow of his former self as he lies, day after day, in that hospital bed, unable to speak, hardly able to move. It still feels too recent, too raw. I inch away, feigning tiredness, and turn my back.

I lie still, waiting until I hear his rhythmic snores, his limbs heavy against mine, before grabbing my dressing gown from the back of the door and tiptoeing downstairs to sit at the kitchen table in the dark. I pour myself another glass of red wine. The smell of beef stew still lingers in the air. The little red light on the dishwasher flashes and beeps to let me know it's completed its cycle. It sounds strangely alien in the dark empty room.

I've tried so hard over the years to keep my life in order, to be successful, to move on, to not think about you every day. It's as though I've been cocooned inside a ball of wool, but now that wool has started to unravel, and when it does I'll be laid bare for all the world to see.

Jason. His name pops into my head, unbidden.

I take a large slug of wine but it doesn't stop my heart palpitating. Because the truth is bound to come out, Soph, and with it the dark secret we kept back then; the one thing we could never tell anyone else. Ever.

2

Sophie

Thursday, 26 June 1997

It's late as I write this. I doubt it will make much sense, I'm a tad wasted. But I have to scribble it down now so that I don't forget it in the morning.

Frankie's back!

I saw her tonight. She was standing at the bar in Mojo's, flanked by two guys I didn't recognise (one of whom was totally lush – just saying!). She had her back to me but I knew straight away it was her. I'd know that hair anywhere. It still hung in a perfect dark, glossy sheet. Doll's hair, that's what it's always reminded me of. The thick, luscious hair of a china doll. She was wearing a camel-coloured fake fur coat (at least, I hope it was fake) and long, black knee-high boots and as I watched her through the crowds I felt that familiar twist of envy in my gut because she's even more bloody beautiful than I'd remembered. I immediately felt under-dressed and dowdy in my jeans and Adidas trainers (although they're new, the navy blue Gazelle ones that I've wanted for ages!).

Then she turned, her eyes locked with mine and

her face broke out into a huge grin. She excused herself from the honeys she was with and parted the crowd towards me like a glamorous film star from the 1960s. Francesca Howe. Frankie. My best friend. And instantly everyone else seemed to fade into the background, as if they were all in black and white and she was in colour.

'Sophie! Oh my God, I can't believe it! How are you?' she shrieked, jumping up and down and waving her arms about excitedly. I think she was pissed, although it was only 8.30 p.m. She never could take her drink. She pulled me into a fierce embrace, engulfing me in the heady cloud of YSL Paris, her signature scent even when we were at school. My nose was pressed into the shoulder of her vintage fur coat. It smelt musty, of mothballs and second-hand shops.

She pulled me away from her so she could survey me, holding me at arm's length. 'Wow, you look so different. Truly amazing,' she said and I know she was taking in my highlights, my eyebrow wax, my contact lenses. 'And look how tall you are! I feel so short,' she laughed. I didn't want to admit to her that I felt hefty compared to her delicate petite-ness. She's as tiny as Kylie Minogue but with huge boobs. I always was jealous of her chest at school. I'm still ironing-board flat.

'What has it been?' She raised a perfectly plucked eyebrow while contemplating how many years must have passed since she left our school. I remember exactly. It was 1993, four years ago. 'That long?' she said when I told her.

She'd left at the end of Year 12. Her parents pulled her out of our under-achieving sixth form to send her to a posh boarding school in Bristol to finish her A-levels. We'd promised to keep in touch, and we did for a while, but then her trips home became less and less frequent. In the end I worried that my letters would seem boringly provincial and inane compared to the exciting life she was living with the Millicents and Jemimas of this world away in a big city like Bristol. How could the housing estate I lived on (still live on now that I'm back from uni) with Mum and Daniel compare to that? Eventually the correspondence petered out and I didn't see her again until we left school. We hung out a few times that summer but things were a bit strained between us when I got into Warwick and Frankie had to go through clearing. She didn't say it, of course, but I knew she was thinking it should have been the other way around, what with her private education. Whereas I was the first person in my family to even go to university.

I expected to see Frankie in the holidays, but she hardly came back home. I bumped into her mum once in Safeway and she told me Frankie and some 'wealthy pals from her course' had rented a house where they could live all year round and not just in term time. Maria had looked annoyed about it and made reference to it being Frankie's father's idea and how he was always spoiling her. I never blamed Frankie for staying away, not really. If I'd had somewhere else to go in the holidays I wouldn't have come back here either.

Sometimes I wondered if she stayed away because coming back was too painful. It reminded her – I reminded her – of what happened with Jason when we were sixteen. Our friendship had never been quite the same after that summer. We'd always been able to talk about anything and yet we were suddenly unable to talk about him, because just mentioning his name would voice the awful thing that we had done.

'So how was Warwick?' she added. 'You always were the brainy one. You did English Lit., didn't you? Like you always wanted.'

I nodded. I was beginning to feel embarrassed by her attention. That was the thing about Frankie. She always had this innate way of making you feel like you're the most important person in her world. 'What about you?'

She waved a hand at me. Her nail varnish was a pale blue, like a corpse. 'I got into Cardiff in the end. Did Business Studies.' She shrugged. 'It's what my dad wanted me to do.'

'That's great,' I said, but thinking how boring. 'Are you staying for the summer?'

She looped her arm through mine. 'I am. Dad wants me to have a career in hotel management.' She threw her head back and laughed. 'As if. What about you?' Her voice sounded posher than it once had, more clipped, as if her boarding school had filed down all those harsh West Country Rs.

'I don't know. I'm applying for jobs. I'd like to get into publishing.' I didn't want to tell her of the doubt that gnawed away at me late at night, that I'd never find a decent job, that I'd be stuck in Oldcliffe like my mum and brother for the rest of my life working in that greasy kiosk near the beach with pervy Stan, despite my 'good brain'.

That wouldn't happen to Frankie. I might have done better in my exams, gone to a highly regarded university, but that didn't mean anything. Not when your parents were well off and threw money at you like Frankie's parents did. Those three years in Warwickshire might have been the only chance I had to get out of this town.

'Aw, I've missed you, Soph,' she said, suddenly serious while she appraised me fondly. 'It wasn't the same – school without you.'

I agreed with her. The weight of her absence bore more heavily on me than I cared to remember. She was my first best friend. My only best friend.

She frogmarched me to the bar, pulled out a wad of cash and ordered two Diamond Whites. Then we spent the next hour talking non-stop about those missing years; the music we liked, the bands we were into. Typically we have the same taste. And as we chatted, the last three years fell away and it was as though I'd seen her only yesterday. She told me about this new club called The Basement that's opened up in the high street and plays indie music, promising me that we would go together and, before I knew it, the staff were calling last orders. I looked around for Helen, the friend I had come with, but she had long gone. Frankie ordered another Diamond White and as we clinked the bottles together she said, 'Cheers, Soph! Here's to one last summer of fun. One last summer before we're forced into the real world, where we have to be grown-ups, with jobs and responsibilities.'

We didn't go home straight away. We zigzagged towards the beach, arms linked, giggling and tiddly and overflowing with Diamond Whites. We perched on the sea wall, watching the water lap against our feet. The air was still humid after a hot day. We couldn't stop talking.

I didn't get home until gone midnight and now I can't sleep because I'm too excited.

She's back. My best friend is back. I've missed her so much. I had fun at uni and met some great friends. But nobody has ever compared to her.

She's in some of my most treasured childhood memories: her teaching me to roller skate; sleepovers in her cosy loft room at her parents' hotel; brunch in their formal dining room with views of the sea (which made a change from me, Mum and Daniel eating tea on our laps in front of the TV); drinking cans of lager on the old pier; making up dance routines to Madonna and Five Star in my (much smaller) bedroom; giggling in the back of the classroom at Mr Marrow's toupee.

And she's in some of my worst. That's the downside of knowing someone as long as I've known Frankie. But I won't let that spoil my mood, I'm still buzzing.

This is going to be the best summer ever!

Friday

3
Frankie

The sky is grey and oppressive as I drive through the centre of Oldcliffe-on-Sea, the clouds so low it feels as though I could reach out and touch them. To my left the sand is as brown as mud, the sea the colour of dirty dishwater and so far out I have to squint to determine where the shore ends and the waves begin. There are a few solitary people in wellies dotted about on the beach, their coats pressed firmly against their backs by the wind, throwing sticks for scraggy, wet dogs.

I pass what was once the outdoor lido, where we spent most of our summers as kids. It was where my dad taught us to swim. It's now boarded up; abandoned and sorry-looking, like a lover who has been stood up on a date. The Grand Pier, further along the coast, has hardly changed, with its opulent art-deco facade and bright red lettering.

Rearing up on the other side of the road, facing the sea, are the Victorian terraces of hotels and guest houses. I pass what was once our hotel, the one I grew up in, its candy-pink walls now a more refined powder blue.

The centre has been gentrified a little – a few upmarket cafés and smart restaurants have popped up amongst the discount shops and greasy spoons – but for the most part the town is unchanged, as if time stopped somewhere in the mid-1950s. Unfortunately the amusement arcades are still here, with their loud, grating music and garish, flashing lights. We loved them as kids. We would spend all our pocket money on those ten-pence machines.

I imagine in the summer the town is bustling, just as it used to be, full of tourists; couples strolling along the front, kids building sandcastles, pensioners squashed on benches and gazing out to sea with their flasks of tea and home-made sandwiches, teenage lovers clasping hands as they ride on the big wheel. Today it's like a ghost town. Today it brings back every unwanted memory of the past that I've ever had.

I drive away from the centre of town and follow the coastal road around to the left. And then I see it. The Victorian relic rises out of the turbid sea like a decaying monster with steel legs that look as though they're about to buckle under its weight. The old pier. The place where you disappeared. You were fond of the pier but I hated it. And I hate it even more now. It's obvious, as I drive closer, that it has become even more dilapidated since I left. If I drive further on, I will reach the sprawling estate where you and Daniel grew up. It's all still so familiar to me, as though I have a map of this town tattooed on my brain.

I pull my Range Rover into a lay-by, turn off the engine and sit and stare at the pier, letting the memories wash over me of all the times we went there, as teenagers with Jason and later with Daniel and his friends. It closed to the public in 1989 but that didn't stop us. It was a great place to hang out away from the main town, somewhere we could sit and drink our Red Stripe lagers in peace, listen to Blur and Oasis on my portable CD player. We made sure never to venture too far onto the pier and certainly never as far as the old deserted pavilion at the end. We had heard whispers of ghost stories bandied about in pubs: the builder who had fallen from the pavilion and now roamed it at night; the woman dressed in Victorian nightwear who threw herself and her new-born baby into the sea after her husband left her. We doubted any of these stories were true, but we liked to scare ourselves nonetheless.

Now the pier is cordoned off and deserted, with a large, red DANGER: DO NOT ENTER sign at the entrance, although it would still be easy enough to climb through the makeshift fencing; if it had been there in our day, I'm sure that's what we would have done.

I sit for a while longer, listening to the rain tap-tapping on the roof and windscreen, watching the waves whipping themselves into a fury like rabid dogs frothing at the mouth. On the journey down I stopped at the petrol station on the outskirts of town. It's no longer an Elf garage like it was in our day, Soph – it's now Shell. Newspapers lined the entrance. HUMAN REMAINS WASHED UP ON BEACH was emblazoned across the front page of the local rag. It seemed so impersonal somehow, so wrong, to talk about you in that way.

I'll never forget when you first went missing. The next day your mum raised the alarm after realising that you had never been home. To begin with she thought you might have stayed with me or Helen, so she waited and waited and, after calling all your friends to no avail, she rang the police. By then nearly twenty-four hours had elapsed since anyone had last seen you. The police interviewed all of us, the coastguard searched for a few days, but you had simply vanished. Nobody could understand it. The only thing they found was your trainer at the edge of the old pier. After that, the investigation tailed off. The police clearly believed that you had fallen off the pier and drowned. There was no official ruling. Your family never requested an inquest, so you're still a 'missing person'.

And now . . . the newspaper headline flashes in front of my eyes again and I blink it away.

I need to go. It's nearly 3 p.m. and I can't put off meeting Daniel any longer. Reluctantly I turn on the engine and I'm about to leave when something on the pier catches my eye. A figure is leaning so far over the railings it looks as if any minute they could tumble into the choppy sea. It's just a dark silhouette, but with the long hair whipping a heart-shaped face it looks like a woman. It looks like you. My stomach lurches. It can't be you. It can't be anyone. The pier is fenced off, the planks rotten and full of holes. Nobody could walk on that pier now without falling through the boards.

Suddenly the low sun breaks apart the grey clouds, shining down on the pier and almost blinding me. I'm forced to close my eyes, black dots swimming behind my lids. When I open them again the sky has reverted back to greyness and the pier is once again empty. Just the light playing tricks on me.

The holiday apartment is high up on the cliff top overlooking the old pier. My mouth is dry as I turn right. I'm no longer on the coastal road but driving up the steep Hill Street, my car making light work of the potholes. The road levels off and I kerb crawl until I spot Beaufort Villas, a lemon and white Victorian apartment block with huge bay windows and ornate, pointed roof gables. It stands in a row of almost identical buildings in ice-cream colours, facing Oldcliffe Bay and looking down on the old pier like a line of disapproving aunts in their Sunday best. This part of town has always been more prestigious, with its grand houses and residents-only park, in spite of the now decrepit pier.

I pull into the driveway, my tyres crunching over the gravel, and park next to a gold Vauxhall. A man is sitting on a low wall by the front door, one leg crossed over a knee, scribbling something in a notebook. I know it's Daniel even after all these years: the curve of his chin, the line of his long nose and the cowlick which meant his dark hair never sat straight but flopped over his forehead, so that he was continually forced to push it out of his eyes. He looks up at the sound of my car, his face expectant, and places the pen behind his ear.

My hand trembles slightly as I pull on the handbrake. Why does coming back here make me feel so nervous? Holding meetings, appeasing difficult clients, dealing with disillusioned staff is all a breeze compared to the way I feel right now. I get out of the car, making an effort to be graceful in my skinny jeans and stiletto-heeled boots. The cold air that greets me is like a slap in the face.

'Frankie?' He leaps off the wall and ambles towards me, still slim and rangy and extremely tall. He's wearing black jeans, a long dark overcoat and a striped scarf pulled up to his chin. He slips the notebook into the front pocket of his coat. From a distance he looks like the twenty-three-year-old he was when I last saw him, but as he approaches I can see that age has softened and plumped out his once-sharp features, and streaked his nearly-black hair with the odd flash of white. His skin looks rougher, less translucent. My first memory of him is on his BMX, riding around the estate and trying to impress us with his wheelies. He was nine. Now he's forty-one and very much a man. The thought makes me blush.

We hug awkwardly. Then he appraises me with a wry smile and I wonder if he's disappointed that I'm not as he remembers. 'You've hardly changed a bit, Frankie Howe,' he says, as charming as ever. 'You still look like a lady.' And I'm there again, in your bedroom, with Daniel lounging on the bed and teasing us with that sardonic raise of an eyebrow, his grey eyes glinting.

I laugh. 'I forgot you used to call me Lady Frankie.'

'Well, you were posh.' He pushes the hair out of his eyes and the gesture is so familiar, so endearing, that I well up. I blink back tears, annoyed with myself. I've never been a crier, that was your domain. I always used to tease you that you lived too close to the well.

'I was never posh,' I say, my discomfort making me sound harsher than I intended, but I know it will fall on deaf ears. It always has. I was the girl from the big hotel whereas you and Daniel were from the estate, with its late-1960s terraces and tatty garages.

He fishes a key from his pocket. 'Come on then, Lady Frankie,' he teases. 'Let me show you your castle.'

I follow him down the long hallway. The ceilings are high, with elaborate cornicing. The stairs are carpeted in a soft biscuit-coloured wool. There are two doors on either side of the staircase with numbers on them. 'Yours is on the first floor,' he says, noticing me pausing outside the door on the left. I follow him up the stairs to a wide, square landing. There are two more doors facing each other with a small arched window in between. I go to the window and look out over the bay.

'Wow, fabulous views,' I say, although my heart sinks. I don't want to have to look at that pier every day, to be reminded of the place where you went missing. *To the place where you died*, I correct myself.

I sense him as he moves closer, to stand behind me.

He places a hand on my shoulder. 'I'm sorry that it overlooks the pier,' he says as if reading my mind. 'I didn't think you'd want a hotel in the centre and these apartments are amazing, perfect for Lady Frankie,' he jokes, lightening the mood. I turn to face him, our noses inches apart.

'It's fine,' I lie. 'You did the right thing, and I'm only here for a bit . . .' I trail off and our eyes lock. The air between us changes, becoming thicker with everything that's been left unsaid over the last eighteen years.

He breaks eye contact first and turns towards the door on the left. A chrome number 4 glints against the white painted wood. Silently he inserts the key into the lock and throws the door open. The air is stale, as if it's been shut up for too long.

I shadow him as he shows me around the apartment. It's pleasant, with large, airy rooms and neutral painted walls. The bedroom is a small double, overlooking the dustbins in the courtyard at the back. There's a modern galley kitchen next door. The sitting room's large bay window overlooks the rough grey seas. The floors are mahogany and creak under my boots. It's stylishly furnished and obviously for couples rather than families with small kids, judging by the pale grey velvet sofa and low glass-topped coffee table. A widescreen television sits in the corner and there is a cast-iron fireplace opposite the sofa with a stack of logs piled next to it. It's a luxury place but has an unlived-in vibe, a musty smell that reeks of weeks standing empty.

'It's only a one-bedroom but my mate says you can

stay until next Friday. It's booked out after that, surprisingly. Someone coming for a long weekend. Otherwise you could've stayed longer.'

I try not to blanch. The thought of staying here for a few days fills me with dread, let alone a whole week.

'I'm not sure how long I'll be here, Daniel. I'm in charge at the hotel now, my dad . . . he . . .'

I feel Daniel stiffen beside me. 'I read about your dad,' he says, turning to look at me. 'Must have been a huge shock, for all of you.'

I stare at him in surprise. There was only a small piece in the national press, squashed between the business pages. I was hoping nobody would see it, least of all the residents of Oldcliffe who remember us. Dad's still so proud, even now.

'It was. The stroke was quite severe . . .' I swallow the lump that's formed in my throat.

His fingers brush my arm and then he takes his hand away and shoves it in his pocket, as though he doesn't trust himself.

I don't tell him that I think my dad will die. That the responsibility of taking on two hotels and opening a third is weighing heavily upon me. That I haven't got the time to be here on some wild goose chase and that I'm only doing it for Daniel, for old times' sake. And for you. *For us.*

'How many apartments are in this block?' I say as I go to the window. It's nearly dark outside. He follows me.

'Two upstairs and two down. It's out of season so I think it's just the downstairs one that's occupied this week.' He pulls a face. 'You'll be OK, won't you? All alone in this big, spooky building?' He laughs. I feel like I've been punched. His laugh is so familiar. It's so much like yours.

'I don't believe in ghosts,' I say with a dismissive sniff.

'Not even Greta, wailing for her newborn baby, wanting to punish her cheating husband?'

'Oh, piss off,' I laugh and punch his upper arm playfully. 'You haven't changed, have you? Still acting like an annoying older brother, trying to wind me up.'

He shrugs, but I can see he's pleased. And then it hits me. He must miss that relationship since you disappeared. Maybe having me here reminds him of you, of our childhood. Does he really need my help to uncover the truth about your disappearance after all this time? Or does he want me here because I remind him of all that we had?

And all that we lost.

While Daniel's fetching my bag from the car, I go to draw the curtains in the sitting room. The pier is a black silhouette against the darkening sky, the two old-fashioned lampposts near the entrance illuminating some of the broken boards and decaying structure like spotlights on a stage. The dome of the pavilion looms in the distance; an ink stain on the horizon. A shiver runs down my back and I pull the curtains closed.

I retreat into the kitchen to make us a cup of tea and

I'm touched when I notice that either Daniel or the owner went out and bought a few things, like bread, milk and teabags.

'I can't remember if you have sugar,' I say as I return to the sitting room, carrying two mugs. He's lounging on the sofa with my bag at his feet. The fire has been lit.

'No, I'm sweet enough,' he grins, taking the mug from me. 'Thanks.'

'Did you put the milk and teabags in the kitchen?'

He shrugs. 'Thought they'd come in handy. What have you got in that holdall? It weighs a ton.'

'Wouldn't you like to know?' I tease, perching next to him. 'Thank you, for the milk and teabags . . .' I touch his arm but he stiffens so I take my hand away, the rest of my words dying on my lips.

His long fingers cradle the mug and he blows onto the tea before taking a sip.

'So, what have you been up to all these years?' I say, trying to keep my voice light.

He frowns and grips the mug tighter. I notice a plain silver ring on the third finger of his right hand and I wonder who gave it to him. At first he doesn't answer and I worry that I've offended him somehow. I'm usually intuitive to people's moods and feelings, knowing when to ask the right questions or issue the perfect compliment to break the ice. In fact, I pride myself on it; it's an invaluable tool in my line of work. But I'm not sure what the etiquette is for a situation like this. What do you say to the brother of your best friend the day after you've learned that her remains have been found? What is the appropriate conversation to have?

He looks up at me over the rim of his mug. 'Well, I went off the rails for a bit.' He shrugs, but looks shamefaced. 'You know how it is.'

I nod, remembering your worries about him. His failed GCSEs and lackadaisical attitude to finding a job. Your concerns that he'd stay in Oldcliffe-on-Sea for ever. 'And then I decided that I needed to follow my dream. Music.'

My heart falls. 'You're still in the band?' I remember the band – mainly because they were rubbish, but that didn't stop them trekking to Bristol most weekends to play in backwater pubs. Daniel wasn't a bad guitarist; it was mainly that the lead singer, Sid, couldn't actually hold a tune, but nobody had the heart to tell him.

He chuckles. 'Definitely not. I realised I was better at writing about music than making it. So I went to college, got a degree in journalism, became a music journalist.'

'Wow. You got out of this place?'

He laughs wryly. 'Don't sound too surprised. What did you think had happened to me? That I was working in McDonald's? Or turned to heroin?'

'No,' I say, not very convincingly.

'Anyway, I was a music journalist for a few years, worked for *Melody Maker*, then *Q*. I lived in London, had a great time.' He smiles as if at some private memory. 'Now I'm the editor of the local newspaper.'

'You moved back here?' I can't keep the scorn from my voice.

He glares at me and I notice animosity in his eyes. 'Of course, only recently, but it's my home and I feel close to Sophie here. I can't run away for ever. Neither can you.'

Shame makes me dip my head. 'I couldn't stay,' I say into my lap. 'When my parents bought their hotel in London it seemed best for me to go with them. A new start. Don't think badly of me, Dan.'

His voice is brusque. 'I don't think badly of you. You're here now, aren't you? When it matters.'

I look up and he's staring at me in that way he always used to. Like he could see right through me. You always joked that he had a crush on me, and there were times when I thought so too. I never even entertained anything happening between us. Oh, I flirted with him, of course. And there was a time, a very short time, when I considered the idea of letting him kiss me. But that was the summer we met Jason.

I take a sip of my tea, my cheeks burning.

Daniel eventually breaks the silence. 'What about you? What sort of charmed life have you been living?' He grins at me but I find it hard to return his smile. A charmed life. I'm sure that's what everyone else would think to look at my life. I have money, a lovely home, a good job as the director of a chain of hotels. Yet part of me died the night you disappeared.

Daniel is staring at me expectantly so I spout the usual story: of my marriage to a hedge-fund manager who I'd adored, of our desire to have children, of my failure to conceive, of his clichéd affair with his co-worker and our subsequent divorce. I fail to mention that the alimony I received helped buy this new hotel and I don't add that I find it hard to trust men now, even solid, dependable Mike.

As I talk, Daniel sips his tea and nods encouragingly. 'I'm sorry to hear that, Franks,' he says when I've finished. 'I've never been married. The right one just never came along.' My eye flickers to the ring on his finger again. There must have been someone special once. He smiles sadly and my heart flutters. What is it about him? It's like his grief and love for you has matured him into a man with an emotional intelligence that he lacked when we were young. He might have looked like a tortured artist back then, with his black clothes and morose music, but it was at odds with his happy-go-lucky demeanour. Not like your ex-boyfriend, Leon, all brooding and serious as he recited his angst-ridden poetry.

'I've got a plan,' he says suddenly. 'We need to talk to everyone who was around that night. I know it's a long shot, but they might remember something, however small. You've only got a week so we'd better get on with it, first thing.'

I open my mouth to say I've got less than a week, that I have to get back to London as soon as possible. But something about his expression makes me close it again.

'Any objections?' His eyes bore into mine and it feels

as though he can read my deepest thoughts. I have lots of objections; I have so much to do that I can't afford a day off let alone a week. But how can I say this without sounding heartless? Without sounding like I don't care about you?

So I gulp down my tea and shake my head, telling Daniel that, no, I don't have any objections.

'Good,' he says, 'because I had a call earlier from the police. They have more information about what they've found.'

My palms immediately start to sweat. 'And?'

'After years in the sea, Sophie's body would have decomposed, Franks. But they've found a foot. They think it belongs to a woman due to its size. It's still in its trainer. Adidas. Apparently floating feet can survive for decades in rubber-soled shoes because the fish can't get at them.'

'Oh God.'

His face is paler than usual. 'I've given a DNA sample and they've asked if I'll go into the station on Wednesday morning for the result. And of course they need to see if the trainer matches the one they found on the pier after she disappeared. It's still in police files. Will you come with me? I . . . I don't think I can do it on my own.'

He looks so vulnerable and, despite everything, I like that Daniel needs me, that he wants me to go with him. 'Of course I will.' I think of the trainers you were wearing that night. You'd loved those Adidas Gazelles.

He stands up. 'I'd better go. But I'll be here tomorrow nice and early.' His voice is unnaturally bright. 'Shall we say nine thirty? I think Leon should be our first stop. Don't you?'

I nearly spit out my tea in shock. Leon? Daniel must be mistaken. Leon left Oldcliffe just weeks after you went missing. 'I don't think so,' I say with faux regret, also standing up. 'The last I heard, Leon was working abroad. Never mind, who's next on your list?'

Daniel raises a quizzical eyebrow. 'I've heard he's back in town, Frankie. I thought you knew.'

My scalp prickles in horror and I sink back onto the sofa.

If I'd known I'd be forced to see Leon again, I'd never have agreed to come back.

4
Sophie

Friday, 4 July 1997

The hot guy who was with Frankie last week is called Leon McNamara. He's half Irish, like me, but with chocolate-brown hair and the most amazing blue eyes I've ever seen. They are the exact same colour as my indigo Levi 501s.

'Leon'. I love the way it sounds. So unusual. So much cooler than Daniel, or James, or Simon, or any of the other boring boys' names that I can think of. And it's not just his name that's cool. He's an indie kid, but there is more to him than what music he's into (which is not just Oasis, by the way. He likes bands I've never heard of, bands with animal names: Buffalo Springfield and the Byrds. The Animals even!). He's quiet and serious. And he reads. Not *Playboy* or *NME*, like Daniel, but books, classic novels like *The Great Gatsby* and *Persuasion.* I mean, he's read Jane Austen, for fuck's sake! But he's not pretentious, he doesn't bleat crap because he thinks it sounds good – like some people I could mention from my uni. He's intelligent without being taught. He grew up on an estate, much like this one, but in Brean. He's full of contradictions; he's doing an HNC in computers, yet he writes poetry and reads Jane Austen.

And he's totally lush!

There is just one downside. I will explain.

It was at The Basement last night when Frankie introduced me to him. I've seen her nearly every day since bumping into her. It's just like old times, as if those three years apart never happened. Maybe that's how it is when you've known someone for as long as I've known her? When you meet again it's like you saw each other yesterday.

She works in her parents' hotel from 10–2 p.m., changing bedding and getting rooms cleaned for new customers. She's getting paid well for it too, much better than I get at the kiosk in town serving slimy fish and greasy chips to tourists. That's the bonus, I suppose, of working for your parents. I finish at 3 p.m., so we then have the afternoons to ourselves. I feel like a teenager again when I'm with Frankie. We do all the same things we used to: walks on the Grand Pier, playing games in the arcade, ambling along the beach with candy floss and chatting about life and the future. We often go to the pub at night, usually the Seagull because the beer is cheap even though the place smells of wet dog, but towards the end of this week, when our wages started to run out, we went to the old pier with Daniel and his mates, Sid and Ade from the band, armed with cans of Red Stripe. We sat there for hours, telling each other ghost stories, particularly the one about Greta and her lost baby. In the end I started to feel so frightened that I was glad I had Daniel to walk home with me.

Anyway, I'm digressing. Back to tonight. To Leon.

The Basement was impressive and because it was a Thursday night it was cheap to get in. I still can't believe that while I've been at uni, Oldcliffe has become up to date enough to have such a cool club. It's (funnily enough) in the basement of one of the big restaurants, with its own entrance below ground, and plays all the music I love. It's small and smoky. Frankie seemed to know everyone; I'm not sure how, but she's as popular as ever. Especially with the guys. And then she introduced me to Leon.

He was standing at the bar, nursing a pint. He was wearing a tan leather blazer, dark jeans and desert boots and when he looked up at me with those brilliant eyes it was as though my breath was knocked out of me. But he barely registered me. He sort of snuffled a hello into his pint. Frankie draped herself all over him and ordered us some Diamond Whites. Then she got talking to some guy, leaving Leon and me standing awkwardly next to each other in silence.

'Do you come here often?' I asked eventually, before realising what I'd said. I was mortified, my cheeks burning. He looked shocked for a second but then his face relaxed and his eyes twinkled. We both started laughing at the same time, which broke the ice.

'I'm sorry, I'm such an idiot,' I muttered, chewing my fingernail. 'I didn't mean it like that.' I never have been very good at chatting to guys I find attractive.

‘’S OK.’ Then he looked at me as if for the first time. ‘I haven’t seen you around here before.’

‘I’ve lived here since I was seven. But I’ve been away, to uni.’

‘That would explain it,’ he said, passing me the Diamond White that Frankie had pushed in his direction, his hand brushing mine and sending an electric current through me. I could see Frankie over his shoulder, making kissing faces and causing me to blush.

‘I’ve only been living here a few years,’ he said, hopefully unaware of my discomfort. He told me then about growing up in Ireland, and moving to Brean when he was eight. ‘I moved to Oldcliffe last year. I live with my brother and his girlfriend in Dove Way.’ I had to stop myself squealing in excitement (that’s just not cool!) because he lives two streets away from me. ‘I quite like living with Lorcan. It’s kinda fun, they just let me do my own thing.’ He explained that he has nearly completed his HNC in computers, going to college in Bristol one day a week and working the rest of the time in the IT department of an insurance company. I could detect the slight Irish accent in his West Country twang. I told him my mum was from Ireland too.

I sipped my Diamond White and listened while he talked. And then I opened up about my ambition to work in publishing.

‘Do you want to be a writer then?’

I brushed my hair away from my face and tried to look nonchalant. ‘As long as I’m surrounded by books and words all day I don’t mind.’

'Have you got anything lined up now you've finished uni?'

'I'm applying for jobs. I did some work experience last summer so at least I have something for the CV and I've got an interview with a small publishing company on the outskirts of London in a few weeks' time.'

I could tell by his expression that I'd impressed him.

'That's amazing. What's the job for?'

'Editorial assistant. I want to be a commissioning editor eventually, but it's so competitive.' I couldn't bring myself to tell him of the two interviews at other publishing houses for jobs that I didn't get, not to mention the endless speculative letters that I send out every week.

'I'd love to be a poet but my parents wanted me to get a "proper job".' He used his fingers as quotations. 'They don't see the point of college or university.'

'But they don't mind you doing an HNC?'

He shrugged. 'That doesn't bother them because I'm getting paid. Although I had another job before this one. But the HNC, according to them, has prospects. Computers are the future, don't you know,' he said in a voice that I took to be him mimicking his parents. Despite his jokey tone a shadow passed over his face so that he looked sad, wiser, older. I had the sudden urge to hug him.

'Shall we sit down?' He indicated a small table in the corner that had just become vacant. I nodded, relieved to get away from Frankie, who was still standing behind him chatting to a group of guys but every now and again leering at me over Leon's shoulder and making lewd faces.

'So, you write poetry?' I said as we both settled ourselves at the table. We were squashed in the corner. His shoulder was pressed against mine and I could smell his aftershave – CK One by Calvin Klein. I always have had a good nose for scents.

He nodded and took another sip of his pint. 'Poems, song lyrics. Although I can't play a musical instrument, unfortunately.'

'Do you know my brother, Daniel Collier? He can play the guitar but he taught himself. He's in a band.'

He frowned at the name. 'I've heard of him,' he said, which sounded ominous, but most people in Oldcliffe have heard of my brother, just like most people seem to know Frankie. They're gregarious, able to make friends easily, unlike me.

We chatted about music and took it in turns to list the bands we loved. When I told him I'd never heard of Buffalo Springfield he promised to lend me one of their albums.

'I have to say, Jez is a knob but he knows his music,' he said as the DJ put on a Bluetones track.

I laughed. 'Why do you say he's a knob?'

Leon shrugged. 'Look at him.' He was leaning over his decks, earphones clamped to his head, chatting up a pretty blonde in a very short skirt and platform boots. 'There's always some girl hanging around him. Just because he's a DJ.'

'You sound envious,' I laughed.

He scoffed and supped his beer. 'Not when I'm sitting here with the best-looking girl in the place.'

'You charmer.' I swiped at his shoulder and he turned towards me with an intense stare. I held my breath, his eyes fixed on mine, his face edging closer.

'There you are!' Frankie stood over us imperiously, hands on her hips, breaking the moment between us. 'You've been nattering, like, for ever. Come on, Soph, we need to dance. You love this song.'

'Babies' by Pulp. I hadn't even noticed. Before I could protest, she dragged me from the table and away from Leon. I glanced back at him and he shrugged and laughed and carried on supping his pint. But I wanted to kick Frankie.

'Why did you have to interrupt us?' I hissed when we got to the dance floor. 'We were getting on well.'

Her green eyes were suddenly serious. 'He's bad news, Soph. He's not for you.'

Anger swelled within me. 'How do you know who is and isn't right for me, Frankie?' I stopped dancing to illustrate my point.

She waved her hand dismissively, still clutching her bottle of Diamond White. 'He's a bit of a psycho, that's all. Very intense. Doesn't take no for an answer, if you know what I mean.'

Shock rippled through me. 'What?'

'Oh, I don't mean in that way, he didn't try it on or anything,' she said when she noticed my horrified expression.

'What do you mean then? Is he an ex?'

She shook her mane of dark hair and took a swig of her bottle. 'He wishes,' she laughed, infuriating me further. When she saw that I wasn't joining in, the smile vanished from her face. She stopped dancing. 'It's just . . .' She hesitated. 'Look . . . I quite fancied him when I first saw him. We had a snog a month or so ago and he was just a little too intense afterwards, that's all.'

'He wanted to go out with you?'

'Of course. He's good looking, but not my type. He has no prospects, ambition.' I opened my mouth to protest, to stick up for him, but she ignored me. 'He sort of harassed me. In the end I had to tell him in no uncertain terms that I wasn't interested. Threaten him a bit. He got the message. Eventually.'

My heart sank at her words.

'But you're friends now?' I said, recalling that she was with him last week in Mojo's, when I first saw her again.

Her lips turned up into a half-smile, almost as though she was harbouring a secret. 'Well, it wasn't his first choice. But I suppose you could say we are friends now.' Oblivious, she carried on dancing, her eyes closed, with all the confidence in the world.

I was tempted to stomp off in a strop, but I wasn't sure why. It wasn't Frankie's fault that Leon fancied her. As we danced I let my gaze sweep over her in her short black and white dress and long black boots. Like a sex kitten from the 1960s. Of course Leon was going to fancy her. I didn't stand a chance.

I tried to pick him out in the smoke-filled club but despite searching through the hordes of people, I didn't see Leon again. We left just after 1 a.m., Frankie chatting all the way home about Jez, who (naturally!) had asked her out.

It wasn't until this morning that I found a note in my coat pocket. A folded ticket stub with a cloakroom number printed on the front and a short message squeezed onto the small space on the back. He must have bribed one of the cloakroom staff to put it in my pocket. In small blocked writing, it read: MEET ME. OLD PIER. FRIDAY 7 P.M. L.

5
Frankie

I'm alone in the apartment for the first time since I arrived, and despite not seeing him for nearly eighteen years I'm missing Daniel's reassuring presence, his banter. He's the only thing worth coming back to this godforsaken place for.

Shadows move and shift on the high ceiling, and the sitting room feels chilly, the wooden floor cold under my feet. I throw some more logs on the fire and huddle around it as the flames dance higher and higher, licking up the chimney, and I breathe in the woody scent of burning logs, tasting it at the back of my throat.

Daniel's parting words are still fresh in my mind. Leon is back in town, and, even worse, tomorrow I'm going to have to face him again. I think of all the excuses I could use to explain to Daniel why I had to return home: one of the hotels is in trouble, my father needs me, Mike's burnt the house down. But even as these thoughts swill around in my head, I already know I have to accompany Daniel tomorrow, because if I don't Leon might reveal things I'd rather keep hidden. Things about the past. And I can't risk that.

I just hope you kept our secret like you promised.

That you weren't foolish enough to unburden yourself to Leon.

A breeze brushes the back of my neck. Why have I got this feeling that I'm being watched? A sudden gust of wind rattles the window frames and howls down the chimney, flattening the fire, and I jump back in alarm. It sounds as though a ghost is trying to break in. I try not to think about the view behind the heavy cream curtains. The dark, hulking shape of the decaying pier, the memories of what took place there all those years ago. Rain slashes against the glass like a maniac with a knife.

I desperately need a glass of wine.

I go to the kitchen and retrieve a bottle of red from beside the microwave. I knew this was going to be a stressful few days so I made sure to bring enough bottles of vino. I settle myself in front of the television, but the weather causes the picture to fizzle and crackle and, frustrated, I turn it off. Spending a night here is going to send me insane. Why did I agree to this? But I know the answer.

Maybe I should have booked a room at one of the hotels in the centre that overlook the gaudy Grand Pier, the promenade and the beach. Like the one I grew up in. These apartments might be more prestigious than the guest houses and B&Bs in town, but being high up on the cliff tops in winter isn't for the faint-hearted, especially considering my past. I feel isolated up here. Why is it that when I'm on my own all of the scary movies and television programmes I've ever watched play out as if I have the DVDs on a loop in my mind?

I think longingly of my house in Islington. It's not as though I'm unused to solitude. Apart from my brief marriage and a few short co-habitations I've always lived alone. But in London I'm comforted by the city's familiar sounds – the almost constant hum of traffic in the street, the honk of a horn, the blare of police sirens, the shouts of teenagers, the faint roar of an aeroplane – that tell me I'm never too far away from people, from civilisation. London is never quiet, even in the dead of night. I'd forgotten how deafening silence can sound.

And then I think of Mike in his dusty work trousers and muddy boots, making a mess of the kitchen and walking dirt through the hallway, and the thought of him in my home suddenly irritates me.

As if he's read my mind, my mobile trills and his name flashes up on my phone.

'Mike?' The reception is sketchy but I can hear the background noise of people, glasses clinking, faint music that indicates he's in a bar.

'Just wanted to make sure you got there OK?' he says. It's a lovely gesture but it signifies everything that's wrong in our relationship. Mike wants things from me that I can never give him. Commitment, children. We've never talked about love, but I know he feels it; it lingers between us in his kisses, the surreptitious glances when he thinks I'm not looking, the way he lovingly twists the ends of my hair around his fingers while we sit listening to music, or watching TV.

And I can never reciprocate his feelings. How can I admit that I fancy him but I'm not capable of anything further? At least, not with him. Deep down I know he's not the right man for me. The truth is, Soph, I felt sorry for him when I met him. You know what I'm like – I never could resist a lost soul.

I tell him I arrived safely and start to describe how remote the apartment is but he interrupts me, excitement in his voice. 'I was thinking, why don't I come down for a few days to keep you company? I don't like the thought of you in that place by yourself. It sounds lonely. We never spend much quality time together, you're always working late and I haven't got much on at the moment . . .'

The thought of him coming here fills me with dread. 'I've come back to help Daniel, for crying out loud, Mike. I'm not in Oldcliffe to have a romantic break with you.' It comes out harsher than I intend.

'Fran . . .' The line breaks up and I move to the window to get better reception, but his words fade in and out: '. . . pushing me away . . . not want to be with me? . . . tell me honestly . . . so cold to me sometimes . . .'

'The line's bad. I can't hear you,' I cry, then the phone goes dead. I slump onto the sofa, still gripping the mobile as the wind howls outside. Then I pour myself another glass of wine, and for some reason my thoughts turn to Jason.

Do you remember when we first met Jason? My mum recruited him to help her in the hotel kitchen cooking bacon, black pudding and overdone baked beans. He wanted to be a chef. He was seventeen, a year older than us, and he was the best-looking bloke that our sixteen-year-old selves had ever seen in real life. He had dark wavy hair and sun-kissed skin. It was an unusually hot June and we had come straight from the beach. We still had sand in the turn-ups of our denim shorts and sea salt in our hair. We smelt of candy floss and sun cream, trailing our towels and beach bags through the dining room, gossiping about boys. He was sitting at one of the pine dining tables being interviewed by my mother, his face serious, trying (as he later admitted to me) to appear grown up and responsible, desperate for the summer job. I can still recall exactly what he was wearing the first time I clapped eyes on him: a khaki T-shirt with a sun on the front and a pair of baggy jeans – and he had those dog tags around his neck. He loved those things, didn't he, Soph. He was wearing them the night he died.

A baby is crying, its wails high-pitched and persistent. The sound shocks me awake. I must have fallen asleep on the sofa, my neck at an odd angle on the purple cushion. I sit up, rubbing my shoulder and flexing my joints. An empty bottle of wine sits on the coffee table in front of me. I look at my watch. It's 2 a.m. The fire has burnt itself out and the apartment is freezing. I wonder where the baby's cries are coming from. It sounds like they are somewhere within the building, although Daniel said the flats are empty apart from the one directly below mine.

I get up from the sofa with great effort; my limbs feel stiff, my feet numb. The curtains to the bay window are wide open, framing the pier as though it's scenery on a stage. A wispy fog swirls around the amber light emanating from the two Victorian lamps that still stand proudly at its entrance. I frown, puzzled. I don't remember leaving the curtains open. In fact I'm almost certain I closed them. I go to the window and look out onto the pier and the rough sea beyond. I'm just about to thrust the curtains shut when, through the ethereal fog, I see you. Standing on the pier, illuminated by the lights, in a long dress, the wind whipping your hair across your face. I blink a few times. I'm mistaken – of course I am. I've drunk too much, I'm still half asleep. When I look again the pier is empty, as I knew it would be.

All those ghost stories we told each other when we were young, I never believed in any of them. But despite my rational thoughts, a chill runs through my body and I hurriedly close the curtains on the pier. And on you.

To take my mind off being back here I unpack my laptop and, balancing it on my knees, try and catch up with some work. With the opening of the new hotel there is so much to do: decorating to oversee, staff to hire. Luckily my dad made sure he employed a hard-working manager, Stuart, but even before his stroke I'd taken on more responsibility so that my parents could semi-retire. My mother is unable to help because of all the hours she spends at my father's bedside. A wave of guilt washes over me that I'm not sitting with her.

Before driving down here I made a detour to visit my dad.

His room was unnaturally warm and smelled of boiled vegetables with an undercurrent of disinfectant. Witnessing him lying there in his hospital bed, hardly able to move, a drip in his arm, brought tears to my eyes. My strong, capable father, who I admired and looked up to, now appeared shrunken, wizened, old. It had been three weeks since his stroke and there was little improvement in his condition.

Mum barely glanced up when I entered, and didn't even register surprise at my early arrival; I usually visit Dad after work. She continued to fuss around him, wiping his brow, smoothing back his greying hair and placing a wet sponge to his lips. I could tell by the rigidness of her shoulders, by her mouth pursed in a disapproving line, that she didn't think I visited enough. I wanted to scream at her that I had the business to take care of, and when I did show up, which was every few days, she made me feel like I wasn't wanted. But I swallowed my resentment, telling myself I was here for my father, not for her. I dragged a chair closer to his bed, the plastic feet making a screeching sound across the floor, causing my mother to wince.

'Did you have to drag it, Francesca?' she said, a pained expression on her face.

Ignoring her I took his hand; it felt heavy and cold in mine. 'Dad,' I said in a low voice. I knew he could hear me because he opened his eyes. 'How are you today? Are you comfortable?' He blinked at me twice, which meant yes. One blink meant no. The doctor had told us a few days before that they'd noticed some improvement to my father's left side, but who knows if he will ever recover further. And if he does, what then?

I smiled at him and squeezed his hand gently, uncertain if he could even feel it properly. 'I'm so pleased.' He tried to return my smile but his lips contorted so that it was more of a grimace. 'I'm taking a few days off work. I'm going back to Oldcliffe. Can you believe it? It's been nearly eighteen years. But Sophie's remains have been found, Dad. Her brother . . . do you remember him? Daniel. He wants me to go back and help find out—'

I was interrupted by a guttural sound coming from my father's throat. He was blinking furiously and I realised he was trying to speak.

My mother rushed over, nearly up-ending my chair, forcing me to stand up. 'It's OK, Alistair, darling. You're OK.'

I felt close to tears. 'Don't worry, Dad,' I soothed, over my mother's shoulder. 'I'm only going for a few days, the hotels will be in Stuart's capable hands. You know how brilliant he is at running things.'

Dad was still continuing to make that awful sound, which echoed around the room and made the skin on the back of my neck prickle.

'I think you should go,' Mum said without looking at me. 'You're upsetting your father.'

*

But now, sitting here in this apartment by myself, I have the horrifying feeling that my dad, ever my protector, wasn't worried about the hotels. He was trying to warn me not to come back here.

The thought of the desperation in his eyes scares me and to distract myself I try to start up the Internet. Typically, there is no Wi-Fi. My heart sinks when I realise that I won't be able to go online. At least I've got 4G on my phone. I fumble in my handbag for my mobile, but I have no signal. I'm unsure whether it's down to the bad weather or the location. I throw the laptop and phone onto the sofa in frustration.

I try not to think about the fact that I've got no reception, no Internet access, that I'm completely cut off from the outside world, from London, from my old life. I find the screams of the baby downstairs a strange comfort. To know that I'm not the only one awake during this storm, unable to sleep, makes me feel more normal. Even after all these years I haven't given up hope that one day it will be my baby crying in the next room. Deep down I know it's impossible, but I can dream.

With nothing else to do I pull on my nightdress and fall into bed, my mind filled with Leon, Jason and you. The ghosts of my past. The baby is still screaming, its cries becoming shriller and shriller. When I do eventually fall asleep I dream of you, standing on the edge of the pier, one foot bare, the other trainer-clad. You're wearing a floaty, white dress that skims your ankles, which makes no sense because you had jeans on that last night. As I approach you tentatively, you turn to me and emit an ear-piercing scream so that I wake up with a start and sit bolt upright in bed, trembling all over, my nightdress soaked in sweat.

The baby in the apartment downstairs continues to wail as if its heart is breaking.

My stomach is churning the next morning and the incessant beep of a car horn does nothing to allay my aching head. I thrust the living-room curtains aside in annoyance, surprised to see Daniel's rust bucket blocking the driveway. He looks up, noticing my nose pressed against the window and gestures for me to come down.

I smooth down my hair in the mirror over the fireplace and add a bit more lipstick, before grabbing my bag and darting out of the apartment. The hallway is quiet, the baby obviously finally asleep after keeping me awake most of the night. There must be a family staying in No. 1, enjoying an out-of-season break, although it doesn't sound much of a break from what I could hear last night.

As I reach the bottom of the stairs I hear the door to the downstairs apartment click shut and I wish I'd been a few seconds earlier to catch my neighbour and introduce myself. Knowing there is a family staying in the place below mine makes me feel less alone, even if I don't know them.

I'm just about to head out the front door when I notice a brown A4 envelope on the mat. It is crumpled, slightly damp. The name on the front catches my eye.

It's been typewritten neatly across the envelope: FRANCESCA HOWE. I pick it up, puzzled. There is no stamp. Who would be writing to me here?

I rip it open, intrigued as I pull out a single sheet of paper. My eyes scan the page, horror dawning. Five words are typed in bold letters. The envelope and the page slip from my grasp and float to the floor face up so that those ominous words are still visible.

I KNOW WHAT YOU'VE DONE.

Saturday

6
Frankie

I stand in the hallway, staring down at the letter. The words swim before my eyes. How can anyone know I'm staying here? I only arrived yesterday afternoon, yet someone has gone to great pains to type this vile note up and hand-deliver it to me. It hadn't arrived when Daniel left around six last night because I came down with him and stood in the open doorway as he made a run for his car, the rain pelting the back of his dark wool coat. Had someone been out there, in the dark, in the storm, watching me? The thought sends a shiver down my spine.

The words can only mean one thing. Somebody must know. We promised never to talk of it, Soph. But someone must know what happened the night Jason died.

A sudden knock on the front door makes me jump and I scoop up the letter and envelope and shove them into my bag before answering. Daniel is standing on the doorstep in the same black coat as yesterday, his chin hidden behind the stripy scarf, exasperation in his eyes. 'In your own time, Franks,' he muffles grumpily. 'I've been sat in the car waiting for you for ages. What are you doing?'

I hesitate, debating whether I should show him the letter. But he's the only person who knows I'm staying here, isn't he? What if he returned last night to post it? Or posted it this morning then fled back to the car and pretended he'd just turned up? Although logic tells me Daniel would never do this, that he's on my side, has always been on my side, I decide to keep it to myself for now. Instead I mumble an apology and follow him across the drive to where he's parked on the road and fold myself into the passenger seat. It's bad enough that I have to face Leon again after all these years, without this added worry. My head pounds and I feel tired and overwrought.

'You know,' says Daniel as he manoeuvres his car along the rain-soaked streets to the coastal road, oblivious to my distress, 'I never really liked Leon.'

I make a concerted effort to push thoughts of the letter and Jason to the back of my mind. Daniel stares at the road ahead, his hands gripping the steering wheel so that I can see blue veins raised beneath his pale skin. 'The girls always mooned over him. I asked Sophie once why she liked him so much and she said he was deep.' He gives a snort of laughter. 'Deep my arse! That's just a euphemism for moody. Or quiet. Or weird.'

I smile at his words. 'You know what she was like. She was a bit of a dreamer. A romantic. She said Leon was like the male hero in her favourite novels, brooding and morose. A Heathcliff or a Mr Darcy.' I never really understood what you meant. I wasn't interested in reading novels, particularly the classics that you and my dad devoured. You always had your nose in a book. It used to irritate me on sleepovers when you would rather read than gossip.

You droned on about how artistic Leon was with his taste in books, not to mention his dire poetry that you found so attractive. I read one once. I'd found it on your bedside table, wedged between the pages of *Anna Karenina* or it could have been *Jane Eyre*, not that I was snooping or anything but when you were in the bathroom I couldn't resist taking a peek. It was intense, dark and a bit twisted, in my opinion. All this talk of being together until you died. It gave me the creeps.

I glance at Daniel. There is definitely nothing deep about your brother. He's always been outgoing and friendly, wearing his emotions like an advertising tabard for everyone to see.

It couldn't be your brother, could it, Sophie? He'd never write an anonymous letter; that's for cowards. Daniel's one of the bravest, most honest people I know. I remember you telling me once how, at the age of eight, he'd taken a punch in the stomach trying to protect your mum from your bully of a father. How, despite your worries that he didn't work hard at school and was directionless, he never bunked off or lied to your mum because he'd seen your dad do that too many times.

I close my eyes and pinch the top of my nose. Daniel is still talking about Leon.

'He was so intense. So possessive. They rowed the night she died. They split up. And then just a few weeks after she went missing he fucked off abroad to work. Anyway, I'm sure he'd talk to you.'

I wouldn't be so sure, I'm tempted to say, but I don't. Then a new thought strikes me: could Leon have written the letter?

My phone beeps. I rummage in the bag at my feet. It's a text from Mike. I open it and then baulk at the words. *I'm glad I know what a heartless cow you really are, Fran. Thanks for the heads-up.* The animosity emanating from my phone is such a shock I exhale sharply.

Daniel turns to me with a frown. 'Are you OK?'

'Oh, just a text from an ex-boyfriend,' I say, trying to keep my voice even as I slip the phone back in my bag. I lean against the seat, closing my eyes and massaging my temples, inwardly groaning as it comes back to me exactly what I did last night; the drunken phone call and, when there was no answer, the angry message I left on Mike's voicemail, informing him that our relationship was over, that I want him to move out of my house by the time I get back. I didn't think he'd get it, the reception was so poor last night, but by the sound of his text message he obviously did. It's true I've been wanting to end our relationship for a while, but after everything with Dad I didn't have the emotional strength to go through with it. It was selfish of me, keeping him hanging on when I could see the relationship was going nowhere. You would have advised me to end things with him months ago, Soph. Being here has given me the perfect opportunity to make that break. But, even so, to do it by voicemail, while drunk, is inexcusable.

'I finished with my boyfriend last night, by phone,' I say, my eyes still closed. 'I was drunk, it was impulsive. He hasn't taken it very well.'

'Ah,' says Daniel knowingly. But he doesn't say any more.

'It's been on the rocks for a while.' I'm annoyed at the judgemental inflection I detect in his 'Ah' and I feel the need to explain myself. I continue to massage my temples. 'But I shouldn't have done it over the phone, and while I was a bit tipsy. I didn't handle it very well.'

I open my eyes just in time to see Daniel smirking.

I sit up. 'What?'

He chuckles. 'You haven't changed, have you, Lady Frankie? Still breaking hearts wherever you go.'

'I'm not . . . I didn't mean to . . .'

'You never do,' he says wryly. I study his profile, his angular jaw, his long nose, the flop of dark hair contrasting with his pale skin. Did I break his heart all those years ago?

'Anyway, Leon doesn't know we're coming so . . .'

'What!' My head pounds. 'What do you mean, he doesn't know we're coming? I thought you'd arranged it?'

He looks shamefaced. 'I know, but I haven't seen him in years, Franks. We're not exactly mates. Don't you remember what happened?' At my puzzled expression he elaborates. 'We got into that fight, I gave him a black eye.' He sounds proud of himself.

I remember the fight. It wasn't long after you went missing but I never did get to the bottom of what it was about. Tensions were running high, especially with that detective sniffing around. Everybody was so worried about you. A few days later, some kids came forward. They were at a beach party by the Grand Pier and saw you walking along the promenade, alone. Then your trainer was found on the old pier next to a broken section of balustrade and the police assumed you'd had too much to drink, decided to walk home and fallen over the side.

'He gave you a split lip if I remember rightly.'

Daniel flashes me an 'I told you so' smile. 'Exactly. Violent tendencies.'

I shake my head, exasperated. 'How do you know he's back? You could be wrong?'

'I'm not. His brother, Lorcan, mentioned it to Sid. Apparently he came home a few days ago. And of course, I did some digging. He's staying with Lorcan on the old estate, can you believe?'

'I don't like the thought of just turning up. I mean, it's been years.' I remember the last time I saw Leon. It was the summer after you'd disappeared and we had just moved to London. Daniel and your mum had left Oldcliffe by then. A new start, they said. Away from the sad memories. I didn't blame them. They were no longer viewed as just Daniel and Anne. They had become the grief-stricken family of 'tragic Sophie Collier'. Everywhere they went they were eyed with pity or fear – after all, bad luck can be contagious.

People crossed the street to avoid them because they didn't know what to say, they were gossiped about in shops and at the local pub. I know how they felt because it was that way for me too. 'There she goes, Sophie Collier's best friend.' Don't get me wrong, Soph, it wasn't that I didn't like being synonymous with you – I loved being your best friend. It was just that Oldcliffe wasn't the same without you. And we all found that we couldn't stay in the place where you had been so alive, so vibrant. We couldn't pretend that everything was as it had been because your death had changed our world.

Leon must have felt the same because just weeks after you disappeared he upped and left. There were rumours that he'd gone travelling. I bumped into him in a bar in Soho nine months later and we'd talked about you. It was all about you, Soph, I promise. We didn't mean to sleep together; we were drunk and morose, reminiscing about the past. He couldn't leave my bed fast enough the next morning. He left me a note propped up on my bedside table, saying it had been a mistake and that he was sorry. I haven't seen him since.

I'm sorry, Soph. It felt like the ultimate betrayal.

Daniel doesn't understand anything. Especially about Leon. And how am I going to explain it all to him without it sounding so . . . *sordid*. So wrong.

I stare out the window to avoid talking to him. The old pier is shrouded in fog so that just a faint outline is visible. The sea in the bay is greyer than further down the coast. The Victorian houses slowly disappear to be replaced by more modern, semi-detached homes. And then there it is, the Birds Estate. We turn into Starling Way with the row of shops on the corner – a hairdresser's, a pet shop and a small Co-op in an ugly concrete grey block, a group of youths hanging around the dustbins. It's only their clothes that differentiate them from the youths of our past.

I frown. The estate is even worse than I remember. Or maybe it's just degenerated even further over the years. Despite everything, I wanted better for Leon. A sudden thought hits me. 'You don't live here any more, do you, Dan?'

He turns to me, an expression of scorn written all over his face. 'No, I don't actually. But even if I did, so what? Don't be a snob, Frankie.'

His words make my cheeks grow hot. Is that what I'm being? A snob?

Daniel makes a left turn into Dove Way. I remember it well, only a few streets from where you grew up.

He pulls up outside No. 59, the end house in a terrace of three. Next to the garage is a rusty green Renault on bricks. I notice the missing wheels. In our day it was a clapped-out Ford Cortina. How you hated it.

'Let's just hope Leon's still staying here,' he says. He goes to open the door and, in a panic, I swing my arm out to stop him, grabbing the sleeve of his coat.

'Daniel . . . there's something you should know . . .'

He pauses, his fingers on the door handle. 'What is it, Franks?' His voice is gentle and I long to tell him everything in that moment but I can't bear shattering his illusion of me when he hears the truth. He notices me hesitating and takes his hand away from the door. 'You know you can tell me anything, don't you? I'd understand.'

I bite my lip. I'm not ready to tell him yet and I just have to hope that Leon keeps quiet.

'Frankie?'

'It doesn't matter, it can wait.' I notice a flash of disappointment cross his face before he wordlessly climbs out of the Astra. I have no choice but to get out of the car as well, despite every instinct screaming at me to stay where I am.

I stand on the pavement in front of the house. A fine rain has started to fall. The red paint is flaking off the garage, revealing a tin colour underneath. It's all much greyer, bleaker, smaller than in my memories, as though everything around me has shrunk.

The estate has been built so that you have to walk past the garages and through the rear gardens to reach the houses. I follow Daniel through a large wooden gate, feeling like I'm trespassing as I enter the garden tentatively, that I'm being watched. A child's swing has been left to rust in the overgrown grass along with a discarded bicycle wheel. A thick Leylandii hedge separates the garden from its neighbour on one side and a fence runs along the road on the other. A low wall divides the postage stamp of a patio from the wild grass. I shadow Daniel down the concrete pathway and hover behind him as he raps his knuckles on the glass of the back door. I realise I'm holding my breath.

I count. One, two, three, four . . . The door swings open.

And he's standing there. His hair is still dark and wavy, threaded with a few grey streaks, his skin tanned. Would you still fancy him if you could see him now? I think you probably would.

For years, living in London, I dated bankers and lawyers, doctors and businessmen, glossy metrosexual men. Until Mike came along. I liked him because he exuded that same raw sex appeal as Leon and Daniel. It comes naturally to them, they don't have to spend hours in the bathroom waxing and shaving, pruning and gelling.

He fills the door-frame with his height, assessing Daniel with those familiar piercing blue eyes. 'What do you want?' he says.

'To talk.'

Leon turns to me and there is a moment's silence as we each take in the subtle, and not so subtle, changes that have taken place in the intervening years. And then, with a slight jolt, he comes to. 'Frankie. I heard you were back.'

So he already knew. My stomach twists. Could the letter be from him? You would never have told him about what we did, would you, Soph?

'Hello, Leon.' I try to smile but it's as if my muscles are frozen and it takes all my efforts to force my lips to curl upwards.

'You'd better come in,' he says. And he steps aside to allow us over the threshold.

'How long have you been back?' I say as the three of us hover in the kitchen. It's old-fashioned, with wooden farmhouse-style units and magnolia-woodchip walls. There is a child's painting of a cat stuck to the fridge with a Stena Line Ferries magnet. The kitchen smells of damp dishcloths and bleach.

He sticks the kettle on. 'A few days, that's all. I'm not staying long. Lorcan and Steph have barely got the room.' He grimaces at us. 'Five kids and one grandchild.'

I want to ask him why he's back here, what he's been up to since I last saw him, but I can't bring myself to form the words.

As if reading my mind, Daniel speaks for me. 'What are you doing back, anyway?' His voice is gruff, begrudging.

Leon shrugs. 'My contract came to an end. So I thought I'd come home, regroup, and see what the future holds.' Regroup. The Leon of my past would never have used that word. It's too corporate, too businesslike. There is something rehearsed about his words, as though he knew we would be coming. 'Go through, I'll bring in the tea.' He waves us towards the door that leads into a hallway. I pause, hoping to talk to him alone, but he turns his back to me and I have no choice but to follow Daniel into the living room. It's a lounge-diner, much like the one in your old house, with a stone fireplace and a widescreen television attached to the wall above it. The floral curtains that I remember from the 1990s have been replaced by wooden Venetian blinds.

I need to tell Daniel about me and Leon. What if Leon blurts it out? Would Daniel think it was strange that I'd never told him? Would he stop trusting me? Yes, he might see me differently if he knew, but he would think I'm a liar if he found out from Leon. 'Daniel,' I say in hushed tones as we sit on a beige sofa, 'there's something you should know – about me and Leon.'

He glances at me and I notice for the first time the purple smudges around his grey eyes. 'What is it, Franks?'

I open my mouth to speak but Leon walks into the room with a tea tray.

'Help yourself to milk and sugar,' he says, indicating the tray with a wave of his hand. Then he reclines on the chair opposite us, crossing an ankle over his knee. It's a gesture I remember well, curiously delicate. I help myself to milk and sip my tea.

'Sophie's remains have been found,' says Daniel without preamble. I didn't expect him to be so blunt.

Leon leans forward, grasping a mug. I notice his hands are lined and calloused. You used to say he had artistic hands, smooth and fine-boned. 'Her *remains*?' he says. 'What do you mean?'

Again, he sounds rehearsed, as if he already knew. This is a small town; I'm sure the news would have spread like a forest fire. After all, it's on the front of the local newspaper. So, why the pretence?

Daniel rolls his eyes. 'What do you think I mean? She's dead, for fuck's sake, Leon.'

Leon stares from Daniel to me, his face white, his eyes tired. The atmosphere in the room is heavy with unsaid words, like the swell of a cloud before it rains. He runs a hand over his face. The only sound to be heard is the ticking of a clock on the mantelpiece. He places his head in his hands and for a horrible moment I think he's going to break down and lose control. I move forward to replace my cup on the tea tray and then crouch in front of him. I put my hand on his knee.

'You must have suspected she was dead?'

He lifts his head, his eyes fixed on mine. His face is unreadable. 'I never gave up hope.' A shadow passes across his face, and he shrugs my hand away from his knee, as though he's offended by my touch.

As I sit back down I catch Daniel's eye. He looks furious.

'This is all very touching,' he says sarcastically, 'but, Leon, I need you to tell me everything that happened that night.'

'Why? Why are you going through all this again?'

'I think she was murdered.'

'And the police?'

'They've always assumed she fell into the sea and drowned,' I pipe up. 'The pier was unsafe. It should have been boarded up like it is now.'

Leon clears his throat, ignoring Daniel but looking at me. 'And maybe she did just fall in.'

Daniel scoffs. 'You'd like us to believe that, wouldn't you?'

Leon stands up, his fists clenched by his sides. 'What's that supposed to mean? If you've got something to say, Danny Boy, then say it!'

Daniel stands up so that they are facing each other over the coffee table. Their little stand-off is almost theatrical.

'Give it a rest,' I snap. Under any other circumstances it would be funny, the way they're so ready to square up to each other. Does Daniel really believe that Leon did something to hurt you all those years ago? Or does it run deeper than that? Does Daniel's hatred of Leon stem from jealousy? Does he think I'm going to take one look at Leon and run off with him into the sunset like in some corny film? Just because you fancied him, Soph, doesn't mean everyone did.

Daniel has the good grace to look ashamed as he slumps back onto the sofa. He's still holding his tea cup. It has a picture of Eeyore on the front. The ridiculousness of it makes me want to giggle. Instead I throw Leon a warning look and he also returns to his seat.

'Please, Leon,' I say, 'just tell us what happened and then we'll go.'

'I told him everything at the time. And the police,' he replies sulkily.

'But there's never been an inquiry. I know it was a long time ago. We're just trying to work out what happened to her. Why did she go to the pier? Was she meeting someone? And if so, who? Don't you care at all?' says Daniel.

Leon sighs. 'Of course I care, but I don't know anything. I thought we were in love until . . .' He fixes me with a hard stare and I squirm. I know what that stare means. It means he knows, doesn't he, Soph. He found out about what we did to Jason and he couldn't forgive you.

'Until?' prompts Daniel.

'Until a huge argument finished things between us.'

'What did you argue about?' urges Daniel.

Leon shrugs, his eyes still on me, dark curls falling into his face. 'I think you know, don't you, Frankie?'

7
Sophie

Saturday, 5 July 1997

I've found out something awful. About Leon. Something I wish I didn't know.

Everything had been going so well. Last night we met as arranged, at 7 p.m. by the old pier. We sat on the beach and talked about music, our upbringings, our hopes and dreams, our desire to one day leave Oldcliffe behind. As we sat with our six-pack of cider he asked about my dad. Even though I knew this question would come up eventually, I still felt the sudden pain of it strike me under the ribs; the horror as I remembered him towering over my mum, yelling and punching, the relief as he slammed out of the house, the fear as Daniel and I watched the blood oozing from my mum's swollen face and onto the mushroom-coloured carpet. I'd been six and Daniel eight. It was one beating too many for my mother. We fled that night, packing up all our meagre belongings and driving the 300-odd miles from Durham until we reached the women's refuge just out of town. We changed our surname to Collier (Christopher Reeve's surname in *Somewhere in Time*,

Mum's favourite film) and as far as we're aware my dad never tried to find us.

I could sense Leon's eyes probing me, waiting for an answer. 'My parents split up when I was really young, I haven't seen him since,' I said. He must have sensed I didn't want to talk about it because he squeezed my hand gently, as though he understood and no other words were needed. We walked onto the old pier after that, and kissed as the sun made its descent into the sea. I haven't felt as close to a guy in years. It felt so right.

And now it feels so wrong after what Frankie told me today.

After work I went to see her. I know it's ridiculous, but I was nervous about telling her about me and Leon. We arranged to meet at her hotel after my shift at the kiosk. It was another hot day; the pensioners and tourists were out in force, so I was running late. By the time I ambled over to the hotel it was getting on for 4 p.m.

The Grand View Hotel would have been elegant once, but someone, probably around the 1950s, had the bright idea of painting it the sickly pink of a Wham bar so that it stood out amongst the many other hotels that lined the main road for all the wrong reasons.

Frankie's dad, Alistair, answered the door. I haven't seen him in three years but I've always been fond of him. When I was a kid he went to great pains to welcome me into their home. I think it was mainly because Frankie is an only child and he wanted her to have company, and being without a dad myself, I looked up to him. He was – is – attractive, clever, with a dry wit and good dress sense (for a dad!). I have to admit to having a bit of a crush on him when I was a teenager.

'Sophie Rose Collier!' he exclaimed when he saw me. 'The wanderer returns. And all grown up.'

The last time he'd seen me I'd been a gawky, shy eighteen-year-old, just about to leave for university, with glasses and knobbly knees. He ushered me into the hallway, all the while asking me questions about university, what my course was like, which books I'd read for my English degree, what mark I got, what my future plans were. And it reminded me how much interest he always took in my studies.

Just being in the hotel again with Alistair took me right back to my childhood. It hasn't changed a bit: the red carpet with the swirly gold pattern still covers the hall, stairs and landing; the cream walls, the heavy wooden furniture in the lounge-bar area, the huge glass chandeliers hanging from the high ceilings, the smell of red wine and beeswax.

Alistair sat me in a chair by the window in the lounge, so I had a view of the beach beyond, crammed with bodies. The net curtains floated in the open window, which let in the cacophony (my new word for today!) of voices, traffic and faint music from the arcades. The lounge was empty; the guests must all have been out on the beach, or mooching around the high street. Even though I wanted to stay there talking to him, part of me was desperate to speak to Frankie, knowing I had to tell her something she'd be unhappy about.

'Too early for a glass of wine?' he asked to my surprise, walking over to the curved bar at the other end of the room. Despite being twenty-one, my mum never offers me alcohol, being a teetotaller herself. That's the thing about Alistair, he always treats me as a grown-up and with respect. Even when I was a kid he listened to my opinions as if they meant something. It wasn't as if my mum didn't listen to me – my mum is great – but she's always worked so hard. She's never had the luxury of time, bringing two kids up on her own.

I opened my mouth to answer when Frankie came swanning into the room, diverting his attention. As usual she looked stunning, in a short floral sundress that skimmed her thighs, her thick hair braided down her back, her skin already tanned thanks to her Italian heritage (her mum's from Naples). I felt pale and lanky in comparison. Alistair used to refer to me as the English Rose and Frankie the Dusky Beauty. I always wanted to be the Dusky Beauty.

I stood up to greet her. She bounded over to me, her eyes wide with excitement, and I wondered what she was dying to tell me, because she looked like she could hardly contain herself. I didn't want to be the one to dampen her mood.

'I'll leave you girls to it,' he said, but I noticed that he poured a glass of wine for himself. As he headed out the door he turned, surveying me as he lounged against the door-frame. Oh yes, Alistair definitely liked to lounge!

'You don't fancy a job, do you, Sophie? We could do with an extra pair of hands. The schools will be breaking up soon and this place is booked up solidly for the next two months.'

My heart fluttered with excitement. I knew how much Frankie got paid. 'What would I need to do?'

He waved a hand casually, 'Oh, making beds, putting clean cups on the tea trays, a bit of hoovering, that kind of thing.'

Frankie flung her arms around me. 'We can work together, it will be so much fun, Soph!'

Alistair flashed her an indulgent smile and I felt envious of their relationship in that moment, that she had a dad who, with a click of his fingers, could make things happen. Could brighten his daughter's day.

'Great. Can you start tomorrow?'

I thought of the kiosk, of my lecherous boss, Stan, all big stomach and bulbous nose, leering at me – and all the young women of Oldcliffe – over the haddock, and I eagerly agreed.

With a parting grin Alistair disappeared and Frankie looped her arm through mine as we headed to the beach. I was only half listening as she chatted away about how Jez was yet to phone her, because I was thinking of Leon and how I should broach the subject with Frankie.

'And look what my dad bought me,' she said, stopping suddenly in the street and causing a woman with a pushchair behind her to tut angrily. Frankie didn't even notice. She was too busy rummaging in her straw beach bag. She pulled out a Nokia phone and I felt a twinge of jealousy. 'A mobile phone! I've got my own phone at last. I've been begging him for ages. Aren't I lucky?' She handed the phone to me and I examined it like it was a species from another planet. 'It's pay as you go. Dad's put a tenner on it for me, to get me started.'

I think it's interesting how she always refers to her dad as the one who buys her things, rather than her parents together, as though it doesn't mean anything that her mother frantically runs around the place, cleaning, tidying and cooking. As much as I like and admire Alistair, he's the one usually to be found standing around chatting to customers, glass of something alcoholic in his hand, while his wife slaves away in the kitchen. He often wears a perplexed expression on his face, as though he's wandered into his own hotel by accident and is slightly bemused by the gatherings of people that he finds there, but able to effortlessly socialise and converse with them nonetheless. It's almost as though he's constantly thinking that his life hasn't turned out in quite the way he'd hoped. Frankie admitted to me once that it was her maternal grandparents who owned the hotel, and when they retired to Italy they passed it on to her mum, their only child. Alistair was an English lecturer when they met. I wonder if he regrets giving it up to run a hotel, despite the obvious rewards.

He knew how much I loved reading as a kid. Frankie wasn't so interested so he would pass me all his classics, eagerly pressing them into my hands. I still have his copies of *1984* and *Great Expectations* on my bookshelf. It was a highlight of my week, receiving a novel from Alistair, and I'd pore over each one carefully, trying to second guess the discussions we would have once I'd read it. I've always thought it a shame that he gave up lecturing.

I handed her back the phone. 'It looks great, but who else do you know with a mobile phone? Who are you going to call on it?'

'Not sure, but people can phone me from their home phones, can't they?'

'Don't ask me, I haven't got a clue how they work,' I laughed. She dropped the phone back in her bag and linked her arm through mine again as we continued to walk. We reached the sea wall and sat overlooking the beach. The town felt loud to me; the shrieks of children paddling in the water, the screeching of seagulls swarming around for food, the grating music of the arcades behind us, the whoosh of the waves lapping at the shore, the indecipherable chatter, the tinkling tune from the big wheel further up the beach, erected especially for the summer. It was enough to give anyone a headache. I sometimes longed for the peaceful, green fields of Warwickshire. It made me all the more determined to get out of this place permanently.

'Do you like my new nail varnish?' asked Frankie. She had taken off her flip-flops and was stretching her toes, which were painted a deep lilac. 'It's called Dolly Mixture. It's cool, isn't it?'

I knew I had to tell her there and then.

'I got off with Leon last night,' I blurted. Next to me I felt her stiffen – even her toes seemed to freeze mid-stretch.

She turned to me, her cat's eyes narrowed, her nostrils flared. 'You got off with Leon? When? How?'

So I explained. About the note, about our meeting up at the old pier. 'He lives two streets away from me too, isn't that amazing?'

She pulled a face. 'Not really. This is a small town.'

'Well, yes, I know . . . but –'

'You don't know what he's like,' she interrupted, her voice cold. She twisted a strand of hair around her finger and pulled hard. It's a habit that I'd forgotten about. At school she used to do it when she was stressed.

Her instant dismissiveness grated. 'I think I do,' I replied.

'Why? Because you spent a few hours with him last night?'

Yes, actually, I wanted to say but didn't. 'He seems like a good bloke,' I said instead.

'Have you shagged him?'

I bristled. 'That's none of your business.'

Of course I haven't shagged him – what, on the first date? – but I didn't want to tell her that.

Her eyes widened. 'We used to tell each other everything.' Her voice was reedy, petulant. 'Remember when you lost your virginity to James Forrester? I was the first person you told.'

I opened my mouth to explain that three years had passed since we'd last confided in each other about our sex lives, that I was no longer the geeky, bespectacled girl with braces and bad hair who used to hang on her every word, that I was my own person now, that I had stepped out of her shadow, moved away to university, made a life for myself without her help. But she looked so down that I closed it again. And was I lying to myself? All through that last year of sixth form and the three years at university it felt like a part of me was missing. I hate to admit it, but having Frankie by my side makes me feel more confident, as though I can do anything. I know that if she'd been at uni with me I would have had much more fun, taken risks that I didn't dare to without her there.

'I wanted to tell you –'

'So, you don't care about what happened to me?'

'But what did happen to you?' My voice was high with exasperation. 'It's not like he assaulted you, is it? He fancied you, you turned him down, he was a bit persistent. So what?' I hate confrontation, especially with Frankie.

'So what?' she said in a pale imitation of my voice. She swivelled her body so that she was facing the boulevard and jumped down off the wall, thrusting her feet back into her flip-flops. She hoisted the bag further up her arm so that it sat in the crook of her elbow. 'Well, if you think that's OK then fine. But remember, I've warned you about him.'

I turned to face her, swinging my legs over the wall. 'Thanks, but I'm a big girl. I can look after myself,' I said, trying to keep my voice even. Frankie and I have had enough rows in our lives, I've known her since we were seven after all, but since meeting up again we've been on our best behaviour, like lovers in the first flush of a relationship.

She paused, her eyes scrutinising my face as though wondering if she should be honest with me. She frowned. 'Are you going to go out with him?'

I shrugged. 'I really like him, Franks. And he likes me too.'

'Then there is something that you should know. About him,' she said.

I sighed, expecting more dramatic revelations about the way he chased her. 'And what's that?' I folded my arms across my chest as though to protect myself from her words. But I wasn't prepared for what she said next.

'He's Jason's cousin.'

8

Frankie

Daniel is quiet on the drive home. It's still spitting with rain, the sky a white, thick duvet of continuous cloud that has swallowed up the rear end of the old pier.

He pulls up outside the villa, the engine still purring, and stares straight ahead. The house is in darkness, the thick bushes that separate it from its neighbours prickly and black.

In the far distance I notice a woman in a long raincoat walking towards us, holding an umbrella over her head. I turn to Daniel. His expression is unusually dark and I mentally replay the conversation at Leon's house. Did I say or do something wrong? And what had Leon meant when he said he thinks I know why you split up? Was he alluding to Jason? Did you tell him, Soph?

I can understand if you did. Under Leon's electric gaze it felt as though the oxygen was being sucked from the room. You once said he had the type of eyes that could see into your very soul and in that moment I knew exactly what you meant.

Who knows what I would have said if my phone hadn't rung when it did. I had pulled it from my bag with relief, and when Stuart's name flashed up on screen I muttered my excuses, telling them it was an important work call, and hurried from the house.

I stood in the garden, my feet freezing in my impractical boots. Stuart was all apologies for disturbing me on the weekend but an important order had been messed up which could potentially put the new hotel opening back weeks. I talked him through his options, trying to remain calm despite Leon and Daniel inside the house waiting for me to return. It felt strange taking a work call while in Oldcliffe, as if my two separate worlds were merging, and it unsettled me. I had to push you, Daniel and Leon from my mind and concentrate on what Stuart was telling me as we brainstormed through our options. I don't know how long I was on the phone for, but eventually I sensed someone behind me. I turned to see Daniel toeing the edge of the grass with his boot and doing his best to look as though he wasn't listening to my conversation. 'I'll call you back later,' I told Stuart. 'But remember to call the supplier. Plead ignorance if you must. And put Paul on a warning. This isn't the first mistake he's made.' I dropped the phone into my bag, Daniel's presence pulling me away from my familiar corporate world and back into Oldcliffe.

'Come on, let's get out of here,' he said, his face grave as he strode up the garden path, leaving me to jog after him to keep up.

He hasn't said a word to me since.

'Is everything OK?' I ask him now, my voice sounding too loud in the silence of the car.

'What did he mean?' Daniel asks. 'Leon. When he said you knew why he finished with my sister?'

He's still not looking at me and I know I have to be honest with him.

Except how can I? Leon might not have been alluding to Jason at all. He might have been talking about something else entirely.

'Why don't we go somewhere and get some lunch?' I say. 'And talk?'

He finally turns to look at me and I can see that he's softening. 'I don't know, Franks . . . I'm supposed to pop into the newsroom at some point today . . . and . . .'

'Oh, come on. We need to eat.'

'Really? Well, in that case how can I say no?' He laughs, but it sounds forced.

'What's bothering you, Dan?'

His shoulders sag so that he appears deflated. 'I don't know, Franks. I'm just worried that all this –' he throws his arms wide '– is for nothing. That I'll never find out what happened to my sister.'

'Daniel . . .' I pause. 'We might never know what happened to Sophie,' I say gently. I reach out and touch his arm.

His eyes cloud over and he shrugs my hand away. 'No, I can't bear that thought. I need to know, Frankie.' His expression is pained and I suddenly have the urge to kiss away his grief.

A thought occurs to me. 'What happened to your mum?' I have this mental picture of Anne in my mind, although over time it has become hazier, like a photograph that has faded with age. I'm remembering a woman in a blue nurse's outfit, with premature lines on her face and dyed blonde hair that was always a little too harsh for her skin tone. A hard worker, a single mother, a bereaved parent.

'She's OK, considering. After Sophie went missing she moved back to Ireland to live with her sister. On the farm. Then she met Tim. He's a good guy. They're married now. I visit, but she's not interested in ever coming back here. Anyway, she believes that it was a tragic accident and that Sophie slipped and fell. Just like the police do.' He sounds sad, jaded.

'Maybe that is the truth,' I say quietly. 'Maybe it was just a tragic accident.'

'There was more to it.'

'How do you know?'

'Because I know – *knew* – my sister, Frankie. We were close, I *knew* her. And she wasn't herself before she died, something was bothering her. Something was wrong. And I wish –' he shakes his head sadly '– I wish that I had paid more attention at the time. But I didn't, I was too busy with my own life. But looking back now, with hindsight, there was definitely something wrong.'

'Hindsight is a wonderful thing. But you were a kid yourself, just twenty-three. And what about me? I was her best friend, and I didn't know there was anything wrong.'

Which isn't strictly true.

He sighs in answer. 'What did Leon mean? What did they argue about?' he asks again.

I fidget in my seat. I can't reveal the truth. But I need to tell him something. 'I warned Sophie about Leon. I told her he was no good . . .' I hesitate, feeling sick.

'Why?' His eyes are hard.

'Because . . . because he came on to me, and when I turned him down he harassed me, stalked me even. He was pretty bloody scary, Dan.'

His face darkens.

'There's more.' I have to force the words out, I feel so ashamed.

'I slept with him. Nearly a year after Sophie went missing. It was just the once, we bumped into each other. In London. We bonded, over her. I was drunk and . . .'

'He took advantage.'

I sigh. 'I don't know. We took advantage of each other, I guess.'

Daniel turns away from me again. We both watch as the woman with the umbrella gets nearer. She has wiry grey hair and glasses. She marches in front of the car and heads towards Beaufort Villas. She's struggling with the umbrella, as though she's having a game of tug of war with an invisible person. She pauses outside the front door and fumbles in her bag. Could she be the anonymous letter-writer? She retrieves a key and opens the front door. She must be one of the guests downstairs. Maybe she's the grandmother of the baby I heard screaming last night. Her eyes flick towards us as she shakes out her umbrella and discards it on the step. Then she closes the door. A few minutes later the light in the downstairs apartment comes on.

'Let's go to the pub,' I say. 'We can talk about the next stage of the plan. I've only got a few days, remember? I can't stay any longer than that.'

He smiles and it transforms his face so that he's the cheeky, happy Daniel of my memories. 'OK, you've persuaded me like always, Lady Frankie.'

He pushes the gearstick into first and I re-fasten my seat belt, relieved that I get to kill a few more hours before having to return to the apartment. As Daniel turns the car, something at the bay window of my apartment catches my eye. I look up, startled. A face is pressed to the glass, gazing down at us. My blood runs cold. Is it you? I crane my neck to get a better view but it's too late, Daniel is already heading away from the house, to the coastal road below.

The Seagull has hardly changed in twenty years. The old-fashioned paisley wallpaper, the ruddy-faced old men nursing pints at the bar, each with a malodorous dog in tow, the smell of chips and vinegar with the faint undercurrent of wet fur hanging in the air – all is exactly as I remember. Even the fake birds hanging from the ceiling and the stuffed seagull on the windowsill are still in residence. It's like stepping into a time capsule.

The pub is on the edge of the town, overlooking the stormy seas and the strip of beach, which narrows the further you go along the coast so that by the time you reach the old pier it's disappeared. A middle-aged man sits alone at the table in the corner reading a tabloid and drinking a pint. His dark hair is thinner, his stomach has expanded but I recognise him straight away. It's Leon's brother, Lorcan.

Daniel nods greetings to the men at the bar and the woman serving them pints. She's buxom, older than me, mousy hair springing out from her parting in corkscrews. I hover behind him, hoping that I'm not recognised by Lorcan.

'Awright, Daniel, my love,' the woman sing-songs in a strong West Country accent. 'Haven't seen you in a while. The paper keeping you busy, is it?'

Daniel grins. 'You know what it's like, Helen. All work and no play.'

She cackles and then notices me for the first time. Our eyes meet and with a thud of recognition I realise who she is.

Helen Turner. Your friend from the estate.

Her jolly face falls. 'Frankie? Well, well, well,' she tuts and shakes her head disbelievingly, 'so the rumours about you being back are true.'

I know I shouldn't be surprised that gossip about my return is already rippling through Oldcliffe like a Mexican wave, but I am. I'd forgotten what it's like living in a small town. And then it hits me, and I suddenly feel too hot in the stuffy pub. Anyone from my past who still lives here could have sent me that letter. They're obviously all aware that I'm back.

Helen glowers at me over the pint glass that she's cleaning, reminding me of how much she disliked me at school. I always suspected her animosity was because she wanted to be your best friend and was jealous of me. She must have been overjoyed when I left the sixth form to go to boarding school. I remember how grumpy she seemed when I bumped into you again in that bar, and like before, we became inseparable. I know you felt sorry for her so we let her tag along when we went to The Basement on a Saturday night, but for the most part Helen was a hanger-on, a bit part in your life.

She was never particularly attractive but the years haven't been kind to her; the sea air has taken a toll on her once-smooth skin, enlarging her pores and reddening her nose. 'How are you, Helen?' I say, my accent-less voice suddenly conspicuous in this backwater pub.

'Aw, don't you talk posh,' she sniggers, the men at the bar joining in with a chorus of guffaws. 'And look at you in all your finery.' I feel overdressed in my black trousers, red wool coat and silk scarf. 'What are you doing back 'ere then?'

To my annoyance I feel my cheeks flame. 'I, um, well . . .'

'Spit it out, love,' says one of the men, the short, squat one with a bald head and glasses. He looks like a character from that game we used to play when we were kids, Guess Who?

'She's come to see me,' Daniel interjects.

Helen's face darkens. 'Really? I didn't know you two kept in touch.' She shrugs as if answering her own question. 'Oh well, nothing as strange as folk, I suppose. Why don't you sit yourselves down over there and I'll bring your drinks over. What can I get you, Frankie?'

'A white wine please,' I say. 'Just a house white will be fine,' I add, before she has the chance to make any cutting remarks or ask if I'd prefer champagne.

'And I'll have a pint, thanks, Helen.' Daniel steers me by the elbow away from the bar, whispering in my ear, 'She might be good for information. She was quite friendly with Sophie, wasn't she?'

'Not really,' I say stiffly, still irritated by Helen's behaviour, her put-down about my accent and clothes, her inverted snobbery.

We have no choice but to walk past Lorcan's table and he glances up, our eyes meeting. He puts down his newspaper and wipes his mouth with the back of his hand. 'I thought it was you,' he says, his loud voice making Daniel stop and turn back. 'Frankie Howe.'

It's Francesca Bloom, I want to shout; then I imagine the caustic response from Helen and the men at the bar, and the words die in my throat. I look at him sitting there in a pair of paint-splattered overalls. Despite being Leon's brother, and Jason's cousin, he doesn't share their good looks. Instead, it's as if all the worst parts of his parents were handed down to him while Leon got the best. He was vaguely attractive once, I suppose, in his mid-twenties. And he had that cocky Irish charm that many women seem to fall for. But his eyes, although as strikingly blue as Leon's, are too close together, his nose too hooked, his chin too big to be considered handsome.

And then a memory hits me. Of us at The Basement, of him pinching your bottom, of you pushing him away good-naturedly. Or was it good-naturedly? Am I remembering it wrong? We were drunk, it was eighteen years ago, but now my memory of your face is morphing into something else, your teasing expression becoming serious, your laughing eyes panicked. And then Leon coming over and pulling him away, punches thrown, Lorcan slinking off into the smoke-filled crowd.

Lorcan fancied you. I can't believe I'd forgotten that. He fancied you and he made a move on you, the girlfriend of his brother.

'Are you OK, Franks?' Daniel's concerned voice cuts into my thoughts. Lorcan is staring at me, a quizzical smile playing on his lips.

'I heard you were back,' he says, flashing a missing tooth.

'Leon told you?'

But he just smirks and taps the side of his nose. 'It's a small town. Word gets around.' Don't I know it. He folds his newspaper up and wedges it under his arm. 'Well, I best be off. Can't stand around all day gassing to the likes of you. I've got work to do, houses to paint.' And then he gets up and I'm startled at his height – I'd forgotten how tall he is. He's taller than Daniel, and broad, strong-looking.

I step aside so that he can get past and we watch as he lumbers out of the pub.

'I don't envy the person whose house he's painting,' says Daniel dryly, staring after him. 'He's half cut.'

I laugh, relieved that he's left. We sit at his vacated table and Helen brings the drinks over and takes our food order. When she's gone I lean towards Daniel and murmur, 'I've remembered something, about Lorcan.'

Daniel takes a swig of his beer. 'God, I needed that. What have you remembered?'

'He fancied Sophie. He tried it on with her once, at The Basement. He was pissed. Leon punched him.'

'Wasn't he married back then?'

'Yes, but that didn't stop him. I remember Leon telling me his brother was a player.'

He assesses me over his pint glass. 'What are you saying? That you think Lorcan had something to do with Sophie's death?'

'I don't know. Look, you said yourself – she was scared of someone. Could it have been him?'

A shadow passes over his face. 'Maybe he was obsessed with her, and followed her out of The Basement. Was he there that night?'

I probe my memory. 'I don't know . . . I can't remember. I always thought . . .'

'What?'

'I don't know, that she was meeting someone at the pier. Someone who wasn't at The Basement.' He frowns so I add, 'Why did she leave the club to go there without telling us? It's odd, don't you think?'

'Yes I do think,' he says, the exasperation evident in his voice. 'That's why I've started this whole bloody thing, Franks. It was out of character for Sophie to go off on her own like that.'

He takes another sip of his pint. We fall silent, each wrapped up in our own thoughts. Helen ambles over with our jacket potatoes. I notice that she places mine in front of me with more force than she does with Daniel's so that some of the side salad slips off my plate and onto the table. I pick it up and return it to my plate pointedly, although Helen seems not to notice as she moves away.

'You know,' Daniel says through a mouthful of food, indicating Helen with his head, 'we need to talk to her.' Helen's humming to herself while wiping down tables. 'She was at The Basement that last night. I know because Sid got off with her.'

'Sid?'

'Don't you remember? Big bloke, a few years older than me. He was in our band. Shite singer. Anyway, she's married to him now. They own this pub.'

'I remember him. Who could forget his singing?' I prod my potato with my fork. 'I'm just surprised she got off with him that night, let alone married him.' Not only was he tone deaf but we always said he had a face only his mother could love.

'Oh, he's all right. Anyway, Helen might remember something useful. It's worth a try.'

Was it possible that Helen knew more about what was going on in your life than I did?

'It's so frustrating,' says Daniel in a loud whisper as we leave the pub.

It has started to rain again. The sea is fierce, the waves

crashing against the slimy, seaweed-covered rocks. He strides ahead of me to his Astra and I trot after him in my heeled boots. He stops when he gets to the car. 'Why do I get the sense that people know more than they are letting on?' He has to shout to be heard over the wind and rain. 'Leon, Lorcan, even Helen. I feel that they're hiding something from me.' I sense his frustration coming off him like steam, yet why do I get the feeling he's angry at me? It's not my fault Helen wouldn't talk to us.

When we asked Helen about that night she insisted she couldn't remember anything, then her face seemed to close in on itself and I knew we'd get nothing more from her today. But there was something in her expression, in the way she fidgeted and avoided eye contact with me, that made me think she knew more than she was letting on. I never trusted her, she bullied me at school and it doesn't seem that she's changed.

'Try not to get paranoid,' I tell him. 'It was a long time ago.' How can I explain to him that for some people you are just the girl who went missing years ago? To us, you mean a whole lot more.

'I think we should pay Lorcan a visit tomorrow. I want to find out more about him.'

I blanch. 'Daniel, tomorrow's Sunday. Lorcan will be with his family . . .'

'Somebody's robbed me of my family. And it could be him. I need to know.'

He indicates for me to get in the car but I shake my head. 'I'm going to walk, I fancy some fresh air,' I say. It's not even three o'clock yet, it's too early to go back.

'Are you mad? It's pissing down and it's already getting dark.'

How can I tell him that I'd rather walk miles in the rain than go back to that lonely apartment? He'd think I was ungrateful. It's a nice place; it's just too remote for my liking, not to mention its sinister view.

'I'll be fine,' I insist.

'I'll ring you later,' he says as he gets into the driver's seat. He slams the door and winds down his window. He frowns, his face and hair wet from the rain. 'Are you sure you're going to be OK?'

'I'm a big girl, Daniel,' I laugh, remembering you saying exactly the same to me once when I expressed my concern over Leon. If only you had listened to me.

He smiles warmly, his eyes twinkling. 'You've always been stubborn, Lady Frankie,' he laughs and my heart contracts. What I'd really like is for him to come back to the apartment to keep me company, but I feel too shy to suggest it. He's already said he's not married but that doesn't mean he's single. That ring on his finger suggests to me that there is someone special in his life. An image of him kissing me, undressing me, flashes in my mind and I shake my head trying to dispel it, feeling guilty for having these thoughts about your brother.

'I'll pick you up in the morning, about ten thirty,' he calls out as he pulls away from the kerb.

The streets are deserted, the air redolent with the smell of fresh rain and seaweed. The taunting cackle of seagulls circling overhead makes me flinch. I'd forgotten how much I hated those blasted things; vermin of the sea, as my dad used to say. An image of him from yesterday, prostrate in his hospital bed, that awful guttural noise emanating from his throat, pops into my head. I can't shake the feeling that he was trying to tell me something.

As I walk along the pavement I have to keep tussling with my umbrella to prevent it turning inside out. In the end I give up and shove the wet umbrella in my bag, letting the rain brush my face and drench my hair. There is a strange kind of freedom in it, I think as I breathe in deeply and then exhale, allowing all the stress of the last few months to dissipate into the rain.

When did life become so complicated?

I stop outside the Grand View, our old hotel. You wouldn't recognise it now – I hardly do. Gone are the lace curtains that I remember from my childhood, replaced by white wooden shutters. The soft blue of the building is a vast improvement on the bright pink. Still, if I squint I can almost see my dad standing proudly beside the front door, surveying the street, nodding to passers-by, relaxed in chinos and a linen shirt, young and handsome. *Oh, Dad.* I hoist my bag over my shoulder and quickly walk on, past the neighbouring hotels and guest houses until I reach the bright, flashing lights of the amusement arcade. I shelter in the doorway for a few minutes watching a group of teenagers crowd around a young, spotty youth on one of those motorbike games, shouting instructions at him in unison as he veers first left and then right.

I head back into the downpour, the heavy beat of a dance tune and the shrieks of the kids following me as I cross the road to the sea front.

Sand blows across my path as I amble along the empty promenade, past the clock tower with the gold-painted spire, and the boarded-up lido. The stretch of beach that has the trampolines, big wheel and helter-skelter in the summer months is now empty. My heels clip the pavement as I round the corner, the hulking, dark shape of the old pier ahead of me. This stretch of the town is quieter, the shops and cafés falling away so that only a few larger hotels remain before the path winds up the hill to my apartment. I decide not to cross the road yet. Instead I stay on the promenade, dotted with the odd metal bench, the old pier looming in the distance. The rain drenches me, but I don't care.

My phone vibrates in my pocket, not that I can hear the ringtone over the growl of the sea and the patter of rain. Mike's name flashes up on the screen. With a sinking feeling I answer it. He deserves more than a drunken voicemail message.

'Hi,' I say, my voice wobbling slightly.

'Fran? It's me, Mike,' he says unnecessarily. The reception is bad and I turn away from the sea, pressing my finger in my other ear to try and drown out the exterior sounds. 'Are you OK?'

Despite his anger, he still cares enough to ask about my welfare. 'I'm sorry,' I say into the phone, fighting back tears. 'I'm sorry for that awful voicemail I left you. You're right, I am a coward.'

'You've been through a lot lately,' he says, and I brace myself for his pleas to reconsider, for me to take him back. Instead he says, 'I understand. I just wanted to ask if it was OK to stay in your house for the rest of this week. While you're away?'

I hesitate, swallowing my disappointment. I don't want him, but my pride is hurt that he's not putting up more of a fight. Ideally I'd like him to move out now, but how can I say that without sounding heartless? You always did think I treated my boyfriends badly, didn't you, Soph. It was only because I hadn't found The One. Except I thought I had . . . but he didn't want me.

'I'm hoping to be back soon,' I say weakly.

'My mate has a room I can move into, but not until next weekend.' The phone starts to break up. I shout into it that it's fine, he can stay until the weekend. Then the line goes dead. I stand and stare at it for a while, the rain pooling on the screen. Then I thrust the phone back into my pocket.

It's definitely over, and despite his obvious anger at the beginning, deep down he knows it too. I oscillate between relief and disappointment.

I continue walking, the solitude of the empty streets matching my mood. It can't be much past 4 p.m. but the torrential rain has brought dusk early; I'm starting to feel conscious that there is no one else around. In the distance I can see the lampposts flanking the entrance to the pier, their soft amber lights a pair of haloes in the charcoal sky, illuminating the rain. I hear footsteps behind me and quicken my pace, although I will myself not to panic. It might be dark but it's not late, and I walk around London by myself all the time. What is it about this place that gives me the creeps?

I glance over my shoulder, but I can only make out a hooded figure through the downpour, in a dark raincoat, trousers and sturdy walking boots. It could be a man or a woman, although their height and slim build makes me think it's more likely to be female. I don't know what spooks me; maybe it's the aggressive stance or unfriendly demeanour, the way they hurry towards me with purpose. Instinct makes me break out into a run and I dart across the road and up the steep incline towards Beaufort Villas. The footsteps behind me also quicken and my heart pounds. Am I being followed?

I continue to run, but my high heels make it difficult to gather much momentum as they keep getting caught in the potholes and I trip more than once. The sound of feet pounds the pavement behind me. I think I hear my name being called, but it could just be the howl of the wind. Panting and sweating, I reach the brow of the hill, but don't stop to pause for breath. The footsteps are closing in on me. I need to get away. My legs feel weak as I stumble along the road but I keep running and don't look back until I reach the front door. My hands are shaking as I rummage in my bag to retrieve my key, imagining icy fingers reaching out to clutch my shoulder. I suppress a scream as I fumble with the lock and then, thankfully, the door gives way and I fall into the hallway with relief.

As I go to close the door I see the figure standing at the end of the driveway, partly obscured by my car, the hood of their anorak pulled firmly over their head, hands thrust into pockets. And even though I can't make out their features, I'm sure I notice a strand of blonde hair whipping against a heart-shaped face.

9
Sophie

Saturday, 5 July 1997

Leon is Jason's cousin. I'm devastated. I still can't believe it.

Maybe, subconsciously, I'm attracted to Leon because he reminds me of Jason. They have the same dark hair and blue eyes, that Irish look that I've always found so irresistible, the same intensity. There was a time when I thought about Jason every day, after he died. The guilt gnawed away at me until I felt like a shell of my former self. And then I moved away, went to uni and tried to put Jason out of my mind as though he was a once-loved toy that I was responsible for breaking, yet couldn't bring myself to throw out so shoved to the back of my wardrobe. I knew it was there although I tried not to think about it.

But since I've been back, the incessant, relentless thoughts pop into my head when I least expect them. While I'm innocently watching *Neighbours*, or drying my hair. When my mind drifts from the book I'm reading.

How terribly ironic that I kissed Leon for the first time in the same place his cousin died.

I'd questioned Frankie, of course. 'How do you know? Are you sure you're not mistaken? Did he actually say he was Jason's cousin?' And, most importantly, 'Does he know what we've done?'

She was pissed off with me – even more than she had been already. 'Of course he bloody well doesn't know,' she hissed. 'Do you think I'd be stupid enough to tell him?' She grabbed my arm and pulled me forcefully along the promenade away from the centre of town, all the while muttering in my ear that she'd found out from her mum, that she definitely wasn't mistaken, that I needed to stay away from Leon if I wanted to keep our secret safe.

But the thing is, I don't think I can stay away from him. Can I be with him and never reveal what we did? We were sixteen, just a couple of kids. We were young, we were stupid. We loved Jason, both of us constantly vying for his attention. How could we have known what would happen?

And why do I have this sense of foreboding? Like I already know my past is going to destroy my future?

Because the truth is, it's our fault that he's dead.

We've kept the secret all these years.

Frankie and I killed Jason.

10
Frankie

As I flick on all the lights in the apartment, I tell myself to calm down, to stop being stupid. But I'm unnerved. I can barely bring myself to formulate the words in my head: *It was you who was following me.* Logically I know it can't be you. You're dead. And I don't believe in ghosts. I *refuse* to believe in ghosts.

Yet when I walk into the living room and dump my bag on the floor I instantly know someone has been in here while I've been out. It's hard to explain but the air feels different, *smells* different. More floral. The curtains that I'd opened earlier are now drawn, and the book I'd been reading and left open on the sofa is closed and perched at a right angle on the glass coffee table. My heart starts to race. When I was in Daniel's car earlier I thought I saw a face at the window. I thought I saw *your* face. I'd convinced myself it was just the condensation making shapes and causing my mind to play tricks on me.

My spine tingles. I've never suffered from mental illness, although I witnessed the deep depressions my mum used to experience, particularly when I was younger. They were known as her 'episodes'. That's what my dad would call them, anyway. I never even told you about them, Soph. I tried to block them out. She would take herself off to the bedroom for days at a time, not even able to face getting up or seeing me, until Dad forced her back to the GP to either up her medication or switch it for a different brand. A few times she had to go away somewhere, to recover. Dad never revealed where, because he wanted to protect me, but I suspect she went to a psychiatric ward or hospital. When she returned she would be OK again, until the next time. She treated each episode as if it had never taken place, refusing to acknowledge or talk about it with me. Maybe in her head they never happened. Over the years it became a chasm between us that was so large that nothing could really fill it and I became closer to my dad. I always knew where I was with him. His feelings for me were constant. Unlike the oscillating emotions that my mum harboured towards me, either loving me so much it was stifling or being utterly indifferent towards me. Eventually the indifference won out. But it's always been a deep-seated fear of mine that I might take after her. That, one day, I might experience 'episodes' of my own.

Grabbing my phone from my bag, I call Daniel. It goes straight to voicemail.

I throw the phone on the sofa in a fit of temper. I tell myself to breathe. Focus. I'm not the sort to get hysterical or jump to conclusions. There must be a rational explanation. There always is. That woman I saw probably wasn't following me at all, it was just a coincidence that she looked like you. It spooked me and I panicked.

Maybe I forgot to open the curtains this morning. I was tired and lightheaded from lack of sleep. I probably had put the book on the coffee table. Maybe the person that owns this apartment has a cleaner – although I dismiss this instantly. Cleaners normally blitz a holiday apartment before the new guests arrive, not while they're in residence.

For the next few hours I try to distract myself. I eat two pieces of toast and watch some inane chat show, even though the picture keeps breaking up. I've nearly polished off a bottle of wine but I'm still unable to settle.

I can't get the feeling of being watched out of my mind. Somebody was following me earlier, it can't be a coincidence. They were standing at the end of the driveway watching me as I pushed my way through the front door. The 'London' me would have confronted them and demanded to know what they were playing at, but since being back here I'm morphing into that girl again. I don't want to go back to being insecure Frankie. I'm Fran now, confident, assured, successful. A grown-up.

This place isn't good for me. Too many memories, too many ghosts.

I feel like I'm in a surreal version of *Groundhog Day* when I wake up the next morning. The baby began screaming again in the middle of the night and its every cry was like a stab wound to my heart. I've wanted children so desperately that for too many years the desire overwhelmed me, became an obsession, a longing so great I would have done almost anything to make it happen. But I had miscarriage after miscarriage, then stopped conceiving at all. We tried fertility treatment and when I eventually became pregnant, after the third attempt, I was ecstatic. Until just a few weeks later, days before my twelve-week scan, I had yet another miscarriage. I'll never forget the devastating pain of losing that final baby, both physical and emotional. As the blood and the clots passed violently from my body, so also seeped the final remnants of hope. I was being punished for Jason. I didn't deserve to be happy.

Around every corner after that there seemed to be a fecund woman with a brood of kids, reminding me of what I'd never have. Six months later, Christopher left me for a work colleague. I've often wondered what you would have thought of him – Christopher, I mean. I like to think you would have hated him, called him a smug bastard, or a fool for cheating on me. When I confronted him he promised he'd finish things with her, that he'd be a better husband. But it was too late, I couldn't forgive him, so I told him to move out and that I wanted a divorce. Since then I haven't allowed anyone to get close enough to hurt me. Even Mike. But it's been over three years now, Soph, and I want to fall in love again.

That's what happens when you wake in the middle of the night. It gives you too much time to think, to wallow in self-pity. So to drown out the baby's cries as well as the memories, I took two sleeping pills, downed a glass of wine, and fell into a heavy, drug-induced sleep on the sofa. And now I have a banging headache.

I shower and change into a jumper and jeans, wishing I'd packed other shoes apart from the impractical stiletto ankle boots that I'm forced to wear again. The sight of the three empty wine bottles lined up on the counter in the kitchen reminds me that I need to go to the shops today for supplies.

I'm heating up a bowl of porridge in the microwave when a knock at the door makes me jump. It can't be anyone from outside as they'd need to be buzzed in the main door downstairs. I tiptoe down the hallway, trying not to make a sound in my heels, and peer through the peephole. It's Daniel, distorted by the convex glass.

I throw open the door. 'How did you get up here? I didn't let you in.'

He shrugs, unconcerned. 'The woman downstairs let me in. She was going out and saw me standing on the step. Why are you looking at me like that?'

'I don't like the thought that she's just letting random men in the front door without checking first. How does she know that you're my friend? You could've been anybody.'

'Jeez, Franks. Paranoid much?'

How can I begin to tell him about the letter and the person following me yesterday without divulging more information, about Jason and the past? I suddenly feel very much alone.

'You'd better come in,' I say, opening the door wider. 'I haven't finished my breakfast yet.' He follows me down the narrow hallway into the kitchen. 'Do you want some porridge?'

He shakes his head, the front of his fringe bouncing as he does so. 'No thanks. Had my breakfast.'

I stand at the counter, spooning the porridge into my mouth, feeling self-conscious that Daniel is watching me. After a few mouthfuls I place the bowl, still half full, into the sink.

'Don't let me put you off your breakfast.' The space between us feels close, almost claustrophobic in the small kitchen. Then his gaze falls on the empty wine bottles. 'Blimey, Franks, you've sunk a lot of wine since you've been here.'

'I've been here two nights, two lonely nights where there was nothing to do apart from get slowly pissed. I tried to call you last night. It went straight to voicemail.'

He stares at me, shock altering his features for a second. 'I didn't get any missed calls. But the reception here is sometimes a bit shit.' His face softens. 'I'm sorry.' He moves closer to me and takes my hand. 'I was the one who asked you to come back here –' he hesitates, searching my face '– and you came. I'm so grateful to you for that. I'm sorry for not being a better friend. I should have spent some evenings with you, but it's difficult. You see –' he clears his throat, his face reddening '– I have someone living with me, a woman. It's a recent thing . . .' He tails off.

So he does have a girlfriend. I swallow my disappointment but it lodges in my chest, giving me heartburn.

'I see.' I can't meet his eyes, worried he'll be able to read what's going on in my mind.

His next words are low and husky. 'She knows how I used to feel, about you.'

I glance up and our eyes lock. He's never admitted to me how he felt, although I've always known. You used to tease me about it all the time, and even though I never reciprocated his feelings I liked that he fancied me. Would things have turned out differently had I allowed myself to feel the same? Deep down I know I would never have looked at him that way back then. He was just your annoying older brother. I'm ashamed to admit it, Soph, but I never felt he was good enough for me when we were younger. He wasn't ambitious or dynamic, preferring to loaf about during the day and playing at being a rock star at night. Now I realise what I've been missing all these years; someone who makes me laugh, who's kind and loyal, who's a friend. I know what you're going to say – that Mike is all those things. And it's true, he is. But he doesn't make me feel the way Daniel does.

I move closer and touch his cheek. It feels cold and rough under my fingers. 'Daniel . . .' I murmur. Our eyes are still locked and I inch my face towards his, wanting, needing to feel his lips against mine. Just as my mouth lightly touches his he moves away as though I've stung him.

'Frankie . . . I can't. I'm sorry.' He turns away from me and runs his hand through his hair. 'You're not . . . I'm not . . . Fuck.' He kicks the kitchen cupboard with the toe of his boot. I stand and helplessly watch the internal struggle he is having.

'Daniel – it's OK. I know you're with someone. I shouldn't have tried to kiss you. I'm sorry.'

He swivels around so that he's looking at me again, his eyes accusing. 'I really loved you once,' he says, shaking his head sadly. 'I'll go and wait in the car.'

I wince as the door slams shut behind him.

I spend the next ten minutes composing myself, putting on make-up, tidying the kitchen. Then I'm ready to go. I dread going downstairs, half expecting another letter to have fallen on the doormat. When I reach the bottom step the mat is empty, but wedged in the letterbox, like a tongue hanging out of a mouth, is another brown envelope. Steeling myself, I whip it from the letterbox's metal grasp, not surprised when I see it's addressed to me. I rip it open, my stomach in knots. This time there is just the one word typed in the middle of the page in black, bold letters:

MURDERER

Sunday

11

Sophie

Sunday, 13 July 1997

I've seen Leon three times since Frankie's revelation and each time I couldn't bring myself to finish with him.

Last night, our fourth date, I contemplated ending things. How could I not, after what we did?

I still have nightmares about it. Flashes of memory from that hot August night. We were kids, just sixteen. I was wasted, drunk for the first time in my life thanks to Frankie stealing those spirits from behind her father's bar. The three of us had gone to the old pier to get hammered and listen to music where nobody would catch us. Both of us were convinced that we were the one he was in love with. Now I look back and cringe at the way I acted, the way we flaunted ourselves at him. As if he'd ever have fancied me. Now I know how ridiculous we both were to hope for a romantic relationship with Jason. Maybe if I hadn't been so delusional it would never have happened. He would still be alive.

I already know I'll never be able to tell Leon.

Guilt. It turns you into a liar.

Anyway, I'm digressing. Back to last night.

I arranged to meet Leon at the old pier. As we sat there on the rotten floorboards, bleached by the sun and hot to the touch, all I could think about was that this was the last place Jason was seen alive. Eventually, after a couple of cans of Red Stripe, I felt brave enough to broach the subject.

Leon stared at me when I asked about Jason. 'Did you know him?' he said, his brow deepening into a frown. He listened intently, his piercing eyes boring into me as I explained that Jason had had a summer job at Frankie's parents' hotel, that the three of us were friends.

As I talked he took my hand, rubbing his thumb across my palm. 'His death was a huge shock to us all,' he said when I'd finished. He didn't look at me as he spoke, instead concentrating on a splintered piece of wood by his knee. 'We were close growing up, he was only six months older than me. He wasn't just my cousin, he was my friend. He was found in the sea. He'd drowned. The toxicology report said there was a lot of alcohol in his blood, which contributed to his death. But I often wondered if he did it on purpose, you know? If he took his own life.'

I was horrified and in that moment almost spewed out the whole ugly truth; the guilt of it was inching its way up my throat. I had to bite my lip to stop the words tumbling out.

'Why . . .' My mouth was so dry I could barely speak. I swallowed and started again. 'Why would you think he'd kill himself?'

'Jason was always a piss-head. And he took too many

drugs. His mum, my dad's sister, was an alcoholic. She kicked him out when he was seventeen, that was why he came here. A new start, apparently. But he was troubled, Soph.'

I remembered Jason telling me about his parents, especially his father, who he'd described as a 'waster'. We had a lot in common, that's probably why I'd liked him so much. He was my first love. Frankie felt the same way too, that was the problem.

Frankie was the one he liked, I've always been sure of that. Yes, we had a lot in common, coming from similar backgrounds. We would often sit and chat together – in a quiet spot on the beach or on the old pier. Sometimes I sensed that Frankie felt left out when we got into one of our philosophising sessions. I could tell by the way she'd try and distract us whenever she saw us deep in conversation. (Although she never admitted it, that's not her style. Frankie never has liked to admit to any weaknesses!) But I always knew that Jason saw me as a friend, nothing more.

'What about his kid sister?' I asked. 'He always spoke of her so fondly.' I only ever saw her once, at Jason's funeral, standing forlornly next to an older woman. She would only have been about twelve, pretty with huge blue eyes, like Jason's.

Leon lifted his head to look at me, his eyes softening. 'She came to live with us for a while. She's OK. Happy. She's sixteen now. My parents dote on her, the daughter they never had.' His smile vanished. 'Hey, why so sad?'

I blinked back tears. 'It's just . . . it's tragic, what happened to Jason.'

He squeezed my hand and then pulled me to him so that I was sitting on his lap. I felt safe wrapped up in his strong arms. 'He had his problems, it wasn't easy for him,' he murmurs into my neck. 'He was a teenager who was struggling with his sexuality. Trying to understand himself.'

I sat up straighter and pulled away from him so that I could see his face, my arms still around his neck. 'What do you mean?'

'He was gay. Didn't you know?'

The shock must have been apparent in my expression. 'Gay? But he fancied Frankie. I was sure of it . . . I . . .'

Leon shook his head, his wavy hair flopping in his face. 'No, he didn't. He had a lot of girls as friends, but he wasn't interested in them in that way. He came out to me when he was fourteen. He'd always known, that's what he said.'

I had no clue. All those times we sat and put the world to rights. I wish he could have confided in me about it.

Today at work (I've now jacked in my job with Stan and I'm working at the hotel every morning except Tuesdays!) I told Frankie what Leon had said. I was helping her change the bedding in a double room and she stopped, duvet cover in hand, the colour draining from her face. It was most peculiar. I wondered if she was going to throw up. It took her a few moments to compose herself and I felt sad for her. It's obvious that she'd thought the same as me – that Jason had loved her. Maybe that's what kept her going, what helped assuage her guilt. And I had taken that away from her. When she recovered, she snapped at me that I'd better not ever tell Leon what we did. And then she waltzed out the room, leaving me to change the bed by myself.

She didn't speak to me for the rest of the day, as though it was my fault that Jason had been gay. Either that or she was cross that I hadn't finished with Leon like she hoped. The thing is, I don't know how long my relationship with Leon is going to last. I know it can't be for ever, not with this huge secret between us.

12

Frankie

The hand that's holding the letter begins to shake uncontrollably, and I watch it, shocked, as though it's taken on a life of its own. I feel trapped, like a defenceless animal, with no choice but to wait for my predator's next move.

I've tried to bury the memory of Jason and what we did all those years ago, Soph. I've gone to great pains to turn my life around, to reinvent myself. A new start in London, the growth of the hotels, which was down to me more than my parents. My mother had always been the driving force behind the business – Dad preferred the social side of things – but since their semi-retirement I've thrown myself into making sure the business is a success. And it's worked – we're just a few months away from opening our third hotel. Not the tacky hotels of our youth either; these are boutique hotels with opulent furnishings and Wi-Fi, with white, fluffy robes in the bedrooms and upmarket toiletries in the en suites. The type of hotels that run twenty-four hours a day, with demanding guests and a high turnover of staff, that seem constantly busy – unlike my parents' place, which only ever seemed to get full in the summer months.

I've been running from my past. Now the past has caught up with me and I feel wrong-footed, out of control.

I tried to convince you that dating Leon – *Jason's cousin* – was a mistake. I was terrified that you would be unable to keep the secret from him. You were always so kind, loyal, a soft touch. You trusted people more than I did, believed in them, assumed that they would live up to your expectations. But what if you did tell Leon? Does he know that we were involved in his cousin's death and is seeking revenge?

I take a deep breath and open the front door. I dart through the rain and slip into the passenger seat of Daniel's car, still clutching the envelope. I can't stop trembling.

His mouth is set in a straight line. I might have been embarrassed by our near kiss if I wasn't so worried about the letter. 'I'm sorry,' he says without looking at me. 'Seeing you again . . .' He reddens.

When I don't answer he turns to look at me. His eyes shift to the letter in my hand. 'What is it?'

Wordlessly I thrust the letter at him and he scans it quickly. 'Where did you get this?'

I explain everything, about the letters, the person who followed me last night.

'Why didn't you tell me this before?'

'I didn't know what to say, or whether I could trust you.' I fumble in my bag for a tissue.

His eyes are hard. 'Trust me? You've known me since

you were seven years old. What, you think I sent you these?'

I shake my head. 'No, of course not . . . but . . .' I stare at him, watching for signs that he might have had something to do with it. His right eyelid twitches.

'What?'

'You were there, this morning,' I say. 'Did you notice the envelope in the letter box then?'

His eyebrows knit together in concentration. 'I don't think so.'

'So someone obviously posted it while you were in the apartment with me.'

He runs his hand over his chin. 'Maybe. I don't know. It could have been in the letter box, I doubt I would have noticed, to be honest . . .'

I sigh. 'Someone knows, Daniel. Someone knows what Sophie and I did . . .'

There is a stunned silence as I realise what I've said. The only sound to be heard is the drumming of the rain on the roof of the car and the swish of the windscreen wipers. Daniel turns the ignition off and swivels in his seat to stare at me.

'What did you do, Frankie?'

In that moment, I know I can trust him. If I tell him what happened he's hardly likely to go to the police; it would implicate you too and he wouldn't want your name dragged through the mud.

'It was our fault,' I whisper, shredding the tissue in my lap. 'The night Jason died. It was an accident, it's true. But we were there. We were with him.'

And carefully I tell him what I think he needs to know.

As soon as we met Jason that day in my parents' dining room we were smitten with him, although I don't tell Daniel this part. I don't think I'd even admitted to you how much I'd fancied Jason – although you could probably tell by the way I flirted when I was with him. He was the reason I turned Daniel's advances down that summer. How was I to know he was gay? He never told us, and my sixteen-year-old self wasn't worldly wise or sophisticated enough to realise. He was just a hot, sexy, older boy who was nice to us. To both of us. Equally.

As the weeks progressed we became friends and the three of us would hang around together. He didn't seem to mind being seen with a couple of giggly girls. He preferred that to hanging out with Daniel and his friends. I knew he'd had a troubled upbringing – he preferred to tell you most of this. I think he saw you as a kindred spirt, somebody with a similar background to his own. I never really thought he fancied you though; no offence, Soph, but you were an ugly duckling back then, only later turning into a swan. But you had that fierce intelligence, that analytical brain, and could discuss things with him – philosophical things that I wasn't interested in. You were naive in so many ways, yet you were also mature beyond your years. You and Daniel were left, most of the time, to fend for yourselves while your mum worked all hours. Not that it was her fault, she had a lot on her plate, both financially and emotionally. You hardly spoke of your father except to say he was a violent bully. Your mum was doing her best to make a life for the three of you away from him.

It was a humid evening in late August when the three of us made a plan to meet on the old pier to get drunk. We were under age and the downside of living in a small town is that everybody knew how old we were so wouldn't serve or sell us alcohol. Jason liked a drink – I wonder now, looking back, if he had a problem with alcohol. So, partly to impress Jason, I decided to steal a couple of bottles of spirits from my parents – vodka and rum.

You got drunk the quickest, probably due to your toothpick frame. The alcohol gave you the confidence to act in a way that was totally out of character. I was quite shocked how you began flirting with Jason in the most embarrassing way, sitting on his lap and flinging your arms around his neck. He didn't seem to mind, in fact I thought that he liked the attention. I even experienced a throb of jealousy at the two of you. We were mixing the spirits with Coke, but that wasn't enough to dilute the effects. As the evening wore on we became more and more drunk.

I don't really remember who started the argument – if it was me because Jason was paying too much attention to you, or the other way around. I suppose we were competitive in the way that best friends are. Except I was usually the winner when it came to boys. And I liked to win. After all, you always beat me in class. It was only fair that I came first in something.

Now I twist the tissue in my hands. 'We were squabbling,' I say. 'Me and Sophie. Jason tried to stop us. Sophie pushed him away – not hard, she didn't mean to, but it was enough to make him lose his balance. He was so drunk. He crashed through the rotten wooden barrier and fell twenty-five feet into the sea below.

'We watched, appalled, as he flailed about in the water. He could swim, we knew that because we'd often gone swimming in the sea together. But, maybe because of the tide, or the amount of alcohol in his system, he couldn't keep afloat and we could do nothing . . . he kept sinking . . .' I hesitate, the memory is still so vivid. 'We could only stare in horror as he got swallowed up by the sea.

'We couldn't have saved him, you see, Dan. We couldn't. We were just as wasted – and neither of us had mobile phones in those days. I often wondered if I should have run for help, alerted one of the neighbours from the nearby houses. But we did nothing. We were frozen by fear, scared of getting into trouble. And so we watched a young man with everything to live for drown.'

There is complete silence in the car. It's so oppressive that I feel crushed by it, as though I've taken a sledgehammer to the clean-cut image he's always had of me.

Eventually he asks, 'Did Sophie ever tell Leon?' His voice sounds raw in the confines of the car, as though he's not spoken for years.

I shake my head. 'I really don't know. I think she was tempted. She hated lying to him. But she was scared. Why? Do you think it's him writing these notes?'

He shrugs and turns away from me to look out of the windscreen again. The windows have started to steam up so he starts the ignition, and the lull of the windscreen wipers and melodic sound of the rain soothes me. 'Who knows, Frankie. What happened after . . . after he died?'

I close my eyes, remembering the shock, the horror of it all; you throwing up over the side of the pier and then screaming uncontrollably so that I had to slap you hard across the face; me grabbing your arm and dragging you away, instantly sobering up as we ran as fast as we could towards the hotel. Dad was still awake and sitting in the living room, reading a book and drinking a Scotch. Luckily all the guests were in bed. I still remember the fear that pinched his face when he saw us, bedraggled and crying, you with vomit down the front of your dress, the words, '*What's happened?*' sliding from his mouth as though in slow motion.

I exhale and open my eyes. 'My dad. We ran back to the hotel and told him. He was the one who insisted that we say nothing about what had happened. He didn't want the police involved. It was an accident, he said. A tragic accident. He never even told my mum.'

'Your dad is good at keeping secrets,' he says and I shoot him a look.

'My dad saved our arses.'

'You said yourself, it was an accident. You should've

been honest, for fuck's sake, Frankie! You should have been honest then and maybe none of this would have happened. Then Sophie might be alive.' His voice gets louder with each word, saliva forming in the corners of his mouth. I don't think I've ever seen him so angry.

Tears seep out of my eyes and I don't bother to wipe them away. 'I know that now. Dad just did what he thought was right. We would have been in trouble for stealing his booze, it would have got in the local newspaper, as you well know. Dad could have lost his licence.' I scowl at him as though he was the one responsible for writing the non-existent story despite only being eighteen at the time. 'And he would have lost his business.'

'I can't believe you kept this from me,' he says, his voice quieter now, less angry. But he still doesn't look at me.

'We kept it from everyone.'

His next words chill me to the bone. 'Well, not everyone. Someone knows, Frankie. And it sounds like they want revenge.'

13
Sophie

Sunday, 20 July 1997

I thought it would be fun working with Frankie but she's hardly spoken to me since last week. I know it's because I haven't done what she wants – finish with Leon. I'd forgotten how stubborn she can be, how things always have to go her way. While we were apart I romanticised our friendship. There is hardly a childhood memory that she's not in, just like Daniel. And yet there were times too where she got on my nerves. Even as a kid she was bossy, giving me the silent treatment if I didn't do what she wanted. Once, when we were nine and I refused to go out and play with her, preferring to stay curled up with my new *Malory Towers* books instead, she didn't speak to me for a week.

Yesterday late afternoon I went to the beach with Helen and found myself pouring it all out to her: Frankie's annoyance that I was going out with Leon, her cold-shouldering, the awkwardness of us working together – although being careful to omit anything to do with Jason.

I've been feeling guilty that I've jettisoned Helen

now that Frankie is back. Helen was a lifeline for me at school after Frankie left. And we'd stayed in touch while I was at university and she was at the local college, making sure to see each other when I returned to Oldcliffe for the holidays. She could be a little grumpy at times, she wasn't bubbly like Frankie, but I admired her straight-talking, no-nonsense ways. The only downside to our friendship was how intensely she disliked Frankie. When we were in the second year of senior school they had a huge fight. Frankie had run into the classroom, blue paint in her hair and smudged across her face, and flown at Helen, accusing her of locking her in the arts supply cupboard. Everyone knew how claustrophobic Frankie was. Helen always denied it but Frankie was convinced it was her as they had been the only people in the art room before it happened. Frankie went around telling everyone about it and calling Helen a bully. They weren't exactly friends before then, but after that they were barely civil to one another. Helen always denied it but I'm still not convinced she didn't do it. Helen can hold a grudge!

We were splayed out on towels, in the shade of the helter-skelter. The day was stifling and airless, the sea calm, the tide out. To my right, and much further along the coast, the old pier loomed in the distance, on the edge of things, like a shy teenager at a party.

Helen shuffled on her towel. She was wearing shorts and a bikini top and her chest was already going pink even though we had only been sitting there for fifteen minutes. The beach was packed with bodies: families sunbathing, children paddling, teenagers tossing a Frisbee.

'So you think Frankie is funny with you because you're getting off with Leon?' she said when I'd finished, shielding her face with her hand and squinting. The sun ballooned in the cloudless sky.

I shrugged. 'Yes, she wants me to stop seeing him. She told me he tried it on with her a couple of months back, and he got a bit nasty when she said no.'

She raised an eyebrow. 'Really? Do you think that's true?'

'Why would she lie?'

'The trouble is, Frankie is used to getting all the attention. She doesn't like it now you've blossomed. And she's always been possessive of you.'

'Do you think?'

She snorted. 'Of course. Nobody could ever get near you at school.'

'No boys fancied me at school,' I said, remembering how I used to look with my braces and National Health specs.

'I don't mean the boys. You weren't able to make other friends. She claimed you, right from when you joined at primary school. You were her best friend and that was it. She's never had to share you before. And now she has to share you with Leon, and she doesn't like it.'

I felt a stab of guilt at discussing Frankie in this way. Especially considering Helen didn't know all the facts.

She carried on relentlessly, in full swing. 'It was the best thing for you, when she left. Gave you the chance to step out from her shadow. But now she expects to be able to pick up exactly where she left off. You've changed. It's been three years.'

I sat up, thrusting my hands into the hot sand and letting the fine grains run through my fingers. I knew what Helen was saying was true. Even if Leon wasn't Jason's cousin, I still don't think Frankie would like me dating him, or anyone. She was used to having me to herself.

Helen sat up too, swivelling on her towel so that she was facing me. 'You can't let her push you around any more, Sophie.'

I felt uneasy. 'She doesn't push me around . . .'

'You're too nice and she takes advantage of that. Guilt-tripping you to do what she wants by making you worry that you've upset her. She did it when you were little and she's still doing it.'

I continued to rake the sand with my fingers. 'A friendship is never equal,' I mused, 'is it? There's always one who is more dominant, more controlling. That's just the way it is.'

Helen frowned. 'Friendship should be about give and take. It should be about equality . . .'

'Don't you think that's a bit naive?' I interjected. 'We're all so different so each friendship will be different. Each friend will bring out a different side to our personality. Yes, Frankie was always the more domineering of the two of us, so when I'm with her I suppose

I do revert to being the same as I was when we were kids.'

She rooted in her bag for her bottle of Hawaiian Tropic (which we loved because it made us look instantly tanned and smelled like Malibu), rubbing it into her already sunburnt chest. 'What about with us? Where does the balance of power lie in our friendship?'

'I don't know . . . we're pretty equal. Aren't we?' Although even as I said this I knew I wasn't being totally honest. Sometimes Helen's quick temper scared me.

'Exactly,' she said triumphantly. She moved on to her legs, the oil mixing with grains of sand so that her shins glistened. She had a look of concentration on her face. 'No offence, Sophie, but you were hardly competition before. With men, I mean. Now look at you!'

I felt myself blush and stared at my hands, partially hidden by the sand. 'Hardly, Hel.'

'No, I mean it.'

'Frankie's gorgeous.'

'And so are you.'

I felt uncomfortable with this – no matter what anyone says to the contrary, I will forever feel like that lanky kid with braces and bad skin. So I changed the subject to The Basement and what time we were going to get there that night.

We stayed on the beach for another hour, then we wandered around the town in our shorts and flip-flops, towels and sun oil stuffed in our beach bags. We stopped at the entrance to the Grand Pier to buy ice creams and then meandered on to the main walkway, the faint sounds of 1950s music overhead.

It was then that I saw Frankie pushing her way through the hordes of people, marching towards us in denim hot-pants and a black bikini top that showed off her ample boobs. My brother was trailing after her with that annoying, love-sick expression he adopts every time he sees her lately. He was wearing black, even in the heat, but had swapped his usual jumper and long coat for a T-shirt and jeans. His normally pale cheeks were red and his dark hair was wet at the front with sweat. Frankie has never really seemed interested in Daniel – although she must be able to tell how much of a crush he has on her. It's so obvious he might as well be wearing a placard with it written right across the front.

Seeing them together was a bit of a shock – they never normally hang out on their own.

Frankie seemed flustered as she stopped in front of us, her intense gaze taking in Helen's arm linked through mine, the ice creams in our hands. She scowled.

'Been to the beach, have we?' she said, addressing me and ignoring Helen.

'Yes, if that's OK with you,' I said, annoyed with myself for getting defensive, knowing it was for Helen's benefit. I wanted to prove her wrong, to show her that I don't let Frankie push me around any more.

Frankie's expression softened and her shoulders sagged. There was something vulnerable about her as she stood in front of me, all small and compact, with

Daniel looming large behind her. 'Look, Soph, I'm sorry I've been a bitch these last few days. I've had a lot on my mind. Are you going to The Basement tonight?'

I could feel Helen tense up beside me. She unlinked her arm from mine.

'Yes. Helen's coming too,' I said. I couldn't leave her out just because Frankie had clicked her perfectly manicured fingers and wanted to be friends again. It wasn't fair.

'Great,' she said, still avoiding eye contact with Helen. She leaned forward and gave me a hug. 'I'll see you there.'

We all watched as she sashayed off, Daniel practically salivating.

'So what were the two of you up to?' I said as the three of us walked back through town. The heat was oppressive, not helped by the tourists ambling along as if they had all the time in the world.

'She called me up, wanted to spend a few hours with me.' Daniel shrugged nonchalantly but I could tell he was secretly elated that she'd asked for his company.

'Did you snog her?' said Helen. By now we were out of the thicket of tourists and had nearly reached the old pier.

'None of your business,' he blushed.

'Oh my God, you did snog her!' I cried. 'I can tell by your lovey-dovey expression.'

'Did you feel her up?' Helen teased. 'How many years have you wanted to get your hands on those tits?'

The shock on Daniel's face made us both descend into a fit of giggles.

'Oh, piss off, both of you.' He stalked off, leaving us clutching each other and laughing.

Now, though, I'm worried.

Daniel's been in love with Frankie for years, but she's never returned his feelings. She probably just wanted a bit of attention.

And if she did snog my brother, it would have only been to get back at me.

I'm no longer sure what she's capable of.

14
Frankie

We pull up outside Lorcan's house and I'm suddenly overcome with a sense of fatigue so powerful that my body feels as though it's made of stone.

I can't actually face going into that house again. I can't bear the thought of seeing Leon or his thuggish brother. What is the point of all this? What is Daniel hoping to achieve here? If either of them knows anything about what happened to you they're hardly going to tell us. All I want to do is go home, return to my London life; even Mike is an appealing prospect right now. I should never have agreed to come back. But even as I think it, I know I'm not being honest with myself. How could I have resisted the chance to return here? The chance to help Daniel identify your body – *your remains* – so that I can finally lay you to rest.

'Come on then, what are you waiting for?' Daniel's voice is sharp, insistent. It's obvious he hasn't forgiven me – may never forgive me – for what I've just told him about Jason. He's never going to look at me in the same way. I'm no longer the person he thought I was.

You're out of all this now though, aren't you, Soph? You are gone and I'm left to deal with it all by myself.

To carry that burden. It was always me, I was the strong one, the leader, the one who got us out of trouble, the one who sorted it the night Jason died, the one who's left to face all this now . . .

I'm just about to tell Daniel that I'm not going back into that depressing house when a tall man strides up to the car and bangs on the bonnet. I jump in fright and Daniel's face pales as Lorcan leers at us through the windscreen. He's wearing the same paint-splattered overalls and work boots as yesterday, with a short-sleeved T-shirt underneath. Does the man not feel the biting cold? He bangs on the bonnet again and Daniel leaps out the car.

My fatigue dissipates, replaced by adrenaline, and I follow suit.

'What the fuck do you think you're doing?' Daniel shouts. 'Stop thumping my car!'

'Would ya rather I thumped you?' Lorcan snarls. 'What the fuck are you doing around 'ere? Leon told me you came over yesterday. We've got nuffin' to say to you.' His anger accentuates his strong West Country accent.

I join Daniel's side and squeeze his arm gently, trying to pull him away, but he stands his ground.

'I just want to know about the night my sister disappeared.'

Lorcan's expression darkens. 'We've got nothing to tell you. So piss off.'

I can feel the tension stretching between them and, in a last-ditch attempt, I step in to diffuse it. 'Look,

Lorcan,' I begin, 'I know you fancied Sophie. I remember you trying it on with her at The Basement. Were you harassing her? You were married . . . what would your wife have said about that . . . ?'

He takes a step towards me and shakes a fist in my face. 'Fuck off, Miss High and Mighty. Who the fuck do you think you are? Coming around 'ere after all these years, trying to fuck with me, you stupid bitch.'

'That's enough,' shouts Daniel, standing in front of me to face Lorcan's wrath. 'Leave her alone.'

'She can't go around accusing folk,' he snarls, spittle flying from his mouth.

'She's not accusing anyone. We just want to talk to you . . . we spoke to Leon yesterday and he was helpful, but . . .'

Lorcan shakes his head at us, but his face softens as he assesses Daniel. 'Look, mate,' he says in a conciliatory voice. 'I'm sorry about your sister, I really am. I heard that they found her body. But her death's got nuffin' to do with me. Now leave me and my family alone.'

And before either of us can say anything further he stalks back into his garden, the wooden gate banging in his wake.

We stare after him for a few moments. Then Daniel turns to me, his eyes sad. 'This is a nightmare. It's much harder than I thought. Nobody wants to talk to me.'

'You're a journalist now, maybe that's why.'

'It's not just that . . .' He sighs. 'Look, Franks. I wonder if it might be better if you do this. Without me.'

'What?'

'Like you say, I'm a journalist. And I'm Sophie's brother. But you . . .'

'I'm an outsider,' I exclaim. 'They've not exactly been friendly to me since I've been back. You heard Lorcan. He called me a high and mighty bitch.'

He runs his hands through his hair in exasperation. 'I don't know what else to suggest.'

We stand there on the pavement, both deep in our own thoughts. Then Daniel's mobile trills and he retrieves it from the pocket of his coat.

'Mia? Yes . . . no . . .' He glances at me from under dark lashes and then turns away. 'OK, I'm coming now.' He ends the call and returns the phone to his pocket. 'I need to go,' he says without looking at me. 'I'm wanted . . . at home.'

'So, her name is Mia . . .' I say before I can stop myself. But Daniel's expression darkens at the use of her name, his eyes narrowing so that he looks older, more formidable. I can tell that he doesn't want to involve her in any of this, that me just speaking her name has sullied her somewhat. He's always been able to compartmentalise, has Daniel. I understand because I'm the same. I know he's thinking that Mia doesn't belong in this murky world of death and murder and revenge. She belongs to the other part of him; to lazy Sundays leafing through newspapers and holding hands over breakfast, of romantic strolls and tender endearments. I feel a sharp stab of jealousy that's as physical as indigestion.

He walks to the car and opens the door. 'Come on.'

I'm suddenly angry with him. Jealousy of Mia has made me want to punish him. So I say I'll walk back. He shrugs, tells me he doesn't think that's a great idea after what Lorcan just called me, but he's already left me in spirit, even if his body is still here. He's obviously worrying about Mia. I remember the moment in the kitchen earlier, our near kiss. He was tempted, I could feel it. He wasn't thinking about Mia then. Maybe he's not as in love with her as he thinks, as he tries to tell himself.

Why didn't I snap him up all those years ago?

Everything could have turned out so differently.

I was wrong when I said that nothing had ever happened between us. I'd forgotten until this morning. That moment in the kitchen brought back memories of the summer you died. Just a few snogs and fumbles around the back of the pier. Not sex, never even close to sex. I didn't know what I wanted back then. I wanted what I couldn't have – and Daniel was offering it to me on a plate. And now I can't have him he's more desirable than ever.

'I'll text you later. We need to decide our next move,' he says hurriedly. He's already behind the wheel before I can reply. I watch, speechless, as he screeches away from the kerb.

I walk through the estate. Luckily the weather means it's deserted; no youths hanging around the off-licence today, no children riding their bikes up and down the streets, no men tinkering under the bonnets of cars. I head for Robin Road, the place where you used to live.

It's been nearly two decades but I can still remember the way to your house. It's only two streets away from Leon's. I could be twenty-one again or fifteen, or twelve, desperate to get to your house to sit in your bedroom, listening to music.

I wander through the underpass that leads from the back of one street to the front of another, so that I'm in the leafy, pedestrianised area. Most of the housing estates that popped up in the late 1960s and early '70s were built to a similar format – green areas in front of the houses where children could play without the fear of cars knocking them down, with garages out the back.

Before I know it I've reached No. 123, the middle terrace in a row of three. It looks shabbier than I remember, the white paint peeling in curls from the wooden cladding. The red door has been replaced by white, plastic-looking double glazing. But I still feel a pull of nostalgia in my gut so strong and overwhelming that I can almost see you waving to me from your bedroom window: the little room that overlooks the front with the Pierrot curtains and matching bedspread, where we listened to Madonna and Five Star when we were eight, changing to Nirvana and Pearl Jam, and then Blur and Oasis as we got older.

And I know that I can't be here any longer. In this town, in the past. I feel you so strongly, Sophie, it's almost as though you're standing right next to me, or behind me. I suddenly feel cold and my spine tingles with fear. I need to get out of here.

I turn and hurry back through the underpass and

along the winding streets, until I get to the main road. It will only take me ten minutes to reach the apartment. I've made a decision. I need to return to London. I can't bear to spend one more night here in this town, with just my thoughts and the ghost of you to keep me company.

Daniel's moved on, with Mia. He'll be OK. He doesn't need me here, not really. Mia can go with him to identify your remains. He's come up against so many brick walls I'm surprised he's still standing. And it's not like I'll ever be able to help him.

It begins to sleet, sludgy flakes falling and dissolving into the pavement. The sea is choppy and grey, the waves lashing around the steel legs of the old pier. I shiver as I pull the hood of my coat up, not that it protects me much. The hood is there more for fashion than practicality and it doesn't quite stretch over my head.

I pause to retrieve my phone from my bag and then carry on, clutching it in my hand. I'm relieved that out here in the open I have some reception. When I get to the lampposts at the entrance to the pier I stop and lean against one of them to tap out a quick text to Daniel. *I have to leave, Daniel. I'm sorry. I'm going home. F x*

When I look up I see you through the sleet, standing in the middle of the pier. You're wearing jeans, your fair hair a tangle around your face. I gasp. My eyes are seeing you, yet I know that logically you can't be there.

I blink, hot despite the cold elements, and look down at the phone still in my hand. There is no reply from

Daniel. It suddenly occurs to me that I could take a photo of you, to prove to myself that I'm not going mad, but when I look up, of course you're not there. I'm completely alone. Turning away from the pier I pull the hood of my coat further over my head and trudge up the hill to the apartment, the sleet like cold lips kissing my face.

Why do I keep seeing you when you're dead? I'm either losing my mind or all those ghost stories we were told about the pier being haunted are true. I don't know which prospect terrifies me more.

15
Sophie

Sunday, 27 July 1997

It's the early hours of the morning as I write this. I can't sleep, even though I need to because I have to go to work tomorrow. I'm going to be shattered!

It all kicked off last night at The Basement.

The evening started brilliantly – Leon invited me over to his house as his brother and sister-in-law were out and we had the place to ourselves. I suspected, I knew, what this meant. That we would be able to have sex. Sex with Leon is something I've fantasised about ever since we met four weeks ago. I wore my best underwear (my new black Wonderbra and lacy G-string!) but I felt self-conscious as I walked around to his house. He had fancied Frankie, with her hour-glass figure and big boobs. I'm the polar opposite. Would he find me sexy?

Despite snogging and holding hands for four weeks, Leon's not really tried anything on. He once put his hands on one of my boobs, over my T-shirt. But that's as far as it's ever gone between us.

And then there is the matter of Jason holding me

back. This huge secret that I'm keeping from Leon about his cousin.

Anyway, when he opened the door and I walked into his kitchen the air was thick with sexual tension. We barely spoke to each other as he led me upstairs to his bedroom, with its narrow single bed pushed up against the wall and an old He-Man duvet cover that used to belong to his brother. He undressed me on that duvet cover, slowly peeling off my jeans and T-shirt expertly, so that I lay there, trembling slightly in my bra and knickers.

Afterwards, wrapped in his arms and staring up at the swirly Artex ceiling, I felt consumed by guilt. I knew that this couldn't last, that the ghost of Jason and what we did will always sit between us. I tried to push down these negative thoughts, to concentrate on that moment. I could have stayed there all night but we were interrupted by the bang of the front door and the raised voices of Steph and Lorcan.

'I fucking saw you, you bastard,' she screeched and then the sound of something smashing. Lorcan shouted back, but his voice was too low to be decipherable.

Leon groaned, turning to me and propping himself up on his elbow. 'Looks like they're having another fight.'

'Do they do this all the time?'

'Pregnancy hormones. That's what my brother says, anyway. We'd better get out of here.'

We dressed, the mood in the room turning awkward as I stepped into my knickers, fumbled with my bra, then pulled my T-shirt over my head and slid into my jeans. Leon had his back to me as he dressed, nearly falling over in his eagerness to get his trousers on.

The back door slammed so loud that it reverberated throughout the house.

'It sounds like he's gone out,' said Leon, relieved. He grabbed my hand and smiled shyly. 'Shall we go to The Basement?'

I agreed, remembering I had promised to meet Frankie and Helen there. We stole down the stairs quietly, not wanting to alert Steph, but then through the open door of the living room we could see her perched on the edge of the sofa. Steph is tall and thin, with curly, dark hair held back by a clip; her bump looks like she's just stuffed a watermelon up her T-shirt. She has intense dark eyes and a scowl that would scare off most women, but she is pretty and young, probably not much older than me. Her hands rested on her tummy, her chin on her chest. My heart went out to her. Leon hesitated, then popped his head around the door.

'Are you OK, Steph?' he said, stepping into the room. I hovered in the hallway, feeling uncomfortable.

I heard her sniff and tell him that Lorcan was a bastard. Leon mumbled his agreement. I made my way out of the hallway, through the kitchen and into the garden so that they could have some privacy. Ten minutes later he emerged through the back door.

'There you are,' he said, relief etched all over his face to see me sitting on the wall. 'I thought you'd gone.'

'I wanted to give you some space. She looked upset.'

'She's OK now. But Lorcan treats her like shit a lot

of the time. I mean she's bloody pregnant and he still can't stop perving over other women. I don't know what she sees in him.'

I've only met Lorcan once when I called for Leon. He has a hard face, and his eyes, so like Leon's yet colder, scanned me in a way that made me feel naked and exposed. Then he gave me a lascivious wink that turned my stomach. He and Steph have already been married for two years, according to Leon, and together since she was fifteen and he seventeen. He's cheated on her throughout their relationship, yet she forgives him every time.

'I'm not like my brother,' he said, taking my hand as we walked to The Basement.

'I should hope not,' I laughed. 'I wouldn't be going out with you if you were.'

When we reached the old pier he stopped, his face serious. 'I've written a poem. It's about you.' He rummaged in the pocket of his jeans and pulled out a crumpled piece of lined paper and handed it to me with a self-conscious smile. 'It's about soulmates. No, don't read it now,' he said hurriedly as I went to open it. 'Keep it, until later.'

I pushed it into the pocket of my jeans, touched. I couldn't wait to get home to read it.

He pulled me into his arms. 'I know we haven't known each other that long,' he whispered into my hair, 'but I can't stop thinking about you, Sophie. I think about you all the time.'

I could feel myself blushing and I remembered

Frankie's warning. Intense. But I liked it. I liked that he was honest about how he felt.

'I feel the same,' I admitted, a lump forming in my throat. In that moment I wanted to cling to him, to wrap my arms and legs around him so that our bodies merged into one again, and never let him go. But I knew that was impossible. I knew that I would have to let him go. Eventually.

The Basement was heaving when we arrived. I tried to spot Frankie or Helen amongst the crowd but the small underground rooms were so full of bodies, a fug of smoke hanging in the air like a cloud, that I couldn't make out anyone I recognised. The place smelt of cigarettes and stale sweat.

'She's going to be cross with me,' I said as we wove our way to the bar. My eyes, ever sensitive, were beginning to water. 'I promised her I'd be here. And Helen.'

Leon shrugged. 'Oh, she won't mind. Knowing Frankie she's found an admirer or two to keep her company.'

My stomach curdled with jealousy. It would have been the perfect time to ask him about Frankie, but I was scared of what his answer would be. I don't think I could bear it if he told me he had been in love with her. What if he still had feelings for her? As much as I loved Frankie I didn't want to play second fiddle to her any more. It was fine while we were at school, even with Jason. But not now. Leon is too important to me, even if he can never properly be mine.

We stood at the bar for ages, jostling with everyone else in an attempt to get served. And then, as if from nowhere, Frankie appeared.

'There you both are,' she said, standing on tip-toes between us with her arms slung around our necks. Her breath smelt sweet, like alcopops. 'I've been looking for you for ages. You said you'd be here at ten, Soph.' Her face was in profile, but she sounded like she was pouting. Still, it couldn't dampen my mood. Leon and I had had sex. He was falling for me. Me, not Frankie.

Leon excused himself to go to the loo and I let Frankie lead me onto the dance floor.

'Where have you been?' She had to shout over the Chemical Brothers.

'At Leon's house . . .'

'You've shagged him, haven't you? Despite everything. How could you?'

'Frankie . . .'

She stopped dancing to stare at me, hands on hips. 'It's all wrong, Sophie. You know it is.'

I bit my lip, wanting to cry because she was right.

Then I felt his hands around my waist, his groin grinding into my bottom in time to the music. I felt embarrassed at his display of affection in front of Frankie. 'Leon . . . what are you doing? Get off me!' Then I noticed the smell. It wasn't the CK One that Leon always wore, but something acrid, sharp in my nostrils, unpleasant. I turned my head and was shocked to see Lorcan grinning at me.

I pushed him away, suddenly furious. What the hell was he playing at?

'What have you been up to with my brother, then, huh? Were you fucking when we came in . . .' His breath smelt of booze, his voice slurred. Despite his crude words I couldn't help but notice Frankie widen her eyes in shock. 'Got a nice arse,' he said, tapping me playfully on the bottom. 'No tits, though. Not like your friend 'ere.'

Frankie grabbed my arm and pulled me to her. 'Lorcan, stop being a prick and leave us alone.'

'What?' he said, grinning innocently. 'I'm doing nuffin' wrong.'

It happened quickly. One minute Lorcan was in front of us, leering, the next Leon was punching him and yelling at him to fuck off. Lorcan is a big bloke but he didn't try and defend himself, or punch Leon back. Instead, throwing us a wounded look, like we were bullies in a playground, he slunk off and was swallowed up in the crowd.

'Are you OK?' Leon asked me, ignoring Frankie. 'My brother is a prick when he's drunk.'

'He was feeling her bum and everything,' said Frankie. Leon's expression darkened and a pulse thumped in his jaw. I was furious with Frankie for making it worse.

'It's nothing I can't take care of.' I was annoyed at them both for treating me like I'm made of glass. But really Lorcan's comments about my flat chest stung. I hoped Leon hadn't heard them.

'I could kill him. How dare he do that to my girlfriend,' he said to nobody in particular, like I was his possession. We'd slept together, now he thought he owned me? He hugged me to him and kissed me as though he'd just rescued me from a near disaster, not some idiot with overzealous hands. Over his shoulder I noticed Frankie roll her eyes and give me an 'I told you so' look.

We left soon after that. Leon walked me home, but we were mostly silent as we meandered through the high street, then past the hotels and B&Bs and across the road to the seafront. There was a gang of kids on the beach, laughing and swigging booze from bottles. Shouts from a group of women could be heard up ahead as a hen night dressed in pink tutus spilled out of Odyssey, one skinny woman wearing a veil. That club was a known meat market.

Leon had his arm around my shoulders and mine was snaked around his waist, my hand resting in the back pocket of his jeans, but we were both brooding in our own way. Frankie's words rang in my ears: intense, a stalker. But Leon had been protecting me, hadn't he? He wasn't just acting like a jealous boyfriend. His brother was being a real arsehole.

When we reached my house Leon apologised again for Lorcan's behaviour. 'I just saw red. He had his hands on you, Soph. How dare he?'

'I know . . . but I can look after myself.'

We kissed by the garage. I was tempted to ask him

in – I knew Mum was working nights – but I wanted to be on my own, to think. Because what Leon did has left a nasty taste in my mouth. Punches thrown, noses bleeding . . . it stirred up memories I've tried hard to bury.

Whilst getting ready for bed I remembered Leon's poem tucked in the pocket of my jeans. I retrieved it and spread it out on my duvet cover, tears prickling at the back of my eyelids as I read the words, the intensity of his feelings jumping from the page:

As the setting sun casts its glow upon the pier,
transforming the decaying metal, a distraction
from my fear,
remembering those who graced these rotten
boards before,
forgotten, unknown, and loved ones who are here
no more.
Through my haze of self-reflection, I see your beauty
clear as day,
like a beacon to my soul, there ceases to be
another way,
destined for the crashing waves below, together
until we die,
bound for ever, beneath this orange sky.

16
Frankie

I close the heavy front door behind me and rest my head against it, engulfed by the same lethargy as I experienced outside Lorcan's house. I half hope to see the family who are staying in the downstairs apartment, just so that I know I'm not alone in this old building, with its clunking pipes and unexplained creaks, but apart from that glimpse of an older woman through Daniel's steamed-up windscreen yesterday, I've seen nothing of them.

Last night, huddled on the sofa, waiting for the sleeping pills to kick in, I was sure I heard footsteps on the stairs. The wind was whistling outside, shaking the window frames, but when it paused for breath I heard the groan of floorboards under the weight of a person. The baby had stopped crying by then and I listened hard to try and work out where the footsteps were heading. It sounded like they had paused right outside my door. With my heart in my mouth I'd scooped the duvet up around my armpits and waddled to the door to peer through the spyhole. It was too dark to see clearly. I know from the hotel I grew up in that old buildings can make a lot of noise, so I told myself that

I was imagining it and fell asleep not long afterwards. But two interrupted nights have played havoc with my emotional state.

The heel of my boot knocks against something on the floor and I look down to see a familiar brown A4 envelope sitting innocently on the coconut matting. I bend over to pick it up, hoping that it won't be addressed to me, but not in the least surprised when I see my name printed on the front.

It doesn't feel like another letter. It's heavier and there is something bulky inside.

I rip it open; a glint of metallic silver is nestled within the folds. My fingers close on something cold and hard and a pair of old dog tags fall from the envelope into my open palm.

I'm in the bedroom hurriedly removing my clothes from the wardrobe and stuffing them into my holdall when the front door buzzes. I go to the bay window in the living room and peer out. Your brother is standing in the gravel driveway, in front of my Range Rover, a grim expression on his face. I know he's here to stop me leaving. And then I see what he's looking at. My bonnet has been splattered with what looks like raw eggs, the yolk fluorescent against the black metallic paint. I turn away from the window, furious.

I buzz Daniel in and then wait at my door as he lumbers up the stairs.

'I got your text. You can't go back to London,' he says as soon as he reaches me. He's out of breath, his pale cheeks flushed. 'Oh, and it looks like some kids have bombed your car with rotten eggs.'

Without a word I walk back into the apartment, sensing him behind me as I make my way into the sitting room. My feet are freezing and I've had to put on extra socks. On the glass coffee table is the brown envelope, the dog tags spread on top. I point to them as I sit on the sofa, curling my legs up under me. 'This was waiting for me on my return.'

He frowns and walks over to them, picking them up and turning them over in his hands. 'Dog tags? I don't understand.'

'Jason's.'

'They're Jason's dog tags?' His voice is hard, disbelieving.

'Well, I don't expect they are the actual dog tags he was wearing when he . . . when he . . .' I can't bring myself to say the words. 'But they are very similar. He wore them all the time, remember?'

He narrows his eyes, as if trying to dredge up the memories of Jason buried deep in his mind. 'Vaguely. I thought about getting a pair. They *were* all the rage in the early nineties.' He stares down at the tags in his hand.

I get up from the sofa and snatch them from him. 'Someone in this town is deliberately targeting me.' I put them back on the coffee table. 'Why would someone send them to me?'

'To spook you, obviously,' Daniel says, moving to the window. 'And it's working, by the looks of it. You're high-tailing it back to London.' He has his back to me;

I can just see the sharp outline of his nose and chin. I wonder if he's seeing you on the pier. I go and stand beside him, feeling braver now that he's here with me. But you're gone and the pier is empty, the sleet turning to rain.

'Not because of this.' I'm annoyed he thinks that's the reason I want to go home. 'It takes more than a few letters to unnerve me. And now eggs on my car. Pathetic.'

'That would've just been kids messing about . . .'

'Not the dog tags, though. That's personal, Daniel. That has to be from someone who knows about Jason.'

I don't tell him that seeing you has scared me, Soph. What could I say without sounding like I'm having some mental breakdown? That I'm convinced I'm seeing you, that you followed me home, that you are trying to tell me something? Maybe warn me? It sounds ridiculous. I don't believe in ghosts – that was always your domain. The irony doesn't escape me. You always wanted to get out of this town yet you're still here, haunting it. And me.

Daniel sits down heavily on the sofa, the leather creaking under his weight. 'If you're not spooked then why do you want to leave? You've paid up until Friday. You might as well stay.'

'I've got work to do.'

'You're entitled to a holiday.'

I roll my eyes. 'Some holiday.' I take a seat next to him on the sofa. I'm still wearing my coat. I wrap it further around my body and Daniel gets up to light the fire. I watch as the orange flames begin to dance comfortingly, their warm amber glow chasing away the grey shadows, transforming the room so that it appears more welcoming, more friendly.

We always wondered what these apartments would be like inside. You had a thing about this side of town, that pier. You could see past the decrepit planks and rusting metal, likening it to an aged movie star; faded glamour but still beautiful. When you looked at it you saw the nostalgia of the past: Edwardian tourists, the men in straw boaters, the women in their ankle-length dresses, gliding along with frilly parasols angled over their heads. You saw the romance in the pier; I couldn't see past its ugliness.

Daniel takes my hand and rubs it between his. 'You feel freezing, Franks, are you OK?'

'I'm fine. I was just thinking about Sophie.'

He squeezes my hand, his eyes suddenly intense. 'Don't go. Please. Stay, at least a few more days. I . . .' He swallows as if embarrassed, his face reddening. 'I need you.'

'I don't know . . .'

'Don't you see,' he says, his voice rising, 'that the person who's sent you these things is trying to get you to leave. Because they know we're getting close to the truth.'

I laugh bitterly. 'But we're not. We know nothing about what happened that night. We've learned nothing. It's too late. It's been years. I think we should just leave it. Get on with our lives.'

He shuffles closer so that our knees are touching, and despite myself I feel a frisson of desire rip through me. He's still holding my hand and his face is inches from mine so that I can smell the mint on his breath and his warm, musky scent like mulled wine. I long to reach up and touch him, kiss him. But I daren't. Not after this morning.

'Just you being here is unnerving someone, Franks. You must see that. Just give it a few more days, please.'

'But what if I'm in danger, Daniel?'

His voice softens. 'You're safe here in the apartment. And you're safe with me.'

'This house is practically deserted. This area of town is empty. It's lonely. I'm lonely.'

'There's that family downstairs.'

'Who I haven't seen, except for that older woman yesterday. Although I've heard the baby.'

'They are probably in and out, like you are. At least you know they're here too. You're not completely alone.'

'Gee, thanks.' It's all right for him. He can go back to his girlfriend. He has someone to keep his bed warm at night.

I think of returning to Islington, back to normality, with no time to think of anything but my busy job and the new hotel. Then I remember that I promised Mike he could stay until the weekend. It would mean having to face him; the awkwardness, his questions. My resolve might weaken and we'd fall back into a relationship that isn't leading anywhere. He's right, I am a coward. I can't face him. I have no choice but to stay here.

If I'm honest with myself I know there is more to it than that. I know your brother has a girlfriend, but if I left now it would mean saying goodbye to Daniel, probably for ever.

His voice is cajoling as he says, 'And you said you'd come with me on Wednesday to the police station. It's that same bloody detective. Do you remember him? DI Holdsworth.'

'That's the one who questioned us when she first went missing?'

He nods. 'He wasn't a DI then, of course.'

I remember him well. Tall and fair with one eye a different colour to the other. He had interviewed all of us, asked probing questions – until your shoe was found and they eased off a bit. Well, the other police officers eased off, but I sensed that DS Holdsworth suspected foul play by the way he kept coming back for more. I once got home to find him in our kitchen having a cup of tea with Mum. As soon as he saw me his eyes lit up and then he interrogated me for an hour. Where had I been when you left the club? What time did I last see you? Who had a grudge against you? Questions he'd asked me countless times before. I found out that he'd asked the same questions to everyone else in town, including my parents. After a few weeks he was called off the case by his boss, and that was the end of it. Until now.

'He was like a dog with a bone. It was as if he was

hoping that Sophie was murdered so that he would have something juicy to investigate.'

'But he was right, though, wasn't he,' Daniel says darkly.

I swallow; my throat feels sore. 'We don't know that. Have you told him your suspicions?'

He shakes his head. 'No . . . not yet, but I'm beginning to think I should. Especially now that you've been receiving those letters. Maybe when we go on Wednesday?'

I stiffen. The thought of involving the police petrifies me. They've always made me feel on edge. And it makes me realise that I can't leave, not yet. I can't let Daniel face all this by himself. I owe it to him to stay. He wants me to go with him. Not Mia – me. That must mean something, surely, Soph?

'I don't know if we should involve the police,' I say. 'What can they do anyway? And if someone wanted to hurt me, surely they would have done it by now?'

I go and stand in front of the fire. I choose my next words carefully. 'Do you think the person writing the notes and sending those –' I nod at the dog tags curled up on the table '– is the same person who knows what happened to Sophie?'

'Yes, I do.'

'Then it must be Leon. Who else would know, or even care, about Jason other than his cousin? He's just the type who would get a kick out of this kind of thing.'

He hasn't liked me since I told you he was bad news, Soph, and it's obvious from his attitude towards me that our one-night stand all those years ago hasn't changed that.

Daniel shrugs. 'Maybe. I don't know. Who knows who Sophie told, if anyone.'

I frown. 'What about Helen? She was a right cow to me at school. We had a fight once and she gave me a nosebleed. She locked me in a tiny cupboard knowing that I was claustrophobic. Maybe Sophie confided in her and this is her way of punishing me. She was always hanging around Sophie, wanting to be her best friend, trying to push me out. Sophie was too nice to see it but there was something about Helen, something spiteful.'

His gaze is sceptical.

'Well, she must have told someone, otherwise . . .' I let the implication hang in the air. I've never told a soul.

He hesitates. 'Your dad.'

It's as though he's punched me. 'What do you mean?'

'Would he have told anyone?'

I scoff. 'Of course not. My dad was the one who made us promise not to say anything. Ever. And we didn't. Or at least, I didn't. I can't vouch for Sophie. Daniel, she was dating Jason's cousin! You know how kind and good Sophie was. She wouldn't have been able to keep that secret from him. She would have felt too guilty.'

You were always the sensible, moral one, Soph. You made me a better person.

Daniel frowns. 'That's true. But she wasn't with him

that long. What was it? Six weeks, two months at the most?'

Oh, Daniel. He knows nothing about it. I do, though. I remember how much you loved Leon. You might not have been together that long but your relationship was intense.

'They split up hours before she disappeared,' I say, remembering. 'And when I asked her about it she refused to tell me. She fled to the toilets, crying, and Leon stormed off home.'

He fidgets, looking uncomfortable. 'Do you think she told him about what happened to Jason? And that's why he finished it?'

'I don't know. I mean, Sophie said he loved her but to me it seemed more like obsession. Who knows what was really going on in their relationship or why they finished? But if she finished with him I can't imagine he'd let her go that easily. He said he had an alibi, but . . .'

'Anyone can fake an alibi. Steph? Lorcan? They could all be protecting each other. How well do we know anyone, Franks? Particularly those closest to us? They're the ones who can hurt us the most.'

I raise my eyes to meet his. 'That's really cynical. You never used to be like that.'

'Yeah, well, I've changed.' He stands up and goes to the window. Losing you has altered him more than I thought. It's not surprising, I suppose, the two of you were always close. I envied your relationship, your easy banter, the way you looked out and protected each other. It must eat away at him that he wasn't able to protect you that night.

I leave the room to put the kettle on. When I return, Daniel is looking down at his phone and swearing.

'What is it?'

He looks up, his face drawn. 'It's a text from Mia. I told her I was at work. I know, I know . . .' he says when he sees my expression. 'I shouldn't have lied to her, but she is a bit possessive sometimes and she's worried about me spending too much time with you.'

He looks embarrassed and I shrug nonchalantly, even though I can't help feeling a little thrill that she sees me as a threat.

'Does she know you lied?'

'She must do,' he says, throwing his phone onto the sofa, 'because Helen turned up at our flat wanting to talk to me. Apparently she's remembered something really important and Mia told her I was here.'

I'm not surprised that Helen has 'suddenly' remembered something important. I always told you that she couldn't be trusted. I knew she was lying to me yesterday.

What important thing does Helen know?

17
Sophie

Sunday, 27 July 1997

I've done something so stupid, so unforgivable, and there is no excuse for it. I love Leon and I understand that he only punched his brother last night because he was protecting me. His brother was acting like a lecherous pig. It doesn't mean Leon would hurt me. It's just . . . after what Dad did to Mum when I was a kid I always said I'd never fall for a man who had the capacity to be violent.

I suppose I always envied Frankie for having a dad like Alistair. Someone kind and caring. Passive. My feelings for him have always been complicated. On one hand I see him as a father figure, but on the other he's this attractive older guy, the Kevin Costner lookalike, the first man who ever paid me any attention, who cared enough to ask what I wanted to do with my life, how I was getting on at school and if I was happy.

So, here goes . . . I kissed him. There, I've said it. And I honestly feel awful about it. That's not who I am, or the person I want to be. I don't go around kissing married men or the fathers of my friends. I've never cheated on anyone before.

It happened at lunchtime and I've been feeling sick with guilt ever since.

My shift had just begun and I was straightening the bed in Room 5 and replacing the dirty cups when Alistair bounded into the room. He didn't realise I was in there and muttered a smiley apology, and was just about to leave when he must have noticed something about me, something about my expression perhaps. I've never been very good at hiding my feelings.

'Is something wrong?' he asked, letting the door swing shut and walking further into the room. He placed a reassuring hand on my upper arm and his touch sent an electric shock through me, and in that moment all I wanted was a man like him. Someone mature, someone strong, someone who was jolly, funny, always putting a positive spin on things. Not someone who had behaved as Leon had. I remember so clearly how Alistair helped us out that awful night when Jason drowned. How I'd turned up at his house with vomit down my dress, panicked and shaking so much that I thought I'd never stop. Shock, he'd called it. He'd wrapped me up in a blanket and given me sips of brandy and told me that everything was going to be OK. That he was going to make everything OK. And I'd sat there, shivering and sipping the brandy, his reassuring words calming me down. Frankie was obviously there too, sitting next to me wrapped up in her own blanket, tears streaming down her face. But in the memories of that night I don't think of Frankie, I just see Alistair.

I found myself telling him everything, about Leon being Jason's cousin, about the guilt that I felt at not being able to tell him what had happened that night. About Leon punching Lorcan and how I know that I have to let Leon go. He sat next to me while I poured out my feelings like some messed-up teenager, his arm around my shoulders. And it felt so good to unburden myself. I couldn't be honest with Leon but I could with Alistair. I began to cry and nestled my face into his chest, inhaling the scent of him, of his aftershave – something expensive, mature – and the washing powder on his linen shirt. He smoothed my hair and stroked my back. And then I lifted my head so that our eyes met and before I could even think about it his lips were on mine and . . . we were kissing. I forgot for a moment where I was, who he was, the kiss went on and on and, wow, what a kisser he is. But when his tongue started to probe mine I pulled away, suddenly ashamed. I'd been caught up in the moment and angry at Leon. It should never have led to that. He was mortified too, jumping up from the bed and running his hands through his dirty blond hair, apologising over and over again. I told him it was fine, that it was my fault. I blurted out to him that I'd had a crush on him when I was a teenager. I suppose, deep down, kissing him had always been a fantasy of mine. But that's where it should have stayed – as a fantasy. He made me promise never to tell anyone.

Another promise. Another secret. Another thing to feel guilty about.

But I made the promise anyhow.

I'd betrayed my best friend and my boyfriend. How am I ever going to face Frankie, her mum or Leon ever again, knowing what I've done?

18
Frankie

The door buzzer reverberates through the flat. Daniel, who is still standing by the window, leans forward to get a better view of who is at the door.

'She's here.' He turns around, horror and excitement written all over his face. His silver eyes are alight. 'I wonder what she's remembered?' I can't bear to witness the hope turn to disappointment. I like seeing Daniel this way, the way he was when you were alive. Full of optimism, even if it is misplaced. He always thought that life would work out for him despite flunking his GCSEs and not having a job. What a wake-up call he had. I don't want him to go back to silent, morose Daniel.

I snatch up the dog tags and envelope from the coffee table and dart into my bedroom. I don't know why, but I hide them under my duvet cover. If Helen has been sending the letters – and it is just the type of spiteful thing I can imagine her doing – I don't want her to know how much it's unnerved me. Maybe you told her our secret? How would I know? It seems I didn't know you as well as I thought.

I go to the intercom and let her in. Daniel lurks in the hallway as I open the door and wait for her to come up. It seems like ages before she reaches the top of the stairs, panting slightly as she steps on to the landing, sweat glistening above her lip. Her shoulder-length brown hair is frizzy from the rain. She's wearing a frumpy long skirt and boots, with a brown wool coat which does nothing for her. Her best feature was always her eyes, which are the colour of treacle.

'Frankie,' she says in a monotone when she reaches the landing.

I don't ask her how she knows where I live. The whole town is probably aware. It makes me feel exposed and vulnerable; a sitting duck.

'Helen,' I say in the same tone. 'What can I do for you?'

'Can I come in?'

I open the door wider and stand aside to allow her over the threshold. She whistles slowly as she wanders into the hallway. 'This is posh, ain't it? But only the best for Lady Frankie.'

I bristle. It was only ever your brother who called me that. When did Helen suddenly jump on the bandwagon? Has Daniel been talking to her about me? It's on the tip of my tongue to tell her to piss off. I know she was your friend, and I realise you thought a lot of her, that she was there for you when I was forced to go to that stuck-up boarding school – which, by the way, I hated – but she's always been a bit of a bitch to me. You could never see it though. Or maybe you refused to.

'Daniel!' she says when she spots him over my shoulder. 'You're a hard man to find. I went to your offices and your flat.'

'Really? I thought you knew all our whereabouts, Helen?' I smile at her sweetly but she frowns.

'What are you talking about?'

'How did you know I'm staying here?'

'Stan told me.'

'Stan?'

You always said Stan would perv at you over the fish, his eyes as pale and cold as the haddock he was selling.

'Yep.'

'Who told him?'

'Leon.'

Did I tell Leon I was staying here? Unless Daniel did. Not that it really matters. Any one of them could be sending the notes to frighten me. I'm going to have to pay Leon another visit. But I won't tell Daniel about it. This is something I need to take care of on my own.

Helen wanders into the living room, exclaiming at its loveliness, at the polished wooden floors and the scatter cushions, at the real fireplace and the views of the sea. 'I bet it's costing a bomb to stay here,' she says, going to the bay window. 'What a view!'

'It's not costing much. It's out of season and Daniel's friend has let me have mates' rates.' I wish she would get to the point.

She turns to me and shivers. 'Ooh, it's chilly in 'ere, ain't it? Even with that fire on.'

The apartment is constantly cold, I've noticed. Is it because you're here with us, Soph?

The fire goes out, as though you've answered my question.

'Spooky!' says Helen in awe as she stares at the dead embers at the bottom of the fireplace. 'It went out as quickly as someone clicking their fingers.'

'I'll relight it,' says Daniel, going back to the fireplace. We both watch as he faffs around with logs and a lighter but, despite his best efforts, the fire refuses to be resurrected.

He stands up with a helpless shrug of his shoulders. 'Let's leave it for a minute. Helen, why don't you sit down?'

I offer to make tea. When I return with three mugs of PG Tips (always your favourite, which is probably why your brother bought it), Daniel and Helen are sitting side by side on the sofa. I place the tray on the coffee table and tell them to help themselves to milk and sugar. I take mine and sit on the grey velvet chair by the window. There is a draught; the wooden sash windows are not strong enough to keep out that wind. I cup the tea so that the heat from the mug can warm my ice-cold hands. I really hope Daniel can get that fire started again. The radiators are blazing but it's making little difference to the temperature. The wind howls down the chimney.

'So, Helen, why the visit?' I ask pointedly when it's obvious that Daniel isn't about to.

'Well, I suddenly remembered something. So I went past your offices, Dan. I know how hard you work and thought you'd be there despite it being the weekend, but there was no answer. So I went over to your apartment. Met Mia. Lovely girl, so pretty.' She flashes me a triumphant look. 'Anyway, she told me you were at work. When I said you weren't there she looked a little surprised and then said you'd probably be at Frankie's house. So I headed here. It's a long walk though, Dan.' She gives a little laugh. 'I wish I'd learned to drive.'

Daniel shifts his weight, looking uncomfortable. He knows he's going to be in trouble when he gets home. I assess him over the rim of my mug. Your brother was always so honest. Maybe he's changed more than I thought.

My grip on my mug tightens. I tear my gaze from Daniel to Helen. 'What have you remembered?' I say, trying to keep my voice calm, even though I really want to shout, 'Get to the bloody point!'

She purses her lips as if she can hear my thoughts and then takes a noisy slurp of her tea. I wait, refusing to speak first. Eventually, she says, 'A few weeks before she went missing –'

'Before she died,' Daniel interjects.

'Yes, yes, before she died, well, Sophie asked me for help.'

'What kind of help?' I ask. I find it hard to believe you would have asked Helen for help and not me. Is she deliberately making out she knows more than she does to feel important? To create a little drama?

She clears her throat. 'She wanted money. She was so happy to get that job as an editorial assistant. Do you remember? Anyways, she wanted to leave Oldcliffe a few weeks before her job started but didn't have enough money.'

Daniel frowns. 'OK, so . . .'

'There's more. She said that someone was making her life hell. A man. And that she needed to leave. She sounded pretty scared of this person.'

'Didn't you ask her who it was?' Daniel says.

'Of course. But she wouldn't tell me. But I did wonder if it could be her dad.' She bows her head, looking slightly shamefaced. 'Sophie had told me all about him. I'm sorry, Dan. He sounds like a right arsehole.'

I'm shocked that you would have talked to Helen about him. You'd only ever mentioned him to me a couple of times. I didn't even know his name.

'We haven't heard or seen him since we left, as far as I'm aware . . .' Daniel turns to me. 'Did she tell you any of this?'

I shake my head miserably. You didn't come to me. You went to Helen for help instead. 'When was this?' I ask.

'I'd say this was the end of August. So it might have only been a week before she disappeared –' Helen flashes Daniel a look '– *died*.'

She leans forward and places her mug back on the tray. Then she rummages in the bag that's at her feet and pulls out a length of pink toilet tissue and blows her nose on it. 'I feel terrible that I never said anything. You just don't think, do you? That it could mean something. I even thought she might have meant Lorcan. He's a right one. Even now. Oh, I hear all sorts of things about him. Gossip is rife in our pub.'

I can imagine.

She dabs at her eyes but I'm certain there are no tears. 'I've often wondered if . . .' She glances at Daniel as though doubting whether to continue.

'Go on,' he says.

'I thought maybe . . . she might have killed herself.'

'She would never do that.' He stands up; his restlessness is making me feel anxious. 'There was no note, nothing apart from her trainer wedged between those rotten wooden boards.' He shakes his head. 'Bloody Holdsworth asked that same question but I just can't believe it. I can't . . .'

'Could she have fallen in? Got her shoe stuck?'

I can see that Daniel is bristling with irritation although he's trying not to show it as he paces back and forth. I shiver and pull my coat further around me. He's creating a draught and it's cold enough in here as it is.

'She would never have gone to the pier by herself in the middle of the night,' he says. 'I think – and so does Frankie – that she'd arranged to meet someone there.'

Helen sniffs. 'No, I'm sure you're right. I just want to be able to help.' She turns to me, her face defiant. 'Sophie was always good to me. She was a good friend.'

Her comment sounds barbed as though she's implying I wasn't a good friend to you.

Does she know more than she's letting on?

19
Sophie

Sunday, 27 July 1997

Leon rang. He wants to come over but I put him off. I feel so guilty about what happened with Alistair earlier, I can't face Leon right now.

I hate to admit it but Frankie was right. About everything, but especially about Leon. I should have listened to her. She always was the more savvy of the two of us. She just seemed to know how these things worked, how people ticked. When we were at school she steered me through the social echelons of our year group effortlessly so that, despite how gauche and geeky I was, I didn't get picked on. Because I was best friends with the popular Francesca Howe.

That first day at our primary school – just days after Mum bundled me, Daniel and all our meagre belongings into the back of her old Ford estate and moved us to the other end of the country – I stood in front of my new class, twenty-eight faces staring blankly back at me, and there she was, like a poppy in a field of weeds. When our form teacher asked who wanted to be my buddy I was amazed that she volunteered. I couldn't believe it: this pretty girl with the green cat's eyes wanted to be friends with me. I stuck to her after that like a limpet. And that's what some of the boys called me. Not Four-eyes, or Beanstalk, or even Flea-bag (and believe me, over the years I've been called all those), but Limpet, because I was always glued to Frankie's side.

As we grew up I began to notice that some of the other kids turned against her, thinking that she was stuck-up, that she thought a lot of herself. But it wasn't true. Underneath her glossy image Frankie was as insecure as the next teenager. All she wanted was to be liked.

She protected me. And that's all she's ever tried to do. It's just that at times I found it stifling, that I couldn't breathe without her say so. Then she left, after ten years of friendship, and I was forced to stand on my own two feet. Well, what a fucking mess I've made of that!

I don't know how I'm going to be able to live with myself.

20
Frankie

I watch from the window as Helen folds herself into Daniel's car, thinking how old she seems, a decade older than she really is – although her expression of disdain is the same as when we were twenty-one. Daniel offered to give her a lift home, even though she lives above the Seagull, a ten-minute walk from here. I survey the grey skies. The rain and sleet have stopped but the clouds look swollen and fit to burst. I can't resist a quick glance at the pier, but apart from a plastic bag being blown about by the wind there's nothing there.

I tear my eyes away and see Daniel reversing his car out of the driveway, his tyres kicking up gravel, and I have a sudden, paranoid stab of worry that the two of them are talking about me. What is it about Helen that makes me feel so uncomfortable? Maybe it's because she's always seemed immune to my charms; that however much I tried at school, with my witty quips and sarcastic one-liners, she would just fix her unusual eyes on me and gaze at me coolly, like she knew that underneath it all I was a phoney, a fraud. She never warmed to me; no matter what I tried, she always liked you. I thought that it was because I was pretty and my parents were quite well-off, whereas you were odd-looking, like her. Although that theory was disproved when you turned up again after university, having turned into a swan. Helen still wanted to be your friend.

A figure lurking behind my car startles me. I frown and edge closer to the glass. It's the woman staying in the apartment downstairs. What is she doing? It looks as though she is rooting around in the bins. I watch as she pulls out a newspaper and an envelope – or it could be a piece of paper – both slightly damp and crumpled. She puts them under her coat and heads back into the house.

I turn away from the window. I don't care about Helen or the woman downstairs. The person I need to speak to is Leon. Because I think you did tell him our secret. I don't blame you. I know you wouldn't have been able to help it, it was what I was worried about all along. The reason I urged you to end your relationship with him. Well, that's not strictly true. There were other reasons too. But you didn't want to finish with him. You fell in love with him, as did I. We always did have the same taste in men.

I cruise through the estate like some boy-racer hoping to pick up a date. If Lorcan is outside I'm praying he won't recognise my car. But the driveway of the house is empty, the rusty old Renault abandoned, still on bricks. I pull up in front of the garage. I can't see into the house because of the high fence. The only view I have is the white wooden cladding and the two rectangular upstairs windows, like bespectacled eyes peering at me over the gate. One of the windows must be a bedroom and the other a bathroom, judging by the frosted glass. Could it be the bedroom Leon is staying in? I squint, trying to make out the print on the curtains. Pink?

I turn the engine off and wait. Thankfully the rain has washed away most of the egg from the bonnet of my car, although I can still see some remnants clinging to the paintwork.

I consider risking Lorcan's wrath and knocking on the back door. I need to see Leon. I need to know if he's been sending me those notes. If he's hoping to scare me then he's succeeded.

After a while the warm air in the car begins to disperse, the cold seeping in through the vents. I don't know how long I can bear to sit here. Leon might never come out. Why would he, on a grey, freezing Sunday afternoon? He's probably sat in front of the television.

When I can stand it no longer I get out of the car. With an iron resolve I push open the gate and make my way through the garden to the back door. Despite my bravado my heart is pounding underneath my red wool coat, and I wrap the scarf further around my neck as though it has the power to protect me. As I feared, Lorcan comes to the door.

'What do you want?' he barks, his large frame filling the doorway, blocking the view into the kitchen.

'I've not come to make trouble,' I say in my most conciliatory voice. 'Can I speak to Leon?'

'If this is about Sophie Collier, then no,' he growls.

'I've had enough of it.' He pulls on the straps of his dungarees as though to emphasise the point. His words are slurred and he reeks of stale alcohol.

'It's not,' I lie. 'Come on, Lorcan. We're all old friends. I just want to catch up with him. I'm on my own. No Daniel.' I try to make this sound enticing without it being flirtatious.

He treats me to one of his lecherous winks. 'Ah, I see.' He pats his beer belly. 'Well, you'd better come in then.' He steps back and I gingerly step into the kitchen. 'Steph? Leon?' he bellows and the smell of his breath nearly knocks me out. I step away from him, the kitchen worktop digging into the small of my back.

Steph comes into the kitchen. At least I'm assuming it's Steph because the curly-haired, hard-faced girl I remember is long gone. She's filled out so much that she is almost unrecognisable. Her hair is wiry and streaked with grey and her face is bare of make-up.

Steph was a year older than us at school and always looked down her nose at me, as though I smelled particularly bad. She was the sort of girl that hated other girls, saw them as competition.

Nevertheless, she smiles at me warmly. 'Frankie, how are you, love? It's been a long time.'

I give her a tentative smile, wondering if this is some sort of joke. Is she pretending to be nice to lure me into a false sense of security before kicking the shit out of me? Then I remind myself that we are no longer teenage girls, we are women approaching middle age. She's got grown-up kids. We've changed.

'I'll leave you in Steph's capable hands,' grins Lorcan. 'I'm off to the pub.'

Steph ignores him, bustles over to the kettle and snaps it on. I watch her, fascinated. Is this what happens to all women who stay in Oldcliffe – they get married, put on weight and stop dyeing their hair? But then I realise I'm being unfair. Steph was once quite glamorous in her cheap-dresses-from-New-Look type of way, but she seems happier now. Gone is the permanently furrowed brow and sharp tongue that I remember so well. The extra weight has made her face softer. Does she turn a blind eye to Lorcan's affairs, or does she just not care any more?

She turns to me and hands me a mug of tea. I decline her offer of sugar.

'Come and sit down,' she says and I follow her into the living room and perch on the edge of the sofa. 'Leon!' she calls. 'Frankie's here.'

I can't imagine how it must feel for Leon to be living back here again after all this time. Oppressive. And depressing. I wonder what he's been doing all these years, where he's been working.

'How have you been?' she asks, cupping her mug.

'Good, thanks.'

'I heard about your dad . . .'

I can imagine them all gossiping about it at the local pub.

'Terrible, for all of you. Such a shock. How is your mum coping?'

'Well, it's difficult.'

'I can imagine.'

'And you?' I ask, to change the subject. I don't want to talk about my dad. He would hate being gossiped about. We might have moved from the area years ago but memories are long. My dad wasn't just the local businessman, he was involved with the town council and had 'fingers in many pies', as he always liked to tell me. 'I'm going to see a man about a dog,' he would say when I was a kid, tapping the side of his nose and winking. The first time he did it I was about six and I sat with my nose pressed to the window all afternoon, waiting for his return, convinced that he was going to come home with a puppy. As I grew older I realised it was just a saying he used when he was off to do some business. Everybody in Oldcliffe knew who Alistair Howe was.

Steph chuckles. 'I've been kept busy, what with five kids. Our Caitlin just had a baby, so I'm a grandma. Can you believe it? A grandma at forty-one.'

I smile politely and ask after Caitlin and the baby. She asks me, like I knew she would, if I have any children, and I say, as I always do, that no, it never happened for me, unfortunately.

A shadow in my peripheral vision makes me turn around and Leon is standing in the doorway.

'Frankie. Back again?'

'I . . . um,' I cough, suddenly uncomfortable. Maybe coming here was a mistake. 'Um, yes. I wondered if you were free to go for a drink?'

He looks taken aback. He glances at his watch. 'It's only two o'clock.'

'Lunch then? I'm starving.'

'I could make you a bite to eat?' offers Steph, standing up.

Leon waves his hand dismissively. 'No, you're all right, ta, Steph. We'll go out. We've got a lot to talk about, haven't we, Frankie.'

His tone is light and he raises an eyebrow at me, but I can hear the dark undercurrent to his words even if Steph is oblivious. He takes my arm and steers me out of the room.

'Wait there,' he instructs and I stand awkwardly in the narrow hallway while he grabs a raincoat from the end of the banister. He shoulders it on, indicating with his head for me to follow him, and then practically drags me out of the door.

'Ow, you're hurting my arm,' I say as he wrestles me through the garden gate. 'You don't have to be so rough.'

'What are you doing here?' he says sharply.

'I wanted to see you.'

'I only saw you yesterday. Why are you here again?' His blue eyes are cold and hard.

'It's important. But I can't explain here. Can we go somewhere?'

For a second I wonder if he's going to tell me to get lost. I hold my breath, relieved when he gives a resigned nod. I point the key fob at the car and he opens the passenger door and slides into the cream leather seat. I try not to give him sideways glances as I get behind the wheel and drive towards town.

I find a parking space overlooking the sludgy sand and the Grand Pier. The tide is out but the deserted beach is dotted with little puddles where the sea has been. The clouds decide this is the time to explode, the rain coming down hard, pounding on the roof and the windscreen, obscuring our view. The air in the car feels thick and oppressive. I turn the ignition off.

'What is this all about, Frankie? I haven't got the time or energy to play your little games.' He turns to me, a frown on his face. He dislikes me, that much is obvious, Soph. It's evident in the tension I notice in his shoulders, the steeliness behind his eyes, the scowl that he doesn't even try to hide. He was civil to me yesterday – I suppose he had to be. But today all pretence of friendliness has gone.

He hasn't forgiven me.

'Frankie?' His impatient voice jolts me back to the present.

'I'm sorry.' I shift in my seat. I open my mouth to speak but no words come out. What do I say?

'Are you sending me anonymous letters to try and freak me out?' There really is no other way of putting it.

He appears taken aback. 'What are you talking about now?'

I explain, as quickly as I can, about the notes.

'Why would I do that?'

'I don't know,' I lie. I can't tell him about Jason if he doesn't know. If you haven't told him.

He frowns. His eyes are lined, bruised with shadows.

'What's going on, Frankie? Is there something you're trying to tell me here?'

I can feel myself blushing. 'No, of course not.'

The rain stops as abruptly as it began.

There is an uneasy silence between us. How could I have thought I was in love with him? I was so vain and naive. For years I thought he was the one that got away. Since then, of course, worse things have happened in my so-called 'shiny' life. Like the collapse of my marriage, the discovery that I can't conceive, your remains being found.

'I'm going to be moving on soon,' says Leon, reaching for the door handle. 'I have another contract. Dubai this time.'

'Good for you,' I say.

He narrows his eyes at me as though I'm being sarcastic.

'I don't know who's sending you those letters, or messing with your head, Frankie. Maybe it's got something to do with your dad.'

'It's got nothing to do with my dad.'

He smiles at me but it doesn't reach his eyes and in that moment I can see the cruelness of Lorcan in him. What did I ever see in him? What did you?

'I read all about him. In the newspaper. Nice guy.'

'He is a nice guy.' I feel on the edge of tears. 'It's all untrue, all of it.'

He shrugs. 'Whatever.'

I'm suddenly overcome with this urge to hit him. I clench my fists. 'Get out,' I say.

'With pleasure.' He opens the car door, but he doesn't get out. Instead he stares at me, his mouth twisting cruelly. 'You couldn't stand the thought that I loved her, could you?'

'It wasn't love,' I spit. 'You hardly knew her. It was infatuation, that's all.'

He shakes his head sorrowfully. 'I feel sorry for you. Nearly forty years old and still not happy. Always wanting what you can't have.'

'That's not true.' But I think of Daniel, his one-time devotion. I could have had him. And now I want him, it's too late.

He sneers. 'Believe what you want to believe, Frankie. You always have.'

He slams the door behind him. I wait until he's sloped off along the promenade, his shoulders hunched against the wind, then I collapse in a heap over the steering wheel and let the tears flow.

21

Sophie

Sunday, 3 August 1997

I can't sleep. It's only 6 a.m. but I need to write this down, to make sense of what's going on in my screwed-up mind.

Leon came over on Thursday night, worried that I was cross with him. I considered not seeing him, scared that the fact I'd kissed Frankie's father would be written all over my face. Every time I think of it (and I've been unable to do much else, it keeps playing over and over in my mind), a wave of shame washes over me and I feel queasy. But I'd not seen Leon since it happened and I knew I couldn't put him off for ever.

He came over about seven and we walked into town together, neither of us speaking, the atmosphere between us tense and awkward. He held my hand, more out of duty, I felt, than desire. I wanted to snatch it away but that would have been rude. The sun was still blazing in the sky and as we approached the centre there were people lying out on the beach, trying to eke out the remnants of the sunshine. The pubs were packed, people spilling out onto the main road with beer glasses and fags. The big wheel was going round, lights flashing, and children were shrieking with excitement as they sped down the helter-skelter, no doubt regretting it later as they assessed burn marks to elbows and legs.

When we reached the entrance to the Grand Pier we hovered awkwardly by the ice-cream stall. I could see Frankie's candy-pink hotel across the road and I imagined what Alistair might be doing. Was he thinking about me? About that kiss? Was he regretting it as much as I was?

I felt so confused in that moment that I nearly blurted it out to Leon.

After the kiss I'd managed to avoid Alistair for the rest of my shift. We bumped into each other once, on the landing, me clutching a basketful of dirty towels and him with a cup of coffee in his hand. It was a bit awkward as I tried to pass him, the two of us sidestepping each other while apologising, so it looked like we were taking part in a barn dance. It would have been funny but I was too embarrassed to laugh. Then I scuttled off as fast as my legs would carry me.

And I've not seen him since. Frankie said he had to go and visit his father, but I think he's been avoiding me too.

'You're still angry at me, aren't you?' Leon's voice cut into my thoughts. He leaned against the sea wall, but his expression was serious, worried even. 'You've not wanted to see me since Saturday night.'

'No, I'm not.'

He grabbed my hand. 'I'm sorry I overreacted. I've

apologised to Lorcan and him to me. He admitted he was acting like a twat, and he deserved it.'

'Nobody deserves to get a broken nose, Leon.'

I'd heard, through Frankie of course, that Lorcan had to go to the hospital for an X-ray.

'He'd already broken it twice when we were kids, getting into fights. It didn't take much.'

'Oh, so that's OK then?'

'No, no, of course not. I feel dreadful about it. I'm so sorry. I just wanted to protect you. I hated that he was trying it on with you. I can't stand the thought of anyone doing that.'

As his arms circled my waist I wondered if I'd ever be on the receiving end of his fists. I once read that having an abusive father makes you more likely to fall for an abusive partner, even though my dad never laid a finger on me. Maybe if he'd stayed around he would have done. Leon seems so kind, so doting, so soft right now. But they all must start off that way – charming, devoted. Intense. Possessive.

'My dad was an arsehole who used to hit my mum,' I said. I've hardly told anyone that before.

Leon's eyes widened and then realisation dawned on him. 'Fucking hell. That's why you reacted like you did?'

I pulled away from him. 'No. What you did was wrong.'

He hung his head, his soft brown curls falling across his forehead and into his eyes. 'I know. I'm sorry.' He stepped towards me and gently put his hands on my waist. 'I don't want to fight with you. I've not felt this way about anybody in a long time.'

'Not even with Frankie?' I didn't mean to ask the question, but I hoped he would understand what I was getting at. I braced myself for his answer.

'Frankie? I've never felt anything for Frankie. What are you talking about?'

So I told him. Everything. What she said to me while we were dancing, that first night in The Basement, how he stalked her and wouldn't take no for an answer. His expression grew darker with every word that came out of my mouth, until he looked apoplectic with rage.

'She really told you all that?'

I nodded.

'What a fucking liar!' His anger made me recoil.

'It's not true?'

His arms dropped from around my waist. 'It's the other way around. She chased me, she made a move on me. I turned her down. She began following me. She's a fucking bunny-boiler.'

Would Frankie really tell such dreadful lies? Or is Leon the one making it up?

I convinced him to walk with me along the beach. I took my flip-flops off, the sand soft and warm underfoot, but Leon kept his trainers on. I've only known him just over a month; I've known Frankie for ever, but as we ambled across the beach with the sun on our backs, I realised I wanted to believe him over her.

'You know, I'd never have gone out with you if I'd known she liked you.'

'Really?' He looked disappointed.

'Well, it's that unwritten rule, isn't it? You don't go after the bloke your friend fancies.'

He shrugged. 'I suppose. Then I'm glad she didn't tell you.' He grinned at me, all his anger forgotten. We decided to sit in a secluded spot by a slimy rock, the tangy smell of seaweed strong. The sun was going down, a bright orange ball in the sky. It hurt my eyes to look at it.

Leon took my hand. 'I know we've only known each other for six weeks, but I love you, Sophie.'

I thought of the interview with Little Leaf Publishing on Monday. If I get the job and leave this town, would we stay together? And if we did, how could we spend the rest of our lives together with this huge secret between us? Not to mention the fact that I've cheated on him. Already. And with a man old enough to be my father.

He tried to pull me onto his lap but I resisted.

'What is it? You don't feel the same?'

Tears stung my eyes. 'I do feel the same.'

'Then what is it? Something's troubling you. You can tell me anything, Soph.'

But how could I tell him? He reacted in anger when he thought his brother was coming on to me. What would he think if I told him about Frankie's dad?

The secrets and lies sat between us.

'I'm not sure if I want anything serious,' I said instead. 'I'll be leaving as soon as I get a job. You know that.'

He stroked my hair, relief on his face. 'You don't have to worry about that yet. Who knows what the future holds. But right now I'm happy to be here, with you.' He kissed me slowly, sensuously, and I pushed the doubts to the corner of my mind where they belonged.

22
Frankie

I remember thinking that Leon was so beautiful, so cool with his unusual music tastes. More often than not he was secreted away at a table in the corner of the Seagull, scribbling poetry into his notebook. With his ink-stained fingers and floppy hair, he was different from the beer-swilling Oldcliffe lads who thought they were cool just because they liked Oasis, yet decried anything more avant-garde as being for 'poofters'. That first time I talked to him in The Basement his eyes seemed to see right into my soul. That must sound stupid to you. He was in love with you. Or was he? Was it just infatuation, Soph? You were both so young. There was always something dangerous about him. There still is. Maybe that's part of his attraction.

I'm trembling all over and grip the steering wheel, afraid I'm about to be sick. I take deep breaths and stare out of the windscreen, trying to calm myself by looking out into the horizon, at the black silhouette of Flat Holm Island in the distance.

I made some mistakes back then. We both did. I thought I could escape it all and become a different person in London. A better person. London is perfect for starting again, for becoming who you want to be rather than the person everyone thinks you are; after all, who wants to be remembered for pissing their pants at the back of the class aged seven, or for vomiting in the street at eighteen? You couldn't take an illegal substance or have an underage drink in Oldcliffe without someone knowing about it. The town was full of curtain-twitchers; every move was recorded, talked about. I'd wanted to get away from all that, Sophie. I wanted to get away from the sympathetic faces and the sad eyes when you disappeared. 'There she is, Sophie Collier's best friend. How awful for her.' People gossiping, staring, you ceasing to be just good old Soph but 'poor Sophie Collier' instead. The tragic victim. I wanted to start again. Is that so bad?

But I'm haunted by the past. I'm haunted by you.

I'm nearly forty years old. I'm not Frankie Howe any more. I'm Francesca Bloom – yes, I still use my married name. I'm successful, I'm in control. I have a shiny life. That's what people see in London and that's how I like it. I would do anything to keep it that way.

When I've composed myself, I leave the car and walk across the road to the Tesco Express that replaced Safeway. I know my eyes must look red and swollen, my face pale, my lips puffy. The wind and rain has turned my hair to frizz and my jeans need a wash. I avoid eye contact with the staff stacking the shelves and the pimply-faced youth behind the till, relieved that at least these aren't people who knew me in the past – they would have been toddlers when I lived here. I grab a ready meal from the fridge – I haven't eaten since breakfast and it's nearly 4 p.m. I grab a couple of bottles of wine and push them into the basket.

When I've paid I hurry back to the car, the plastic bag swinging from my arm, the wine bottles knocking my hip, hoping not to see anyone, although the streets are deserted. My car is the only one parked in the spaces by the promenade and looks lonely and conspicuous with its glossy black paintwork and brand-new number plate. I long for the anonymity of London. I slide into the driver's seat and slam the door on the town, instantly feeling comforted by my familiar space, as though nothing can touch me while I'm in the cocoon of my Range Rover.

I contemplate phoning Daniel and telling him about my conversation with Leon. He would sympathise, hating Leon as he does, but I dismiss the idea at once. I don't want to cause any more problems between him and Mia. I think I've caused enough already.

I drive slowly through the town, even though there is no other traffic on the road. The sky is darkening and all the lights in the hotels, guest houses and pubs have been switched on, flooding the wet streets with a warm orange light that reflects in the puddles on the road and pavements. The Grand Pier is also lit up like a firework, green and yellow blurs stretching out to sea. I remember how I used to love the town best at night; it always looked so festive lit up against the black skies, as if it was giving us permission to go out and have a good time.

Two guys and a girl walk along the promenade, laughing and joking. They head towards the zebra crossing and I stop to let them cross. One of the men, extremely tall with brown wavy hair, puts his hand up to thank me, although he barely looks up; he's too busy chatting to the other bloke, who is nearly as tall. They both have their arms linked with the girl's, who walks between them. My heart pounds when I realise who they are: Daniel – and what looks like Leon.

The girl, slim and youngish – definitely younger than me anyway – is attractive, with long, dark hair. She breaks free from them and runs ahead before turning and making silly faces. I can't make out what they're saying because I feel like I'm in a dream. Or a nightmare. Is it Leon? And if so, what is he doing with Daniel? They hate each other. Have always hated each other. And who is the girl with them? Is it Mia?

I watch as they head into the Seagull, for all the world as though they are the best of mates. I'm paralysed with shock. I sit at the zebra crossing, my hands gripping the steering wheel, staring at the pub, even though they've long disappeared through the door. Eventually a car comes up behind me and beeps its horn. I move forward reluctantly, on the edge of tears again as the realisation dawns on me that I can't trust anyone.

Not even Daniel.

*

I pull up outside Beaufort Villas, willing myself to get out of the car and go inside. The light in the downstairs apartment is on and the curtains are open. I can see the yellow painted walls, the flickering of a television. I'd better prepare myself for another sleepless night with the baby screaming into the early hours.

I feel heavy with tiredness. I long to just reverse out of here and head to the M4 and London, but I know I won't leave. I can't. Not yet. There is too much unfinished business.

I get out of the car, thankful it's stopped raining. I'm desperate for a shower and an early night. I plan to microwave my spaghetti bolognese, have a glass or two of wine and then go to bed. Everything will be clearer in the morning. I expect I'll see Daniel at some point, although tomorrow's Monday and I'm not sure what he'll be doing about work.

I turn the key in the front door and let myself in, switching the light on in the hallway. Just as I'm about to close the door I hear someone calling my name. I look up and freeze. Someone is standing at the end of the driveway. Someone in a dark overcoat and walking boots. My heart pounds. It's the person who was following me yesterday. They step forward, pushing back the hood from their head. The light from the hallway illuminates a face and long blonde hair and I gasp.

Because it's you, Soph.

It's actually you.

'Frankie,' you say again, so softly I wonder if you've actually spoken at all. You're about thirty feet away, but you haven't changed a bit. You're still twenty-one, younger than I ever remember you looking, and I know I must be seeing your ghost. I let out an involuntary scream, amazed that the sound is coming from me. I slam the door on you and slump against it, my whole body shaking violently, my legs giving way, and I sink to the floor. How can you be outside? What do you want? Are you trying to warn me? Or scare me?

The door to the downstairs apartment swings open and the grey-haired woman darts out. 'What's going on? Are you OK?' she asks in alarm. She has a soft Yorkshire accent and kind eyes. It's all too much. I burst into tears. She rushes over to where I sit huddled on the floor. 'Oh my love, you're trembling. What's happened? You poor lamb.' She crouches down so that she's on my level but I can't speak for a few minutes, I'm gasping and crying, pointing behind me. 'A ghost, a ghost . . .' I'm gabbling incoherently. I've not felt this petrified since you went missing.

She shushes me, rubbing my arm until I calm down, my sobs receding, then she helps me to my feet, my legs still weak and shaky, and I hold on to her for support.

'I'm sorry,' I stutter, embarrassed. She pulls a tissue from her sleeve and hands it to me. I blow my nose and wipe my eyes, knowing I must look a mess. 'There was someone . . . someone outside. They startled me, that's all.'

She frowns and pushes her glasses further up her nose. 'Someone outside?' She sounds panicked. I nod and she opens the front door a fraction despite my protests. She peers around the door. 'There's nobody there, my love.' She closes the door and turns to me. 'My name's Jean.'

I introduce myself, feeling foolish.

'You've had a fright. Do you want to come in?' She moves towards her apartment and I long to go with her, to have some company. She's about my mum's age, maybe a little older.

But she has family with her. I've already embarrassed myself enough. 'It's been a stressful day,' I say, my hand going to my head to emphasise this point. 'And you've got your family with you, I don't want to intrude.'

Jean frowns and wraps her cardigan further around her thickening midriff. I notice that she's wearing fluffy rabbit slippers. 'I've got no family with me, my love. I'm on my own, visiting my brother. He's in the local hospital you see, heart bypass.'

I stare at her, dread creeping its way around my intestines. Blood pounds in my ears. 'But . . . the baby! I've heard a baby crying for the last two nights.'

'Baby? I'm a bit old to have a baby.' She laughs. 'My children are all grown up. I've not been blessed with grandchildren yet, but my son's just got married so I've got everything crossed.'

'But . . . but . . . I heard a baby,' I say, feebly.

'Maybe it's coming from next door?' She doesn't sound very certain, which isn't surprising considering the walls are thick and this is a detached building.

I can't take any more surprises, I feel like I'm having

some sort of nervous breakdown. Maybe this was all too much for me, coming back here, especially so soon after my dad. I don't want to see you again, Soph, despite how much I loved you.

After I've showered, eaten and sunk a bottle of wine, I slump in front of the television in my dressing gown, comforted by the inane chat of the presenters on a game show. I must eventually doze off because I'm jolted awake by what sounds like fists hammering on the front door. I rush to the window, wondering if the kids who pelted my car with eggs have returned, but there is a man standing in the driveway looking up at the building. It's too dark to make out his features but it looks like Leon. What does he want? I squint, trying to see more clearly. He steps back, instantly illuminated by the security light.

It's not Leon. It's Mike.

What is he doing here? I knock on the window and gesture for him to go to the door. Then I buzz him up and wait, wondering why he's travelled all this way.

When he reaches the top of the stairs, his face breaks out into a huge grin. He's still in his work clothes; his complexion is grey, his eyes tired and there is some sort of powder in his unruly hair.

'Mike?' He shouldn't be here. He's part of my other life.

He rushes up to me and envelops me in a bear hug. He smells of building sites and cold air.

'What are you doing here?' I say into his shoulder.

He releases me. 'Can I come in? It's been a long drive. I'm gasping for a coffee.'

Reluctantly I stand aside to let him over the threshold. He goes straight to the kitchen and switches the kettle on.

'What's going on, Mike?' I want to tell him he's invading my space, but I bite my tongue because the selfish part of me is glad that he's here. After the fright earlier, I can't deny I'd welcome his company. Some normality.

'Where do you keep your cups?'

I tell him to move aside and I make us both a coffee. Then I lead him into the living room, where we sit on the sofa. I pull the dressing gown over my feet. The fire is lit, but it's dwindling.

'So?' I ask, pointing the remote at the television to turn it off. 'Is everything OK?'

He looks shamefaced. 'I know we've split up, but I'm worried about you, Fran. You've had a shock, finding out that your friend is dead. Then you ring me up and finish with me over the phone. It was very sudden.'

I hold up my hand. 'I'm sorry but I haven't changed my mind.'

If I've hurt him with my words he doesn't show it. Instead he adds, 'After everything with your dad, and now this with your friend, I just wanted to make sure you were OK. You're not as strong as you make out. But you never let anyone in. You never accept help.' He takes a sip of his coffee.

I stare at his work boots. I know what he's saying is

true. Since I've been back here I can feel myself crumbling as though all the self-confidence that I've nurtured over the years is turning to dust. Maybe you can never really escape your past.

'You don't look well. You look tired out.'

'It's just been a rough day, that's all . . .'

He inches closer and his voice is gentle when he asks, 'Why are you here? This isn't doing you any good. Your dad has been through a lot. He needs you by his side. Come home, Fran. Come home with me.'

I feel close to tears. 'I can't. Not yet.'

He sighs. 'Why?'

'Daniel needs me. He wants me to go with him on Wednesday to identify . . .' A tear trickles down my cheek.

'Can't he do it by himself?'

I look up at him, aghast. 'That's a bit callous, isn't it?'

He mumbles an apology into his mug. 'Has he got someone else that could go with him?'

I think of Mia. She would go with him like a shot, I imagine. But I want to be the one to do it. I don't know why. Maybe I need to know that it's really you, Soph. That it is your remains that have been found. Maybe I want to feel like I'm needed by Daniel. I can't explain it to Mike or to you. I just know that I can't leave Oldcliffe. Not yet. Not until I've finally laid you to rest.

'He has nobody else.' I take a gulp of my coffee to swallow down my lie.

He reaches out and touches my arm. 'I still love you, Fran. I'm not ready to give up on us yet.'

I move away from his touch. 'I can't do this now, Mike. Not with everything else going on.'

He stands up and goes to the window. The curtains are still open. 'It's a bit lonely here, I imagine,' he says in a strange voice. 'It seems a bit creepy.' He turns to me with hope in his eyes. 'I can't imagine you'll want to stay here long. Why don't you come back with me in the morning?'

It's almost as though he's trying to spook me into going home and I'm suddenly struck by a thought: could Mike have sent those letters in a bid to make me leave? But that's ridiculous. I never told him where I was staying. I stare at him while telling myself to stay calm. Being back here has made me paranoid. Mike would never do such a thing, and he knows nothing about Jason or our past.

23
Sophie

Sunday, 3 August 1997

I was a fool to think things would be the same between me and Alistair. That kiss has changed everything.

There is so much to say about Alistair, to try and explain. The way I feel about him is so complicated. I've tried to block my own father out, but flashes come back to me sometimes, mostly in my dreams, or my nightmares: his dark, hooded eyes always shadowed by anger or disappointment, his Geordie accent, his black donkey jacket with the shiny panel. I remember that shiny panel from the amount of times he had his back to me, usually when he was storming from some room or slamming out the house.

Alistair, in comparison, was the dad I always wanted. Blond and smiley, with a cheerful demeanour and encouraging words. He loved his daughter more than life itself; you could see it in the way he always made time for her, always answered her questions patiently. There were occasions, when we were teenagers, when I thought he was a little unfair, like when he tried to make Frankie feel guilty for going out. He would stand in the doorway to her bedroom while we were pulling on our shoes or brushing our hair, and say, almost petulantly, 'Where are you going? Are you leaving me on my own again?' And he would seem disappointed when we said yes. He would try and make light of it, turn it into a joke. But even at sixteen I could tell he didn't find it very funny. Then Frankie would have to go over to him, her arm sidling around his waist, and tell him that we wouldn't be long, that maybe when she came back they could play a board game. Her readiness to appease him made me want to roll my eyes, but it also made me feel sick with jealousy.

We always had an easy banter. There was a flirtatious note to his voice when he spoke to me that wasn't there with Frankie. I had a crush on him but was too young to really be aware of it. I just knew I liked him, that I thought he was attractive, that I would have happily stayed playing board games with him rather than walking around town with Frankie. Yet I couldn't ever say that to Frankie. She would think it was gross if I ever admitted to her that I quite fancied her dad.

But after I kissed him my feelings for him changed. It had felt wrong, it had felt sleazy. He was twenty-seven years older than me. A proper grown-up.

And today it took another turn.

All week we had managed to avoid each other. I knew things had changed; we had crossed a line and could never go back. He would never just be Frankie's dad again. But when Maria rang and asked if I'd do another extra shift today, I thought it couldn't do any harm. After all, Alistair has been staying with his dad all week and even if he was at the hotel, I knew I'd have to face him sooner or later.

I was pulling the duvet cover across the bed in Room 11, making sure to tuck the edges in under the mattress like Maria had taught me. The room was stifling, right up in the eaves. Sweat pooled in my armpits and my pink T-shirt stuck to my back. I was grateful for the denim shorts I was wearing. I was bending over the bed when I felt a hand slap my bottom hard. I stood up in shock, my bum cheek stinging. At first I thought it was Frankie mucking about, but it was Alistair who stood next to the wardrobe, grinning at me, as if slapping my arse was a normal everyday occurrence.

'Nice bum,' he said, to my horror. Just because we had mistakenly kissed didn't give him the right to touch me. I tried to laugh it off, although my heart began to stutter in my chest. I turned away from him to fluff up the pillows, hoping he would take the hint and go. Instead he grabbed me around the waist and started kissing my neck.

'Oh, Sophie,' he mumbled, his voice husky and full of longing. 'I can't stop thinking about you.'

I tried to pull away from him. 'Alistair . . . stop . . .'

He spun me around so that I was facing him, his hands on my hips. 'Don't tell me you don't want this, I know how you feel about me,' he said. He tried to push his lips onto mine. It was all happening so fast.

'Get off me.' With all my strength I pushed against

his chest and he went staggering backwards, shock in his green eyes.

'What?' He looked panicked as it dawned on him that he'd misunderstood. 'Sophie, I thought you felt the same.'

I pushed my hair back from my face, feeling flustered. 'Alistair, I have a boyfriend. You're my best friend's dad. You're married . . .'

He came towards me again, his face softening. 'I know, I know, there are a lot of things against us. But I can't stop thinking about you. Having to see you around the hotel, in those little shorts . . .'

I swallowed the bad taste in my mouth. What had I started with that blasted kiss?

'I want to touch you, I want to hold you and kiss you. Make love to you.'

If I hadn't felt so repulsed I would have laughed out loud. This was Frankie's dad talking this way. Frankie's dad! It was surreal.

'Alistair, the kiss was a mistake . . .'

He stepped away, confusion all over his face. 'What do you mean?'

Why wasn't he getting it into his thick head?

'I don't feel the same way, I'm sorry . . .'

'But you've fancied me for years. Maria used to tease me about it when you were a teenager. And then you come back here after three years away, an ugly duckling turned into a swan . . .'

What did he seriously think was going to happen? That I'd have an affair with him? That I'd get off with him up here in Room 11 while his wife and daughter were elsewhere in the hotel? I stared at him, thinking he had lost it.

'I did have a crush on you when I was a teenager,' I said finally. 'A silly schoolgirl crush. But that's in the past.'

'Last week you kissed me, Sophie.'

'How many times have I got to say this? It was a mistake, Alistair. I was upset. It shouldn't have happened and I'm sorry if I made you think I wanted more.' I was embarrassed that he was talking to me in this way. He was Frankie's father, for goodness' sake – surely he should be the grown-up here and realise that it was just a moment of madness.

But it was as though I'd slapped him. 'I know you want me, Sophie,' he said in a rush. 'I know you feel the same. You're just feeling guilty. And that's understandable. That's what makes you such a fantastic person. That's what makes me love you.'

Love me? Surely he wasn't serious? How could I tell him it wasn't love he was feeling? It was lust, and infatuation. He probably doesn't have sex with Maria as much as he'd like, a young girl kisses him and he gets ahead of himself, starts believing he's in love.

But I just stood there and shook my head. 'I'm in love with Leon,' I said.

'Leon? That little runt I've seen you with down by the beach? He's just a kid.'

I sighed. 'Alistair, so am I.'

'You're a woman, Sophie. You need a proper man.'

The conversation was making me more and more

nauseous. I moved away from the bed and to the small attic window, desperate for air. The room had a sea view and from where I stood I could see the Grand Pier and the beach packed with bodies. I longed to open the window wide and scream for someone to help me. Not that I felt in any danger, not really; I was embarrassed more than anything else. I wanted to be down on the beach with Frankie, acting like normal young girls, not up here with some middle-aged man with a hard-on.

'Alistair . . . I'm sorry if I've given you the wrong impression,' I said, continuing to look out of the window. I felt close to tears.

The bedroom door slammed, making me jump. When I looked around Alistair had gone.

Monday

24
Frankie

I awake the next morning with Mike curled up next to me in the double bed. Nothing happened between us, Soph. I didn't think it was fair to sleep with him. I wanted comfort, that's all. Is that so wrong?

By the time I'm showered and dressed, Mike is up and in the living room, lighting the fire. He's wearing my lilac dressing gown, which is much too short on him, the cuffs up by his elbows and the hem just reaching his knees.

'Wow, this place is cold,' he says unnecessarily as he blows out the match. 'What do you want to do today? I'd quite like to explore. I've never been here before . . .'

'Mike.'

At the warning tone in my voice he looks up and I see disappointment etched into his features. 'You're going to tell me to leave, aren't you?'

'I'm sorry.'

'And you're not going to come with me?'

'I need a few more days, that's all.'

His shoulders slump. 'Why do I get the feeling I've been used, huh, Fran? I came here hoping to sort things out between us. When you let me stay I thought you might have changed your mind about us.'

I take a step towards him. 'I haven't used you . . .' But my words sound hollow. Of course I've used him. I've not slept so well since being back in Oldcliffe. Even the baby's cries in the early hours of the morning didn't bother me. I felt safe in his arms in spite of any misgivings I had about him yesterday.

I'd asked him how he found out where I was staying, and he said he'd found the note I'd made of the address on the kitchen table. I remember scribbling it down on the notepad but I was sure I'd crumpled it up and thrown it away after I'd typed it into my phone. Did Mike go through the kitchen bin? An image of Jean going through the dustbins outside flashes in my mind. What was she looking for?

I shift from foot to foot, feeling uncomfortable. A weak light filters through the cream curtains. A pool of wine has formed around the base of a bottle of Pinot Noir. It looks like blood.

'I'm going to have a shower,' he says gruffly. 'Then I'll be out of your hair.'

I go to the bay window, pulling the curtains aside. The sky is a dense white, but at least it's not raining. Instead a layer of ice has coated the windscreen and roof of my car. I avoid looking towards the pier because I can't bear the thought that you might be there, watching me.

I can't be depressed – this is nothing like what my mum experienced – but maybe the grief and guilt I feel about your death has manifested in delusions. Since I received that call four days ago, I haven't been able to stop talking to you. Maybe it's being back in Oldcliffe again. This town is so intrinsically linked with you – with our childhood, our teenage years, the accident with Jason and your disappearance – that it's only natural I'm going to be thinking about you all the time, isn't it? I can hardly remember a time when I was in Oldcliffe without you; a brief period before you moved here, and an even briefer time after you disappeared and we left for London. In those first few months you went missing there was still hope; that you would turn up, shamefaced, admitting that you'd had a row with your mum, or were upset by how things ended with Leon and had just gone away for a few days. But you didn't turn up, did you? Until now.

Mike finds me in the kitchen, spooning cereal into my mouth. He looks fresh in a clean jumper and jeans.

'So, you really want me to go then?' he says.

I swallow down the muesli. 'I'm sorry.'

'You don't sound very sorry.'

I take a deep breath. 'I didn't ask you to come.'

He stares at me, hurt in his eyes. 'I can't believe how cold you can be, Fran. I agree with you, this relationship isn't going to work. When you do eventually decide to come home, I won't be there.'

I lower my gaze. When I look up again he's gone, slamming the door behind him.

*

You always said I treated my boyfriends badly and you were right. I didn't set out to hurt them. My relationships always started off well enough, until they fell in love with me and then, in my mind, they became needy and unattractive. Except with Christopher. My ex-husband was fiercely independent and never needy – so much so that he ended up having sex with someone else.

Maybe I would have felt that way about Leon if he'd fallen in love with me. As it is he despises me, that much is obvious from yesterday. And what about your brother? Would I end up treating him badly too if he reciprocated my feelings? You would probably say yes and remind me of how I treated him when we were younger. I'm not proud of it, Soph. I like to think that I've changed, it's just that I haven't found the right person who challenges me yet. Who refuses to take my crap. Maybe that person is Daniel.

At least I thought it might be Daniel until I remember last night. I was sure he was with Leon. Could I have been wrong?

I need to get out of this apartment that still smells of Mike. I shoulder on my coat and wrap a scarf around my neck. With my hand grasping the doorknob I steel myself, as though mentally preparing for a fight. Will there be another anonymous letter or a sinister gift left on the doormat? Or will you be waiting for me at the end of the driveway again? Who knows what I'm going to face. Gingerly I turn the handle and tiptoe to the top of the landing. There is only Jean downstairs, but after embarrassing myself in front of her yesterday I can't risk bumping into her today. I squint, trying to determine whether there is anything on the doormat or hanging out of the letter box. I feel almost giddy with relief when I see nothing. I make sure to lock my door before quietly making my way down the stairs, stopping midway when I see Jean come out of her door. She has her back to me as she bends over the welcome mat.

I clear my throat and she stands up, swivelling on her slippered feet to face me, a newspaper rolled up in her hand. It has a dark stain covering the end. 'Hello, Francesca, love. I just came out to get the local newspaper.' She waves it about to emphasise her point. Is it my imagination or does she look shifty? 'Someone must have a subscription because it came last week as well.' She shakes her head. 'Who would waste money like that? Still, it means I can read it. I like to know what's going on, even though I live thirty miles away.' She chuckles. And then I notice a flash of pink plastic in her other hand.

I run down the few remaining stairs so that I'm standing in front of her. 'Is that . . . a dummy?' I point to her left hand.

She frowns down at it in her palm, as if wondering how on earth it got there. 'Yes.'

'But . . . you said you didn't have a baby staying with you.'

She looks flustered. 'I don't . . . I just found it, sitting on the mat next to the newspaper.'

I stare at her in disbelief. Why would somebody post a dummy through the door? The letters and dog tags I can understand; they were personal to me – to us, Soph. But this? This doesn't make sense. Unless she's lying and she really does have a baby in her apartment. But why would she lie?

'Anyway, must get on. Need to visit our Graham at the hospital later.' She closes her fingers around the dummy and pushes it into the pocket of her cardigan, then, with the newspaper clamped under her armpit, retreats back to her apartment, closing the door firmly behind her.

I'm too shocked to do anything but stand there for a few moments, staring at the door that she's just closed in my face. I need to get out of here.

The air is freezing, the wind slapping my cheeks. As I'm about to get in my car I notice my right wing-mirror has been smashed. I take a deep breath. It looks as if someone has punched it; the imprint of a fist splintering the glass into shards that resemble a spider's web. Mike? Surely he wouldn't have done such a thing. But he was so angry when he left this morning.

Maybe Mike is right and I should just go home. But what if, in my absence, Daniel finds out what happened to you? I get behind the wheel and turn the heater on, watching as the ice on the windscreen slowly dissolves. When it's all melted away I reverse out of the driveway, half expecting to see you in my rear-view mirror. Then suddenly I'm thrown forward in my seat as the car hits something with a sickening thud.

Oh God. Is it you?

I pull on the brake with a trembling hand and dart

out of the car. But thank God it's just a dustbin. Did someone put it deliberately in my path or did I just fail to see it? With great effort I drag it out of the way, rolling it over the debris that has spilled out onto the road. BEAUFORT has been painted on the side of the bin. I haven't taken any rubbish out to be collected yet, which must mean it's Jean's. Was she out here this morning messing with the bin? I dust down my coat and step over the empty egg carton and tin cans to get back into the car.

I need to get out of Oldcliffe, even if it's only for a few hours. I turn left, down the bumpy hill and onto the coastal road. The old pier is on my right as I head through town.

As I pass the last few houses, I feel as though I can breathe again, the tension seeping out of me. I don't know where I'm heading, I just keep driving until the road turns into a dual carriageway, and then a roundabout with directions. I take the exit for the M5 towards Bristol. I need to spend a few hours in a city, and Bristol is the nearest one.

The last time I was in Bristol, you were with me, Soph. We used to catch the train so we could go shopping. There never were any decent clothes shops in Oldcliffe unless you were over fifty. We'd spend hours walking around Broadmead, and inevitably venturing up to Park Street so that we could go into Rival Records.

I switch the radio on, the sounds of 'Begging You' by the Stone Roses shocking me for a moment. You loved this song. My eyes flick towards the radio and I frown. Why is it on Radio 2 when I always have it on Classic FM? You wouldn't understand, you hated classical music. And so did I, back then. But I find it soothes me now. But this song, Soph, it takes me right back so that I'm there, in The Basement, with you on that packed dance floor, the smell of smoke and sweat and bodies filling my nostrils. I can remember how I felt; that surge of adrenaline coursing through me, the beat vibrating through my body as we danced with abandon, alcohol lowering our inhibitions, arms flung in the air, the lights flashing through the smoke. It's so tangible that I'm twenty-one again. I can't breathe. My heart starts pounding and I have to loosen the scarf at my neck before I reach over and turn the radio off.

Bristol city centre is almost unrecognisable since we were last here. I take the wrong exit on more than one occasion as I try and navigate the new streets. The roads by the Hippodrome have become pedestrianised; bars and cafés have popped up alongside the waterfront and there is a huge shopping mall called Cabot Circus, with, can you believe, a Harvey Nics. Oh Soph, we would have loved shopping there. Although I doubt we would have been able to afford much back then. I haven't been here since the summer you died. You found out you got that editorial assistant's job; you were so excited and wanted to buy some smart clothes. I recall the stab of jealousy I'd felt when you talked about moving to London. You were leaving me behind and I sulked as we ambled around Broadmead. I'd followed you in and out of Oasis and French Connection, feeling more and more dejected and abandoned with every shop we went into. It was in Kookaï, in between the combat trousers and strappy tops, that you turned to me and demanded to know what was up. When I eventually admitted how I felt you hugged me and told me that I was more than welcome to come with you, that we could share a flat, that it would be fun. We could get out of Oldcliffe together. We had such plans.

But two weeks later you were dead.

The café in Park Street is large, modern, anonymous. And warm. We're experiencing a cold snap according to the radio.

I settle myself at a small table by the window overlooking the busy street. People are scurrying past with oversized shopping bags, chins hidden by scarves and hats pressed down on heads.

I'm catching up on emails and phone calls when I get a text from Daniel: *Where are you? I've been to the apartment. No answer. D xx*

It's funny how, in a matter of days, we are so familiar with each other we can put kisses after our text messages. Before Friday I didn't even have his number or any idea where he was living. He told me he'd managed to get my number from my hotel website, although thinking about it now he rang me on my mobile. But of course, Daniel is a journalist. He has ways of getting in touch with people, of finding information, that I don't have. Your brother is more hard-nosed than I remember and just because he calls me Lady Frankie and talks fondly of our past, I shouldn't forget that.

I ignore his text and get back to my emails.

Then I'm interrupted by a call from my mum.

'Hi,' I say quietly so that the other customers can't hear.

'Frankie. I've been trying to call you for days . . .' She charges straight in, not even asking how I am. 'Are you still in Oldcliffe?'

'I'm in Bristol at the moment but, yes, I'm still staying in Oldcliffe. The reception isn't always that good—'

'Anyway,' she rushes on, 'I thought you'd like to know there's an improvement to your dad's condition. Isn't that great news? I told you he was a survivor, didn't I? He'll get through this.'

'I'm so happy to hear that, Mum, I really am. But this doesn't change anything, does it? He'll still have the court case to face if he gets better.'

'Why do you have to bring that up now? He's innocent. We all know he's innocent. I'm just about holding it all together, Frankie. And with you a three-hour journey away, well, it's selfish. It really is . . .'

I close my eyes and listen to her tirade, letting her words wash over me. I know by now not to get offended by her criticisms. That her anxiety and depression can make her short-tempered. Of course she's worried about my dad, she would be lost without him. She's stuck by him through everything, I have to give her that. She doesn't ask about you, or even about the hotels; since Dad's stroke, she hasn't taken any interest in them. After semi-retiring two years ago, they've enjoyed the cruises and holidays to far-flung places that the profits allowed them.

You'd be surprised how dedicated I am these days, Soph. It turns out that I enjoy running a business after all. I never thought of it as a substitute for a family, a life, until now. Since my marriage ended I just jogged along, not really thinking of the future, just living day to day, throwing myself into my job, the occasional non-serious love affair. Now I know I was living half a life, waiting, as though I always knew that eventually I'd be exactly where I am now. It was inevitable somehow.

'Anyway, I need to get back to your dad. Just thought you'd like to know.'

'I'll be home in a few days, hopefully. Tell Dad I love him . . .'

She hangs up without saying goodbye.

I order another cappuccino and I'm just about to ring the hotel manager, Stuart, for an update when my mobile buzzes in my hand and Daniel's name flashes up. I contemplate ignoring it and letting him sweat a bit more. Hopefully he thinks I've gone back to London, and if I did would he really care? He only wants me here to help him find out what happened to you. But we are no closer to knowing anything now than we were on Friday. After the sixth ring I relent and answer it.

'Frankie?' He sounds tense.

'I thought you'd be at work.'

'I am,' he says and, as if on cue, a phone rings in the background. I imagine the busy newsroom, although I've only seen it once, when we were at school. It's bound to have changed. 'Where are you?'

'In a café. In Bristol.'

'Bristol? Why?'

I sigh. 'I needed to get out of Oldcliffe. It's so oppressive.'

'There's nothing wrong with Oldcliffe,' he says, his voice laced with defensiveness.

I stay silent; there is no point arguing with him. What was I thinking? I'd never be happy living in Oldcliffe-on-Sea again and he loves the place. It's just as well that he has this Mia. It would never have worked between us.

'Are you OK, Franks?'

I feel a flash of irritation. It's all his fault. I trusted him.

'No, I'm not,' I hiss into my mobile. 'I saw you last night. With Leon.'

'Leon?' He sounds perplexed. 'I wasn't with Leon last night.'

I take a deep breath, vigorously stirring my cappuccino. 'I saw you, Daniel. You crossed right in front of my car. You were with Mia too, heading for the Seagull. I thought you hated Leon. What's going on?'

'I do hate Leon. I certainly wouldn't go drinking with him. I was with a bloke from work. He's a sub. New to the area. I said I'd meet him for a pint.'

'What's his name?'

Is he lying to me?

'Rob.' He doesn't miss a beat.

Could I have been mistaken? It really looked like Leon. Am I imagining him now, just like I'm imagining you?

'What does Rob look like?'

Despite the noise of the coffee machine, I can still make out the note of repressed irritation in Daniel's voice. 'I don't know . . . he's tall. Dark, curly hair.'

Like Leon? I want to ask, but don't.

'I wasn't with Mia either,' he adds sadly. 'We had a row. That was Trish, our receptionist.' I can hear the words he refuses to say. I know the argument was about me.

'I hate Leon,' I blurt out, remembering with fresh humiliation how nasty he was to me in the car yesterday. I fill Daniel in on our conversation.

'You shouldn't have gone to see him on your own,' he says when I've finished. 'We don't know yet if he's responsible for Sophie's death. He could be a killer, Frankie. No matter how good-looking you obviously find him.'

It gives me a small, jubilant thrill to detect the note of jealousy in his voice. 'I don't think he's good-looking. Not any more,' I say. 'And you're right, I think he did harm her. He must have had something to do with her disappearance.'

How could I have doubted Daniel? He's one of the good guys, fundamentally decent with a strong moral code. He might have played up at school and liked a drink, but he was never nasty. I remember how he used to refuse to kill spiders, irrespective of how scared we were of them, and the way he was so overprotective of you. The man of the house, he was always there for you. It would make me feel envious, wishing I'd had a big brother to look after me. He would do anything for anyone. He'd do anything for me. I just wish I'd appreciated it more eighteen years ago.

There's a pause on the other end of the line. If it wasn't for the background noise of the newsroom – the ring of phones, the low hum of conversation – I would have assumed he'd hung up on me. Eventually, he says, 'Listen, someone called the newsroom, spoke with one of my reporters. They didn't leave a name but they suggested we talk to Jez.'

'Jez? He still lives in Oldcliffe?'

I haven't thought about Jez for years. All the girls liked him, mainly because he was a DJ, but he was a coke-head with the brains of a rocking horse.

'Yes. Although I haven't seen him since I've been back. It didn't occur to me to speak to him about Sophie, but he was the DJ that night. He would have seen all sorts.'

I start to cough and have to take a sip of my coffee, now lukewarm. My throat feels scratchy. I hope I'm not coming down with anything. Spending days in that freezing apartment isn't good for my health.

Daniel sounds serious as he continues: 'The caller

left a message, told us to meet Jez at the abattoir at two p.m.'

What he says next sends me into a cold sweat. 'He says he has important information about that night and if we don't go and meet him he'll take it straight to the police.'

25
Sophie

Monday, 4 August 1997

I tried to avoid Alistair for the rest of yesterday. I hung around Room 11 for fifteen more minutes until it was the end of my shift. Luckily it was just Frankie and her mum in the dining room clearing away the breakfast things when I came down. Frankie had her arms stacked with greasy plates, a slither of bacon fat trailing over the edge of the top one. It made me feel queasy to look at it.

'Where have you been, Sophie?' asked Maria.

I stared at her, speechless. Her attractive face was flushed, dark curls escaping from her hairband. She still has a slight Italian accent, even though she's been living in the UK since her early twenties. I could feel my face grow hot and I felt ashamed just looking at her. I had snogged her husband, he had tried to kiss me again, proclaimed his love for me. It was all so wrong.

'I'm not feeling too well, Mrs Howe . . .' She was always Mrs Howe; I sensed that she preferred it that way. Alistair had always insisted that I call him by his first name. He said 'Mr Howe' made him sound old.

Like his dad. Now I realise he wanted me to see him as someone young, funky. Not a dad. And especially not my best friend's dad.

'What's the matter?' she barked. Mrs Howe is not particularly maternal. She loves Frankie, fiercely, although Frankie can't always see that. She says her mum is always putting her down, but I think she just wants the best for her. But she isn't a cuddly sort of mum; she's no-nonsense, sharp. Not like my mum. My mum might work all the hours God sends, but when she's home she likes nothing more than to cuddle up with me and Daniel on the sofa and watch television.

'I feel sick,' I said truthfully. 'And my shift has nearly ended anyway.'

'You'd better be off then,' she said with a dismissive sniff, turning away from me and ushering Frankie into the kitchen. 'See you tomorrow.' Frankie flashed me a concerned look over her mother's shoulder but I couldn't meet her eye. I had betrayed her. I'd betrayed both of them.

I scuttled through the dining room and into the hallway as fast as I could, my head down, my chin almost on my chest, as though trying to disappear, hoping that I wouldn't bump into Alistair. But he was standing at the front door.

He was blocking the entrance. I wanted to scream at him. But Maria might be in earshot.

'What have you been saying?' His green eyes assessed me. They were cold, accusing.

'I've told Maria –' I looked up at him to meet his

gaze '*Mrs Howe* – that I'm not feeling well. My shift has nearly ended anyway.'

'You won't say anything, will you?' He hung his head.

'Of course not,' I said and then I lowered my voice. 'But you have to understand: it was a mistake.'

'I know, I'm sorry.'

I felt a surge of relief. It was a moment of madness, for both of us. A stupid kiss, that's all. No damage done.

He took a step towards me. I could smell his musky aftershave, the faint whiff of coffee on his breath. He must have sensed me softening towards him because he reached out and touched my hair. 'Oh Soph,' he said, his voice full of . . . what? Longing? Regret?

'Alistair,' I pleaded, 'I need to go home.'

'Let me walk you?' He removed his hand from my hair.

'You can't.' I wanted to get away from him.

'You're not feeling well – I want to make sure you get home OK. What's wrong with that? I can drive you. It's perfectly innocent.'

'It's ten minutes away.' I felt on the edge of tears. 'I can walk.' The flocked wallpaper in the hallway was closing in on me. The air smelt musty, the remnants of fried egg and bacon still evident.

'I'm not letting you walk home,' he said, his jaw set in determination. I'd seen that look before, a hardness around his mouth and chin. I remember seeing it the night Jason died, when he convinced us that we couldn't go to the police. 'I'm not letting you out of here until you say I can drive you home. I'm not going to do anything, Sophie.'

I wondered if I should scream. It would make Maria and Frankie come running. I could just imagine their faces, eyes round, mouths open, frozen in horror. But then what? What would I say? That Alistair had tried to kiss me upstairs, that he thinks he's in love? Or that I had kissed him first? Would they accuse me of leading him on? I imagined the hurt in Frankie's eyes and in her mother's. Her parents might end up getting divorced and it would be all because of me.

'Alistair . . .' I tried another tack. 'It would look weird if you drove me home. What would Mrs Howe say?'

He pooh-poohed this at once. 'Nonsense. Maria would want me to drive you home. It would look weird if I didn't. You're ill. You look really pale.'

I felt I had no choice. I was desperate to get out of there. So I let him lead me to his car, which was parked across the road from the hotel, overlooking the beach. He had his arm linked through mine, forcing my body close to his so that our hips touched. People edged past us, laughing and jolly. Families on holiday. Couples enjoying the sun. If anyone saw us who didn't know us, they would think we were father and daughter. He stopped in front of his black BMW.

'Get in,' he said when we reached the passenger side. He smiled sweetly at me but it didn't reach his eyes. I contemplated making a run for it. With every fibre of my being I didn't want to get inside his car.

He reversed and pointed the nose of his car towards the Birds Estate. Traffic was slow, vehicles queuing to get in and out of town, people constantly walking in front of the cars to get to the beach, clutching their bags bulging with towels and sun cream, buckets and spades. The sky was a powder blue, scattered with gossamer clouds. Everybody looked happy, relaxed, but my body was stiff with tension.

Alistair didn't talk to me at first. His eyes focused on the road, his foot stop-starting on the pedals. He cursed softly under his breath every time another person meandered in front of the car. 'Bloody tourists,' he sighed again and again. 'Clogging up the town.'

'It would have been just as quick for me to walk,' I said. The air con was on; I could feel it brushing my toes in my flip-flops. The cold air caused goose pimples to pop up on my arms. A musk-scented air freshener that looked like a set of traffic lights hung from the mirror, the smell making my nausea worse.

'I'm worried about you,' he said. And then he reached over and put his hand on my knee. I slapped it away.

'Stop it!'

His mouth was set in a straight line. 'I'm sorry, I didn't mean that. But come on, Soph. You're lying to yourself if you say you don't feel anything for me. You're here now, aren't you?'

'Because I felt I had no choice.' Why wasn't he getting the hint? My stomach tightened with anger, my legs sticking to the leather seats.

'Oh, but we've always got a choice,' he laughed. It

had a nasty ring to it, reverberating around the car so that the atmosphere between us became something else, something sinister. 'I know how you feel about me,' he said, 'and I won't stop until you admit it.'

I glared at him, fury burning in my chest. How dare he! 'Then what? We go and tell Maria? And Frankie? You leave them, for me? We go and set up house together? What the hell do you think is going to happen?'

His eyes widened in shock. I'd shocked myself too with my outburst. I usually try and take my mum's advice of thinking before speaking. But I was knotted up with anger and the words had just come tumbling out.

'I don't want to leave my family,' he said. 'I love them.'

I breathed a sigh of relief. 'Great. So now you can see where I'm coming from.'

But his next words sent a chill through me: 'No. I love you too.'

I couldn't believe what I was hearing. 'So, what? You want me as a mistress, is that it?'

He shook his head. 'You make it sound so sordid. I can't help the way I feel.'

'But . . .' I said desperately. 'Alistair, we kissed. Once. It was a mistake. You're my best friend's dad. I've known you for years. But you're acting like . . .'

'Like what?'

'You're acting crazy.'

'There was always something between us – we just didn't realise it. Until now.'

I wanted to cry with frustration. What could I say to make him realise he was acting like a deluded fool? A man stepped in front of the car, causing Alistair to slam on the brakes. The traffic was still heavy in front of us. I found the door handle, my fingers quickly feeling for the latch. Relief coursed through me when I realised he hadn't locked it. I opened the door before Alistair could work out what I was doing.

'I'm not interested, so get that into your thick head,' I hissed as I jumped out. The vehicle in front wasn't moving and, unless he abandoned his car in the middle of the road, he couldn't follow me. 'Leave me alone in future.' And I slammed the car door on his stunned face and then ran onto the promenade and down to the beach, safe in the knowledge that he couldn't follow me.

I phoned in sick today, pretending I have a stomach bug. I can't face him, Frankie or Maria. I need to stay out of Alistair's way until he comes to his senses.

26

Frankie

I tug the scarf higher up my neck and over my mouth to protect myself from the slicing cold that penetrates to my bones. I can see my breath bloom out in front of me when I exhale, as though I'm smoking. Do you remember when we were at school in the winter? We would breathe out with our fingers to our lips to pretend that we had a cigarette. We were always so desperate to appear grown up, but we fooled no one.

The frost crunches beneath my feet and I feel precarious on the ice-coated, uneven surface. Every sound I make rings out in the deserted car park. Where is Daniel? He said he'd meet me here at 2 p.m. I look at my watch. It's nearly quarter past. He should be here by now.

This place gives me the creeps even more than the old pier: the scrubland that doubles as a car park, the crumbling railway bridge where the steam trains used to run from here to the next town, the ugly 1950s building that houses the town's abattoir. Tourists would never find this place, conveniently hidden on the edge of town by a dead-end road. Even I had forgotten about it until Daniel reminded me. We came here a few times, me and Jez, to get off together in his souped-up Ford Fiesta with the blacked-out windows. We used to shudder at the thought of working in the abattoir – all those screaming pigs. He was going to be a famous DJ, wowing the crowds on a sun-soaked Ibiza beach. I bet he never thought he'd end up here. The abattoir looms in front of me, solid and squat, its cream, rendered walls streaked with black dirt. It has a sinister look about it, as though all the blood, guts and horror has somehow seeped into the walls, as if it's been permanently stained by death.

I hesitate, not knowing what to do. Shall I retreat back to the safety of my Range Rover, or hover here, in the biting cold, feeling conspicuous? Just as I'm about to head back to my car I hear a clunk as the heavy metal doors are pulled back and a figure emerges. I'm too far away to make out whether it's Jez. The man is slight, not that tall, a grey beanie pushed down over his head, hiding any hair. He has his back to me, and spends a couple of minutes pushing the metal doors shut again, fastening the lock. When he's finished he shoulders his backpack and strides towards me. As he gets closer I recognise his once-pretty face, his keen, hazel eyes. He's aged dramatically, his cheeks hollow, his face heavily lined so that he looks years older than forty-one. I remember the rumours about hard drugs that had rippled through the town, and Jez's dependency on alcohol. He frowns as he comes towards me, and I move back instinctively, suddenly afraid of this man, this much older Jez. He seems more worldly now, which

I know is to be expected but it still comes as a shock. He has an edge to him that wasn't evident eighteen years ago. He stops when he reaches me and takes a sharp intake of breath.

'It's you,' he says, staring. I see myself through his eyes, with my expensively cut red wool coat, black jeans and heeled boots. 'You've cut your hair,' he adds and I touch it self-consciously. It's just past my shoulders now, no longer halfway down my back. 'I'd heard you were running around town with Daniel Collier, irritating everybody with your questions about the past.' He sniffs and wipes his nose on his hand. I concentrate on keeping my face impassive. 'Why you bothering for? She's dead, ain't she?'

It still shocks me to hear you being described as dead. I don't want to be here, without Daniel, standing in this lonely car park in the middle of nowhere with a man I barely recognise.

'He's searching for answers . . .' I say finally.

'Pah! I don't know why. He thinks I'm stupid, that's the trouble. But I'm not.' He stares at me as if challenging me to dispute it.

'I know you're not, Jez. Did you call his newsroom?'

'It's not *his* newsroom,' he spits. 'He comes back here, all swanky now he has a bit of money and a good job. I've known Daniel years, we went to school together. He used to be one of us.'

'He still is one of you,' I say, unable to help myself. 'Can't you see? He loves this place.'

I want to add, God knows why, but I don't.

He scoffs, spittle flying from his mouth and landing on my cheek. 'Don't be ridiculous. Course he ain't. He's only been back five minutes, stirring everything up again. What nobody seems to be asking, though, is what *he* was doing that night.'

My scalp prickles. 'What are you talking about?'

He looks around him, as if expecting Daniel to appear, even though the place is empty.

He lowers his voice. 'I saw him that night.'

I shrug. 'So? He said he was there that night. I saw him too. And you and Helen and Leon. We were all at The Basement.'

He emits a sound from his throat, a mixture of a growl and a laugh. 'Much later, as I was coming home. I saw him. With Sophie. They were at the entrance to the old pier. They were arguing. She was shouting at him. Then I saw her push him. I called out to them, asked if everything was all right, but they ignored me. Probably didn't hear me. I was wasted anyway, it'd been a long night. So I carried on home. Didn't think much of it, they were brother and sister. Who doesn't sometimes fight with their sister?'

A coldness washes over me. 'Did you tell anyone about this? You know, at the time? The police . . . ?'

He shrugs. 'Course not. I wasn't going to land one of my oldest mates in trouble. And I didn't think he'd have done it. I assumed she had an accident later. I forgot all about it, until he came snooping around here again.'

I frown. 'I don't believe Daniel would hurt Sophie. Ever. If he did, why would he be here asking questions, trying to find out what happened to her? He wouldn't. It makes no sense.'

He shrugs. 'It's obvious, ain't it? To throw everyone off the scent. To make sure the truth don't get out.'

I laugh. It sounds forced and high-pitched, quickly dissipating into the cold afternoon air. 'That's ridiculous.' Then another thought hits me. 'You don't think you could have been seeing Leon, do you? Not Daniel? From a distance it would be hard to tell them apart. They are both taller than average, brown-haired. In the darkness it would have been difficult to distinguish exactly who it was, surely?'

He shrugs again as though suddenly bored with the conversation. 'I don't know. I've told the police now, anyway. Daniel's no longer a mate.'

I pull the scarf away from my throat, feeling as though I'm choking. I can't breathe. 'I trust Daniel implicitly,' I say firmly, although this isn't strictly true any more. 'He'd never hurt Sophie,' I repeat. I stare at Jez with disgust, wondering how I could have ever contemplated snogging this little runt of a man with his ludicrous allegations. And now he's told the police they will question Daniel. He's been through enough; I don't know what it would do to him if he knew he was a suspect.

A suspect. It's not true. We both know that, don't we, Sophie? Your brother would never hurt you. He couldn't hurt a fly.

'Was it you? Did you call the newsroom, pretending to be anonymous, urging Daniel to come and speak to you? What were you going to do to him, Jez? Lure him here just so you could taunt him with your accusations? Would that make you feel less jealous of him? Make you feel more of a man?'

He glares at me, disgust written all over his face. 'It's true what they say about you, Frankie. Hard as nails. You and Daniel deserve each other. You're both the same.'

'Why, because we have aspirations? Because we want to better ourselves? What's wrong with that?' I'm so furious I forget to be scared.

He pulls the beanie further down over his head so that his eyebrows are compressed, giving him a sinister look. He sighs and I can see he isn't angry at me, not really. He's just pissed off with the way his life has turned out. 'There's nothing wrong with that,' he says, and his shoulders slump. He looks small and vulnerable now and it makes me want to hug him. Oh, if you could see him now, Soph. If you could see how different he looks, ravaged by years of drink and drugs and disappointment.

'I'm sorry, Frankie,' he says, surprising me. His voice is softer now, as though the bitterness and resentment has seeped out of him. I reach out and touch one of his calloused hands. 'I didn't mean to say those things. You were always all right, you know that? I liked you.'

I smile, feeling shy, remembering those drunken fumbles in the back of his car. 'I liked you too.'

He rubs his five o'clock shadow. I note the purple bruises under his eyes, the sunken cheeks. 'I fucked my life up. But I'm getting back on my feet, slowly. I wish I could turn the clock back, y'know?'

Jez wouldn't be able to see it to look at me – he must think I've got it made, with my nice car and my expensive clothes – but we're not so different. I understand *exactly* how he feels.

When I pull up onto the driveway the sky is darkening, although it's just gone three. I've checked my mobile countless times since leaving Jez and still no word from Daniel. I half expect him to be waiting for me at the apartment but there is no one here. I let myself into the hallway. Surely Jez didn't really see Daniel on the night you went missing – he has to be mistaken. Daniel told me he never saw you again after 11.30 p.m. that night, that you'd 'simply disappeared' from the club. Was Jez making it up to cause trouble and now regretted it?

This town is sapping all my energy; I have a sudden, paranoid thought: is the reason Daniel didn't turn up today because he's already been arrested? I lean against the door, my eyes adjusting to the gloomy hallway. Only four more days before I can go home, until I can return you to the back of my mind, only coming to the forefront now and again – when I hear a song you loved on the radio, or see a blonde-haired, long-limbed girl walking in front of me. I think about you, don't get me wrong, but not every day. Not in the obsessive way I've been thinking of you since returning to Oldcliffe.

I slowly climb the stairs. I have visions of Daniel in an interview room somewhere, being interrogated by two policemen clutching Styrofoam cups of bitter coffee, one pretending to be nice, trying to wheedle information out of him, the other ruthless, going in for the kill, trying to break him. I clearly watch too many cop shows.

As I reach the landing I hear a bang coming from the apartment opposite mine, the one that's supposed to be empty. I listen, poised outside the door. Maybe someone's rented it for a few days. It's out of season, but it does happen – look at Jean. And me. I listen a while longer, straining my ears, not quite sure what I'm hoping to hear. Just as I'm about to cross the landing to my door, another crash punctuates the silence, making me jump. What if someone has broken in? I rummage in my bag and grab my phone, fingers hovering over the 9. But I can't call the police – what would I say?

Still holding the phone in one hand I rap my knuckles on the door, steeling myself. 'Hello!' I call, inching my head closer to the door. 'Is there anybody in there?'

The silence is total. I knock again, louder this time, and the force of my knuckles makes the door creak open. I realise it's just on the latch. Maybe someone's moving in today. Perhaps they've rented it out from Monday to Friday. I push the door and it opens further, revealing a hallway much like mine – polished oak floorboards, intricate coving, high ceilings. I repeat my 'hello', but still no answer and I gingerly step over the threshold. 'Is anybody here?' I ask again, feeling foolish.

It comes out of nowhere. There is a high-pitched screech and a blur of ginger comes flying at me, all scraggy fur and pointed teeth. I stumble backwards in shock as the cat darts past me and onto the landing. I'm trembling all over, my heart beating so fast I can hear the vibrations pulsating in my ears. It must have been trapped in here, although I'm sure pets aren't allowed in these apartments.

I steady myself and then creep into the living room. A gust of air brushes my cheek. The sash window gapes open, letting in gusts of cold, February air. I barely take in the room because my focus is on a glass vase on the floor beside a coffee table, one half of it still intact, the other in smithereens, shards glinting on the dark wood. That must have been the crash I heard. The cat must have somehow got through the window, although I'm not sure how, considering we're on the first floor.

A scan of the room shows it to be empty of any personal belongings; I doubt anybody is staying here. I move to the bedroom; the bed is neatly made and a quick look in the wardrobe proves my theory. There are no clothes hanging on the rail. Maybe the cleaner was in and had forgotten to lock the door and close the window when they left.

I walk back into the living room, deliberating what to do about the broken vase. I bend down and pick up a piece of glass and then drop it again in shock as it pierces my fingertip. Blood oozes out and I put it in my mouth to try and stem the bleeding. As I step carefully over the shards of glass to close the window I notice the computer. The screen is blank. Attached to it is a printer, its green light winking in the fading light. I frown, noticing the familiar brown A4 envelope lying next to it. I pick it up, a smudge of blood from my finger staining the corner, and gasp in shock: the envelope is addressed to me.

27
Sophie

Monday, 11 August 1997

Things with Alistair are getting out of hand. I don't know what to do.

It's been a week since I leapt from his car like a startled cat, and I've tried my best to avoid him by phoning in sick. I had no choice – I needed to put some distance between us, even though I was losing pay, which I can't really afford.

Mum's been on nights, so she's spent most of the mornings in bed, thankfully, leaving me tiptoeing around the house each day. I didn't want her to know that I was taking a mammoth sickie, she'd only ask questions. Mum has always had a great work ethic. She hates layabouts and skivers. Daniel was also in bed, but that was down to a hangover rather than his great work ethic.

When Leon rang last Monday, asking if I wanted to go to the pub that night, I found myself keeping my mouth shut about my sickie. We met on the corner by the Co-op and walked down to the Seagull together, my hand tucked into his. It was still warm, the sky streaked with pink and orange, the sea calm, but my stomach churned with worry. The thought of Alistair's mouth on mine, his declarations of love, made me feel as though I was having an affair, even if it was one-sided.

The pub was quiet so we sat by the window overlooking the sea. It was gone eight, yet a few people gathered in clusters on the beach and the odd couple strolled on the promenade. As I drank my pint of cider I found myself relaxing so that my attention was solely on Leon. I listened with interest as he told me about his day at work and the heated argument between Steph and his brother as soon as he'd got home. He held my hand across the table, sending shockwaves of lust through my body.

'Do you want to stay tonight?' I found myself saying, ignoring my mum's 'No night guests' rule. 'Mum is working and Daniel will keep quiet. Knowing him he won't be home until the early hours anyway.'

'I can't believe you even have to ask me that,' he grinned. 'Can we go now?' He stood up so eagerly that he nearly knocked his pint over. I laughed, standing up too. He reached for me across the table and kissed me so intently that my head spun, his hand in the back of my hair. When he let go I had to hold onto the table for support. I was suddenly desperate for him. We'd only had sex a handful of times, grabbing the opportunity when we could, each time more frenzied and quick than the last, knowing we had a time limit on our passion. The thought of spending the whole night with Leon, taking our time to explore each other's bodies, was a turn-on by itself.

As I went to retrieve my denim jacket from the back of the chair I froze. It was dark by now, the sky the kind of dusky denim that only occurs in the summer, yet I could still see the inky figure standing staring at me from across the street. His face was in shadows but I knew it was him by the way he held himself, the fall of his hair, the line of his straight nose. And I knew that he'd be able to see me, backlit by the harsh lighting like an actress in a play. The starring role.

I had no clue as to how long he'd been standing there or what he'd seen. Had he witnessed the lingering kiss between me and Leon? But I knew why he was there. His presence spoke volumes, there was no escape. I might have avoided him by skiving off work, but he was reminding me that he was waiting.

I turned away from him, slowly, deliberately.

'Are you all right, Soph?' Leon said as he walked over to my side of the table. 'You've gone pale.'

I nodded and forced a smile. 'I've just been feeling a bit off, that's all.' Snaking his arm around my waist he led me out of the pub. Alistair was nowhere to be seen. But all the way home I imagined that he was following us. Every time a car drove past I craned my neck, looking for his BMW and exhaling with relief when it proved not to be him.

I pushed him out of my mind as I sneaked Leon into the house. As I suspected, Daniel was still out. For once me and Leon could really let ourselves go. We made love twice: the first time it was quick, but the second . . . wow! Afterwards, nuzzled against his chest,

I was tempted to tell him about Alistair. I felt so close to him in that moment and I didn't want to keep secrets from him any more. But I knew it was just wishful thinking.

We eventually fell asleep, only waking when we heard footsteps on the stairs just as the sun was coming up. I shook Leon awake and told him to hide in my wardrobe, just in case my mum poked her nose around the door. But she must have been exhausted because I heard the toilet flush, then her bedroom door close and the springs of her mattress creak as her tired body fell into bed. Suppressing my giggles I retrieved Leon from the wardrobe, where he was huddled naked under my clothes, a flowery dress that I'd worn to a wedding three years ago brushing the top of his head.

'Sophie Collier,' he whispered as we climbed back into bed, giggling, a tangle of limbs, 'I love you so much.'

It was such a special night. Leon finally sneaked off home just after seven so that he could get changed and go to work.

Later that morning, as I was coming out of the local newsagent's on the corner of the estate clutching a plastic bag of magazines and cartons of milk, I heard someone calling my name. I turned to see Alistair's car purring by the side of the road, the window wound down. He grinned at me, his eyes sparkling. The toast I'd had for breakfast scratched the back of my throat.

'I thought you were ill,' he called, oblivious to the looks from some of the kids skateboarding around the dustbins. 'You look fine to me. Perfect, in fact.' He pointedly stared at my legs and I pulled the hem of my skirt down.

Tears pricked the back of my eyelids. But they were tears of anger and frustration. 'It's my day off, so why don't you fuck off and leave me alone?' My voice rose in distress, causing the skateboarders to turn and look at me. One of them, a boy of about sixteen wearing a hoody and jeans too big for him, whooped.

Alistair's expression darkened. 'If you're not in tomorrow you're sacked,' he said, his lip curling up.

'You 'eard her. Fuck off, you pleb,' another of the boys, acne-scarred with a pierced eyebrow, called out. 'She don't wanna talk to you, you tosser.'

Not taking his eyes off me, Alistair wound the window up. His jaw tensed as he turned to stare ahead of him, the tyres of his car screeching as he sped away.

'You all right, love?' asked Pierced Eyebrow. I nodded, grateful for their intervention.

The next morning – Wednesday – I contemplated calling in sick again but I knew Alistair would sack me if I did. I had no choice; I need the money. Especially if I get that publishing job and have to move to London. There's no way Mum can afford to give me a month's deposit to rent a flat. I have to come up with it myself.

And, I reasoned as I walked into work, Alistair couldn't really do much to me at the hotel, not with his wife and daughter within earshot. Maybe he'd finally got the message after I was so rude to him the day before.

I was wrong.

At first I managed to avoid him. I helped Mrs Howe in the kitchen clearing away the breakfast things, making small talk with some of the punters who were still lingering over their rubbery-looking eggs. All the while I was keeping an eye out for Alistair. Wednesdays are Frankie's day off, so I knew she wouldn't be working. Maria told me she was still in bed and I idly wondered what she'd been up to since I'd last seen her. She didn't really have any other friends in Oldcliffe.

'Can you go and change the bedding in room seven,' Maria said, her back to me. It wasn't a question. I studied her bent stature, the round shoulders, the thick dark hair so like Frankie's.

Wordlessly I left the room to go to the large cupboard on the first floor where all the clean laundry was kept. It was at the end of the corridor and around a bend. I was standing on tiptoes, trying to reach the shelf where the double duvet covers live, when I felt hands grasp my waist. I could smell him before I could see him. That musky scent mixed with cigarettes. It made me want to vomit. I wiggled away from him, but there was nowhere to go and he knew it. He must have been lying in wait, knowing that if he accosted me here nobody would see.

I slapped his hands away and spun around to face him. 'Why won't you get the message?'

He had that look on his face that I remembered from childhood, a sort of precocious pout like a little boy who's been told he can't have any sweets. He used to pull that face at Frankie when she wanted to go out and he wanted her to stay in and play board games.

'You weren't very nice to me yesterday,' he said in a whiny voice.

I didn't know how best to respond. I prayed that Maria would come up the stairs, but even if she did she wouldn't see us there, hidden by the wall.

'I have to be horrible to you, Alistair, because you're not getting the message. I'm not interested.'

'I think you'll change your mind.'

'Whatever,' I said. I pushed past him but he grabbed my arm.

'I always get what I want, Sophie. One way or another.'

Was he threatening me?

'Not this time,' I hissed, shaking him off. 'I'm out of here, Alistair. I can't do this any more.'

I stalked off, but he followed me, his voice needling. 'Soph, wait! I'm sorry, don't go.'

'Get away from me,' I spat. 'I've had enough of this. I saw you the other night, watching me and Leon. Why won't you leave me alone? You're mental.'

Panic flashed across his face. 'OK, OK, but shhh!' He put his fingers to his lips. 'Please, be quiet.'

'I should tell Maria!' I was in full flow now, all the frustrations tumbling out of me. 'She deserves to know what a bastard you are.' By now I'd reached the landing. Alistair's eyes darted to the staircase that stretched up to Frankie's floor. He was worried that our argument would wake her. What had he planned to do? Snog me in the laundry cupboard?

'Please, Sophie. I'll leave you alone. I'm sorry. I got it wrong.'

'I really hope so, Alistair. You're a forty-eight-year-old man, for crying out loud. I'm sorry I kissed you, it should never have happened. Now get over it.' And then I hurried down the stairs. I didn't go back into the kitchen to Maria, who would demand to know why I wasn't changing room 7. Instead I walked as calmly as I could to the front door and then I ran. And I didn't stop running until I had put enough distance between us.

I already know I'll never set foot inside the hotel ever again.

Mum's calling me, I'll have to finish this later.

28
Frankie

I pull up outside the local newspaper offices on the trading estate on the edge of town, relieved to see Daniel's Astra in the car park. THE OLDCLIFFE ADVERTISER is written in huge letters across the front of the 1960s building. It hasn't changed from when we did our work experience here when we were fifteen – do you remember, Soph? You had aspirations to be a journalist then, although you changed your mind regularly. You just knew you wanted to do something creative. I, on the other hand, had no clue, although went along with it because I thought it would be a laugh. Instead we were separated and I spent most of my time taking phone messages while you shadowed reporters to court.

I've tried to call your brother several times since finding the envelope, but he hasn't answered. In desperation I jumped in the car and raced here, hoping he would be at work. I had to do something because there's no way I'm going to stay in that apartment by myself now.

My legs still feel shaky as I make my way into the offices. There is nobody on reception so I continue into the open-plan newsroom. The strip lights are on but there is only one head bent over a keyboard: a woman with a pony-tail twisted at the nape of her neck. She looks up as I approach and smiles questioningly. She's young, probably mid-twenties, and vaguely familiar. Where is everybody else?

I introduce myself.

'Hi, I'm Trish,' she says. It dawns on me that she is the girl who was with Daniel last night. 'A big story came in. So I'm left manning the phones.'

That might explain why Daniel didn't meet me and Jez earlier. 'Has Daniel gone too? His car is outside.'

She frowns. 'No, he's here somewhere –' She's interrupted by the phone ringing and mouths an apology as she answers it, turning away from me to scribble something down on a notepad. I take the opportunity to wander towards the only glass cubicle in the place. It has a sign saying EDITOR on the closed door so I take it to be Daniel's office. I walk in but it's empty, although his computer screen is on.

Intrigued, I go to his desk to see what he's been working on and my hand flies to my mouth. On screen is an article about severed human feet being washed up on the beaches of the Pacific North-west. 'The reason victims' feet survived,' I read, 'was because they were wearing trainers or boots that scavengers were unable to chew through. This meant they could have come from bodies that had been in the water for years, even decades –'

'Frankie?'

I jump at the sound of Daniel's voice.

'What are you doing?' He pushes past me to click on the mouse to close the page and then stands looking at me, his eyes narrowed. 'Why are you snooping around on my computer?'

My head is reeling. 'I'm not. It was open. And anyway, why are you reading about severed feet?'

'I just want to understand, before . . . Wednesday, that's all.' But he avoids eye contact, instead shuffling papers on his desk.

He's googled 'severed feet' to get more insight into what happened to you, Soph. It's so gruesome. I'm suddenly furious with him. What the hell is he playing at? 'Where were you?' I cry. 'You were supposed to meet me to talk to Jez. You left me to face him by myself . . .'

His expression is dark. 'A big story came up . . . I got waylaid.' He rubs his eyes. He looks shattered, and for the first time I realise how much responsibility this job must be.

'You could have phoned . . .'

'I'm really sorry.'

'There's something else too.' I fill him in on Jean, the dummy and the envelope. 'It had my name on it and it's freaked me out. Can you come back with me? I'm too afraid to go alone.'

'You, afraid? Wow, Lady Frankie, that's something you don't admit very often. Give me ten minutes to finish up here and then we'll go. The deputy editor will be back in a minute and he can take over.'

*

Back at Beaufort Villas, at the top of the stairs, I point to apartment 3 with a timorous finger and tell him what happened. When I've finished he frowns but doesn't say anything. Instead he goes to the door, now closed, and turns the handle. It's still on the latch, exactly as I found it earlier, and creaks open easily. Daniel calls out a hello then disappears inside the apartment. I'm too scared to stand out on the landing by myself so I follow him. Everything is the same as it was when I went in there less than an hour ago.

'There are no belongings,' I say. 'It doesn't seem as though anyone is staying here. It looks like someone has been using this flat purely to type up those poisonous letters to me. Who would do that? Do you know who this apartment belongs to?'

His back is to me and he's leaning over the desk that's been pushed up against the bay window. He picks up the envelope and turns to me. 'This is the same as the ones you've been receiving?' he asks.

I tut impatiently and tell him that, yes, of course they are. He turns it over in his hand, a puzzled expression on his face. 'You said it had your name and address on the front, but there's nothing here.'

I snatch it from him. Sure enough the brown A4 envelope is blank.

Daniel looks irritated. 'You've jumped to conclusions based on a blank brown envelope? A generic envelope that everybody uses?'

'But . . .' I stare at it, confused, as if expecting my name and address to suddenly reappear in the middle of the envelope. 'I don't understand. It definitely had my name on it . . .' I throw it back at Daniel but he makes no effort to catch it and it floats to the floor. I get down on my hands and knees to search frantically under the desk. 'Maybe the wind blew it off the desk,' I say desperately as I scan the parquet flooring in vain. I stand up and dust down my trousers. Daniel is staring at me, perplexed. The disbelieving look on his face makes my eyes swell with tears. 'It was here,' I say in a small voice.

'Oh, Franks.' Daniel's expression softens and he takes a step towards me. 'You look exhausted – I'm worried about you.'

'I'm fine,' I sniff, trying to blink back tears. I can't fall apart now, not after all this time, although part of me would love to bury myself in Daniel's arms, to hide within the folds of his long black coat. I've been strong for so long. Just a little bit longer, Soph.

I turn away from him and swipe at my eyes with my sleeve, careful not to dislodge any mascara, and I freeze. 'The vase . . .' I say, staring at the coffee table. 'The vase . . . it's gone.'

'What vase?'

I don't know what's happening but I feel an overwhelming sense of dread. 'There was a vase . . . the cat had knocked it over. It was on the floor, broken. But now it's gone, someone's cleared it up. Someone's been in here and cleared up, taken the envelope.' I can hear my voice; it's shrill, the type of voice I despise, and I hate that it's coming from me.

'Frankie, you're not making any sense.'

I spin around to face him. 'Don't you see? Someone is messing with me, Daniel. Someone's trying to frighten me. Why?'

He takes hold of my elbow and gently steers me towards the door. 'We shouldn't be in here,' he says in a low voice. 'Come on.'

I feel sick but I let him lead me out of the apartment. He pulls the door to and then I follow him back into my own apartment. I suddenly have the irrational fear that while I've been out someone has been in here. I dart from room to room in a crazed manner, checking under the beds and in the wardrobe.

'Franks, you're being paranoid.'

Daniel's voice makes me jump and I whirl around to confront him. 'You said the other apartments were empty. But they're obviously not. Do you know I hear a baby crying at night? This is a detached house, Daniel. The sound has to be coming from somewhere. The woman downstairs says it's not coming from her flat yet this morning I saw her with a dummy. It's as though someone –' I swallow a sob '– it's as though they know how to push my buttons.' I can't help it, I burst into angry, frustrated tears.

'Franks . . .' Daniel looks stricken but I'm on a roll. All the pent-up fears that I've tried to bury spill out of me. I have no control over what I'm saying.

'I see her, I see Sophie! She's watching me, she's on the pier, she follows me home, she's standing at the bottom of the driveway, calling me. She wants to talk to me, is she trying to warn me? And now the apartment across the hall has a new guest. Someone who's writing me poisonous letters . . . I can't . . . I don't know what to do . . .' I bury my face in my hands, embarrassed at my outburst. I'm so good at keeping it together, even in stressful situations, so why do I feel like I'm unravelling, being back here?

Daniel doesn't say anything but I feel him pull me into his arms. I cry against his chest for a couple of minutes before composing myself. 'I'm sorry,' I sniff eventually, not able to look at him. 'I'm sorry for saying all that about Sophie. I know, rationally, that she's not there, that it's my imagination.'

'Franks,' he says into my hair, 'I think that apartment is empty. I can't explain the vase or the envelope, but it didn't look as though anyone was staying there.' He pulls away from me and tenderly wipes a tear from my face. 'I'm sorry. I'm so sorry for putting you through this. I should never have asked you to come back here. I never realised it would affect you so much. What you said about Sophie . . . I understand. For years I thought I saw her. That's what happens when someone you love dies, you know that.'

I can't tell him that it's more than that. That when I see you, you're as real to me as he is. That it's not just the flick of long blonde hair or a slim pair of legs that fleetingly remind me of you. It is *you*. You're here. I'm as sure of it as I know my own name. I'm not sure why you're here, though. Is it revenge for not being there for you that night? Or are you trying to warn me? To help me? I never believed in ghosts, that was always your domain. But now . . . now . . .

He kisses the top of my head then pulls away. 'I'll put the kettle on. It will be OK . . . I have a good feeling we're getting closer to knowing what happened to my sister.'

When he's left the room I go to the en suite and splash my face, then hurriedly reapply my mascara and brush my hair until I feel calmer. My eyes look huge in my face, the glisten of tears making the green irises brighter.

Daniel is sitting on the sofa when I finally make an appearance. I draw the curtains, deliberately avoiding looking anywhere but at the drapes. All at once I have a sudden, sharp memory of you – your face, your laughing grey eyes – and it's so clear, so intense, that I cry out as though I've been stabbed. The guilt, it's eating away at me. That I couldn't save you.

'Franks?' Daniel's voice brings me back to the present.

'It's OK,' I smile reassuringly. He already thinks I'm losing it, I can't tell him anything else. I rub my chest where my heart is. 'Just a bit of indigestion.'

'Sit down, for God's sake, the last thing we need is for you to keel over from a heart attack.' He's joking but I can hear the note of concern in his voice. I join him on the sofa and sip my tea. He's put sugar in it, but I don't complain. I need the energy spike for my frayed nerves.

'Do you want me to stay here tonight?' he says. 'I could sleep on the sofa.'

I long to say yes, for him to share my bed, to lose myself in him, but I know I can't. My head is all over the place at the moment, and he's got a girlfriend. Sweet, kind Daniel. I'd hate to hurt him like I did back then. 'What about Mia?' I ask instead.

'She'd understand,' he says, but I can tell by his expression that he's lying. I know she wouldn't understand. I know that if he was my boyfriend I wouldn't.

I squeeze his hand. 'Thanks, Dan. But I think we both know she wouldn't like it. I don't want to cause you trouble.'

He stays for another hour and we order a takeaway. He has to go down to the driveway to make the call, the reception in this apartment is so sketchy. I leave the front door open for him but I hover in the kitchen, keeping an eye on the hallway just in case the person who is staying in the opposite flat makes an appearance. Daniel doesn't believe me, but I know what I saw. I'm certain someone is staying in there. Maybe not all the time; they could just be using it to write their nasty letters, for all I know, creeping out in the early hours of the morning, leaving their brown envelopes and their filthy little notes behind. I don't understand what they're hoping to achieve. Are they trying to scare me into leaving? I'd love to up and leave, to run back to the safety of London. But I'm not going yet. I refuse to be driven out of this town by a few cryptic notes.

When Daniel returns, his nose red from the cold, a few snowflakes decorating his hair and shoulders like dandruff, we talk about everything but you. After we've devoured our curries he leaves, pausing by my door for a moment. 'Don't come with me to the front door, I can see myself out,' he says as I begin to stuff my feet into my boots. He kisses me on my cheek and I resist the urge to reach up and kiss him.

I reluctantly close the door on him, the apartment feeling empty now that he's gone. I throw some more logs on the fire and down another glass of wine. I'm going to have to stock up again tomorrow; I'm drinking far too much since I've been back here. My head is full of you, Soph. It's no longer full of the business, like it was before. You've managed to wheedle your way back into my thoughts, just like you did in the weeks and months after you first went missing.

As I've done every night since I've been here, I grab the duvet from the bedroom and curl up with it on the sofa. It still carries the scent of Mike and part of me regrets sending him packing this morning. I could really use the company right now.

The reception on the television isn't too bad tonight and I'm comforted by the chatter of the characters in some period drama. After I've polished off the bottle of wine I fall into a deep sleep, still in my clothes. I'm woken by the howls of the baby. Like clockwork, I think, as I blink at the green lights on the DVD player: 02:00. It's always 2 a.m. when the baby starts crying. I listen carefully, trying to ignore the goose bumps on my arms, the hairs that stand up at the back of my neck as though someone is blowing softly on my bare flesh. It's rhythmic, the crying. Stopping for about five minutes, then starting up again. Stopping. Starting. Stopping. It's almost like . . .

I jump off the sofa and run to the front door. Where is it coming from? I stand on tiptoes and look out through the spyhole. There is a dim light on in the hallway so that the landing is illuminated by a soft glow and shadows flicker on the walls, but I tell myself there is no one there. Am I brave enough to go out onto the landing in the middle of the night? Before I've thought about it too deeply I run back into the living room and grab the silver candlestick from the top of the fireplace. I'm not sure what I plan to do with it, but I feel safer having some sort of weapon. Just in case there is someone out there who wants to hurt me. Who wants – like Daniel thinks – revenge.

I grab my door keys from the granite worktop and close the front door behind me so that I'm standing on the landing in my stocking feet, candlestick in hand. My reflection from the arched window makes me jump, and then I laugh at myself. What an idiot I must look, Soph. Wild hair and wild-eyed.

I pause. One, two, three . . . the baby's screams start up again. Just like they did last night, and the night before, and the night before that. I tiptoe to the door of apartment 3 across the landing. It definitely sounds like it's coming from there, not from downstairs like I initially thought. I inch forwards, pressing the palm of my hand gently on the door. Just like before, it swings open. The cries get louder. I have to do this, I have to go in there. Gripping the candlestick more firmly in my fist I enter the small hallway and flick on the light switch. Everything is exactly how Daniel and I left it earlier. Except for the shrill cries of a baby. If there's no baby in this apartment then what is making that sound?

I approach the living room with trepidation, the screams intensifying so that I have to put my hands over my ears. I scan the room but there is no baby. And then I notice the computer by the window, its screen emitting a ghoulish green glow. I stand staring at it, frozen in shock, transfixed by the green wave patterns flickering across the black screen. The screams are coming from the computer. It's a recording. A recording of a baby screaming its lungs out. What sick fuck would do something like this?

I reach over and press down on the mouse, trying to get the recording to stop. I know a bit about computers, but this seems like quite a sophisticated piece of equipment and I can't halt the recording despite smacking as many buttons as I can. I feel a surge of anger and kick the leg of the desk. What the fuck is going on? I finally manage to find the volume control, turn it off and the room falls silent.

I stand next to the desk. The darkness folds itself around me like a blanket. The only light in the room is coming from the computer screen.

A bang makes me jump and I whip my head around. I thought I was alone in here but what if I'm wrong? What if the person who set this up is in here too? A chill runs through me and I run from the apartment as fast as I can, slamming the door, even though it doesn't close properly, still on its latch. With shaky hands I fumble with my keys and then close and lock the door behind me and sink to the floor.

What does it all mean, Sophie? What's going on?

I have to focus. I need to find out who owns No. 3, I think, cursing the fact that this apartment has no Wi-Fi. I'll go to a café in the morning, I vow, as I get up off the floor and wrap myself in the duvet on the sofa, still trembling. I put my hand to my hair – I can't help it, Soph. It feels so good, the tension easing as I tug sharply. I stare at the thick, dark hairs threaded through my fingers. I haven't done it in years, not even when I split up with Christopher.

At least I've managed to make the 'baby' stop crying, I think with a hysterical laugh.

I fumble for my phone, my hands shaking, and dial Daniel's number. I know Mia will be cross that I'm calling her boyfriend in the early hours of the morning but I can't spend the night here alone. I pray that there will be enough reception to get through, relieved when I hear his voice, thick with sleep, on the other end of the phone. I manage to tell him to come over before the line breaks up and goes dead.

29
Sophie

Monday, 11 August 1997

I've been a coward. I've not been able to face Alistair since I ran out of the hotel. Frankie called the next day, demanding to know what was going on. For a horrifying moment I thought she'd overheard me shouting at her dad on the stairs. But thankfully she just wanted to know why I'd run off home. I had to tell her I have gastroenteritis and that the doctor has ordered plenty of rest. I've been hiding at home, re-reading novels. I know I can't pretend for ever, that I have to leave the house at some point. I wake up in the night in a cold sweat, worrying that Alistair is outside the house or lurking in the street in his car. I can't shake the feeling that he's still around. That he's watching me. And I know it's stupid considering all he's really tried to do is kiss me, but it's the delusion that scares me, his conviction that I have feelings for him when the only thing I feel for him now is disgust. Thinking about him makes my skin crawl.

Daniel came into the living room on Saturday

morning carrying a huge bunch of flowers in his arms. I was wrapped in a blanket on the sofa, still pretending to be ill. 'Look what's just arrived. Leon must be in love,' he grinned as he handed me the bouquet. My heart sank. I knew, without even opening the card, that they wouldn't be from Leon. He doesn't have money to splash out on flowers, especially ones as opulent as these. He's called me a few times but each time I've told him not to come over, that it might be catching. I haven't seen him since the night he stayed over and, despite missing him, I feel too guilty to face him.

I took the flowers from Daniel. They were beautiful, there was no denying it, huge velvety red roses of the kind I've never seen before. My eyes welled with tears, not of happiness like my brother no doubt thought, but disappointment. How I wished they'd been from Leon.

'I know you feel the same,' read the card. 'I won't give up on you.' There was no name. There didn't have to be.

Daniel must have noticed my downcast expression because he perched next to me on the sofa. 'Are you OK? Me and mum are worried about you.'

This was the first I'd heard of it. Apart from the odd glance, Mum hadn't voiced any concerns to me. When she got home from her night shift I'd hear her creep into my room, obviously checking up on me, but I'd pretend to be asleep. And then when she got up in the early afternoon she'd make me some soup, telling me I had to get something down me, even though the thought of eating made me want to gag. I'm beginning to feel as though I really do have gastroenteritis!

'I've just got this bug,' I said by way of explanation. I didn't sound very convincing. Daniel knows me better than anyone, even better than Frankie does probably. 'I need to put these in water.' I sidled away from him and his questions, with the flowers in my hands. Water dripped from the stems and down my arm. In the kitchen I hovered over the bin, contemplating throwing them away. The stench rose up to greet me: rotten cabbages, last night's stew. It hit me in the face with such force that I retched. I had to turn away.

Mum came into the kitchen wrapped in her threadbare dressing gown, her hair standing up on end, moaning that she couldn't sleep. Of course she exclaimed over the flowers. Who wouldn't? And of course I had to pretend they were from Leon. Lie upon lie upon lie. She took them from me, told me I was as white as a sheet and to get up to bed and that she would put the flowers in a vase.

When Leon turned up at the door yesterday afternoon, Daniel immediately started teasing him about the flowers. 'I don't know what you're talking about,' said Leon gruffly, his face flushed. I pulled him back into the hall and barked at Daniel to go away.

'What flowers?' he said as I led him upstairs to my room, where he nearly tripped over the pile of books stacked by my bed.

'Oh, I think they're from Frankie's family. Daniel thought they were from you,' I said, trying to brush over the subject. Leon didn't seem convinced and he kept snatching glances at me when he thought I wasn't looking, as if he was trying to figure me out. I've always been a crap liar.

'You still look peaky,' he said. My hair was scraped back into a pony-tail and I had no make-up on. I knew I wasn't looking my best. I had dark smudges under my eyes and my face was drawn. And because I've hardly been able to eat much more than soup for a week the waistband on my jeans is loose. I couldn't afford to lose weight, not if I wanted to keep 'Twiglet legs' at bay.

'I feel better now that you're here,' I said truthfully. 'I've missed you.'

He sat on the edge of my bed, looking up at me. His eyes were sad and I suddenly felt a rush of affection towards him. 'I wanted to come over,' he said defensively, 'but you kept me at arm's length. I was worried I'd done something wrong when I stayed last week.'

I stood in front of him, suddenly feeling on the edge of tears. 'You've done nothing wrong. I was just worried to come near you in case you caught it.'

He looped his thumb in the waistband of my jeans and pulled me towards him. 'I've missed you too.' Then he fell backwards, me on top of him so that we were suddenly a jumble of limbs on top of my Pierrot duvet cover. Making up for lost time!

And in that moment I felt that everything would be OK after all. As long as I had Leon by my side.

Tuesday

30
Frankie

Faces invade my dreams. Faces from the past: you, Leon, Helen, Daniel, Jason and even his sister. I can't remember her name, just her sad, pinched little face at the funeral and her mass of blonde hair. I haven't thought about her in years, but being back here, the anonymous letters, all of this has stirred up so much heartache, so much emotion – so much *guilt*.

My sleep is fitful; I dream and then wake up with a start. I'm relieved when the first cracks of light appear through the gap in the curtains, surprised to find myself in the bedroom until I remember my frantic phone call to Daniel at 2.30 in the morning, his voice heavy with sleep, the relief when he turned up at my front door fifteen minutes later with bed-head hair and a dazed grin and I realised with startling clarity that I loved him. I'm in love with him, Soph. I'm in love with your big brother. He's been my rock these past few days. He's what I've been missing all these years. If I'm honest I think I've always loved him but I just didn't realise it, believing I needed someone ambitious, enigmatic, independent. My head was turned by intense indie boys like Jez and Leon. Like Jason. When all the time I needed someone solid, someone dependable, someone grounded. I've been so busy trying to escape the Frankie of my past, to run away, when really everything I need has been here the whole time.

But it can never be. You know that, don't you, Soph?

I fling back the duvet and grab my dressing gown from where it hangs on the back of the door and creep into the living room. Daniel is curled up on the sofa, fully dressed, a blanket barely covering his body, his legs too long to stretch out along the length of the sofa. His face in sleeping repose is peaceful, his mouth closed, his breathing shallow. I long to move the dark hair away from his forehead. I stand and stare at him for a while, thinking how lucky Mia is to have him, when his eyes suddenly flicker open, widening in surprise at his surroundings and to see me standing by his side in my dressing gown, open just enough to reveal a glimpse of cleavage. I know, I know, it's a cheap shot. But you know me, Soph. I haven't changed that much.

With a groan he sits up and runs a hand across the stubble on his chin. 'What time is it?'

'Just gone eight. I'll put the kettle on.' I pad into the kitchen but I can already hear his protestations as he throws aside the blanket, the thud of his feet on the wooden floor as he swings his legs from the sofa. He'll be running back to her. Not for the first time I wonder what she looks like, this Mia. He hardly talks about her, yet his silence speaks volumes.

I flick the switch on the kettle and wait. Within seconds he's filling the door-frame, his hair standing up on end, his shirt hanging out of his jeans, the edges creased. 'I'm sorry, Franks, I've got to go. I need to get home and shower before I go to work.' With promises to call me later he blows me a theatrical kiss, unaware of my sinking heart, and then he's gone and the flat suddenly feels huge and empty without him.

I shower and dress, and then force some porridge down my throat, my eyes flicking to the clock on the kitchen wall, the hands moving agonisingly slowly. It's just gone 8.30 a.m. I need to find a café with Wi-Fi so that I can work out who owns the apartment across from this one. I doubt many are open before nine. Something strange is going on here. Why would someone do that to me? And a baby crying . . . it's as if they know, Soph. But how could they? How could anyone?

When Daniel turned up last night I was crying and shaking. He had poked his nose around the apartment opposite and then tried to talk me down as I sat shivering on the sofa. He held my hands in his as he calmly told me his theory: that the computer was on a timer, that someone had forgotten to turn it off, that it wasn't aimed at me at all but was just a coincidence. 'Maybe someone had set it up for research, or for a film. There could be any number of reasons why someone would have a recording of a baby on their computer,' he said.

He had a rational explanation for all of it. But I know, deep down, that this is aimed at me. I saw that envelope with my name typed on the front, even if it had magically disappeared later.

I thought of what Jez said yesterday, the accusations he'd made about your brother. When I'd asked Daniel about it he'd shrugged it off, said that Jez was talking nonsense, that he hadn't been the one arguing with you on the pier the night you went missing. Your brother has always been so open, his thoughts and feelings written all over his face. He usually couldn't wait to blurt everything out. Verbal diarrhoea, you always said.

But yesterday . . . I could tell he was hiding something from me.

The baby crying. It seemed like a cruel taunt, as though someone had set out to deliberately hurt me. I'd told Daniel about my desire to have children, he's the only one from Oldcliffe that I have told. A thought moves and shifts inside my head; a thought so terrible I push it to one side, refusing to voice it even to myself.

I have to trust Daniel. I remember how much he loved me and I know he still cares. I have to hold on to that thought, Sophie, because there is nobody else.

I close my eyes and massage my forehead. My brain feels woolly, a headache tugging at my temples. I know it's lack of sleep; too many nights curled up on that blasted sofa after downing a bottle of wine. The week stretches out in front of me like a traffic jam on a motorway. I can't even go home unless I'm happy to share my house with a hostile ex-boyfriend – that is, if Mike did go home. I've heard nothing from him since he stormed out yesterday.

I down the rest of my coffee and then snatch up my laptop and phone and squeeze them into my large handbag. I pause at the door, my mind racing, suddenly afraid of what I might find out on the landing. Will the person who terrorised me last night with those eerie recordings be there, watching me through the gap in the door?

I pull back the door gingerly and peer out onto the landing. A weak winter sun struggles through the arch-shaped picture window, illuminating the usually dark landing. The door to the apartment opposite is closed and I wonder if it's still on the latch or whether someone came up here and locked it while Daniel and I slept. Relieved that the landing is empty, I step out of the apartment and close the door behind me.

Something crumples underfoot and I look down, my heart sinking when I notice the brown envelope stuck under the heel of my boot. I bend down and pick it up, noticing straight away the smudge of blood on the top left-hand corner, like a macabre stamp, and I immediately know it's the envelope that was on the desk yesterday. The envelope that mysteriously disappeared.

I rip it open, pulling out a single sheet of plain paper.

I'M WATCHING YOU

The hairs on my arms instantly stand to attention and I whip my head around, half expecting somebody to be lurking in the doorway of the apartment opposite. But there is nothing except the white painted door and the silvery number 3 glinting in the weak sunlight.

'Fuck you!' I say to the door, sticking up my middle

finger for good measure. I resist the urge to flee down the stairs as quickly as my legs will carry me. Even though my instincts are screaming at me to do just that, I descend the steps, trying to remain calm and not think about being followed or a hand on my back, pushing me to my death. I grip the banister, swallowing my fear.

It's not until I've wrestled the heavy front door open, crunched over the gravel to my car and slid into the driver's seat that I allow myself to release my tears.

I can't deny it any more, Sophie. I'm scared. I'm really, really scared.

Miraculously, I manage to find a café with Wi-Fi near the high street, down a cobbled side street, almost behind the hotel I grew up in. It's small and practically empty. Although it's away from the seafront, as I perch myself in the corner by the window I can hear the screech of the gulls, smell the salt in the air that reminds me I'm still in Oldcliffe.

The waitress tries to engage me in conversation as she brings me coffee and a croissant. 'I've not seen you around here before,' she says in a thick West Country accent as she places my milky coffee in front of me. I had asked for an Americano but she gave me a blank look so I settled for a normal coffee. I'm surprised she doesn't know who I am. Everybody else in this town seems to.

She stands at my table, brushing down her apron and assessing me through narrowed eyes. She's trying to place me, I can tell. I look up at her. She's about my age with red hair and freckles. Her name tugs at the corner of my memory. Did I go to school with her?

'Frankie? It's Frankie, isn't it? I thought it was you.'

I smile, trying to conjure up her name.

'Jenny. Jenny Powell. I was in your class at school, remember?' She fiddles with her notepad and pen, her jolly face clouding over. She's remembering. It reminds me of how people used to look at me after you disappeared. 'Terrible business,' she shakes her head. 'You know the town never really got over it, Sophie Collier going missing like that. And now I hear she's dead.'

She's still shaking her head while looking at me, and I see something else in her eyes, a glint at the possibility of the gossip.

'Is that why you're back? To find out what happened?' I open my mouth to speak but she rushes on. 'It's been so long . . . what is it now? Eighteen years?'

I nod.

'Terrible business.' She chews her pen thoughtfully, her eyes never leaving mine. And it suddenly occurs to me who she is. She had plaits at school, so tightly knitted together that I always imagined her mother must have done them in a temper, grabbing the hairs and winding them around each other so deftly that none dared escape. It gave her a severe appearance. She had been friends with Helen and I think she would have liked to have been friends with you too, if it wasn't for me.

'I really liked her,' she said, almost to herself. 'She was kind to me at school. And to Helen. We were the oddballs, the geeks.' She laughs but I can sense remnants of hurt behind her words.

You always did have a way with strays, being one yourself until I took you under my wing.

'She was lovely,' I say. 'Everybody loved her.' I always thought you were a nicer person than me. You didn't deserve what happened to you, Soph.

Jenny touches my shoulder in sympathy, seeing my distress. 'I'm sorry,' she says gently. 'It must be hard being back here, what with all the memories.'

I tell her that it is. Not least because you're here with me, but I keep that to myself.

'They should pull that old pier down, it's an eyesore,' she says with feeling. 'Not to mention dangerous. I don't understand why they've kept it standing all these years.'

I know you won't agree. You loved anything old and from the past.

'I wish they would.'

She throws me another sympathetic smile and then thankfully leaves me in peace to go and tend to another customer.

I take a sip of the sickly coffee, forcing myself to swallow it down, and then I click on Safari, relieved that there is a connection. I bring up the Land Registry website and find the section on owner information. It's surprisingly easy. I type in the address of the flat opposite the one I'm staying in. I wait, my heart banging against my chest. I need to pay a small fee. I bend down and ferret in my bag to retrieve my purse. I look over my shoulder to make sure I'm not being watched but there is only one other customer, an older gentleman reading a newspaper. I quickly key in my card details and wait for the name of the owner to appear on the screen, my palms damp, coffee churning in my stomach.

I gasp, causing the man to look up from his newspaper. The words swim in front of my eyes.

Address: Apartment 3, Beaufort Villas, Hill Street, Oldcliffe-on-Sea, Somerset
Date of purchase: September 2004
Property owner: Mr Leon James McNamara

31
Sophie

Tuesday, 12 August 1997

My lies are causing a rift between me and Leon, their toxicity sucking all the goodness out of our relationship. And I feel so guilty because I started all this with my stupid teenage crush. With my ego. What had I been hoping to achieve, kissing Alistair? I was flattered when he first kissed me, like all those teenage fantasies had finally paid off. I did it for the skinny, spotty girl I had been. To make myself feel better, to make myself feel wanted. What an idiot. I hate myself for it. All the insecurities I've ever had, about my looks, about Frankie, about playing second fiddle, manifested themselves in that one moment of madness. And now I'm paying the price.

I'd managed to avoid Alistair thanks to my gastroenteritis story, and then yesterday lunchtime I found out I'd got the publishing job in Ealing. I was so relieved when I tore open the envelope and read the letter that I burst into tears. Mum came running into the hallway, worry etched on her lovely face, until she realised they were tears of joy. I made her and Daniel promise not to tell anyone yet.

Receiving the letter gave me the impetus I needed to leave the house. I needed my old job back on the fish stall. Even working with Stan was preferable to going back to the hotel. As I walked down to the seafront I tried to quash the feeling of unease that threatened to overwhelm me. Alistair wasn't following me, there was no sign of him or his car, yet I still felt horribly exposed and anxious.

Luckily Stan said I could have my old job back and I thanked him, relieved that I could start earning money again. I needed as much as possible if I was going to move to London.

I was due to meet Leon at the old pier. I moved through town in a daze, dreaming about leaving, worrying about how I was going to break it to Leon, scared that Alistair would find out. It meant I'd have to keep it from Frankie, of course. Another lie, but I can't risk her spilling the beans to her dad.

As I walked along the promenade I heard a car pull up. I knew, without even looking, that it was him. It was in the middle of the afternoon. There were people all around – sitting on the sea wall eating pasties and ice creams, sunbathing on the beach – so I knew I wasn't in any danger. It was a no-parking zone, yet it didn't stop him abandoning his car. Why did he think he was above the law? I carried on walking briskly, already knowing that he was going to catch up with me in a few easy strides.

'Hello, Sophie,' he said, falling in next to me. 'Feeling better?'

'Much,' I said, staring straight ahead, thinking that if he tried anything on I'd just scream, right there on the busy promenade in front of all the nice old ladies and kind old men, in front of the young families and the rowdy teenagers.

'I take it you're not coming back to the hotel. I've missed you.'

There was no talking to him, I decided. Best to ignore him.

'I'll take that as a no,' he said, regret in his voice. 'That's a shame.'

I carried on walking. Ignore, ignore, ignore, I told myself over and over again.

'I know you love me,' he said. 'I know you want to be with me. I'll wait for you, Sophie. I won't give up. Did you get my flowers?'

Ignore, ignore, ignore.

Was he going to follow me all the way to the old pier? What would Leon say when I turned up with Alistair at my heels?

'You know,' he said, as though chatting about something as anodyne as the weather, 'I think I've proved my love for you by keeping your secret. Back in Ninety-two.'

I refused to take the bait but his intention was clear enough. Blackmail.

I kept up a purposeful stride, and a few moments later I sensed that Alistair wasn't walking beside me any more. I glanced over my shoulder to see him a little way behind me, standing in the middle of the pavement and waving.

'See you soon,' he called cheerfully. Five minutes later a car cruised by, beeping. I didn't have to look to know it was him.

As I rounded the corner out of town the crowds thinned, the streets becoming quieter, the only sound to be heard was the gushing of the sea as it exploded onto the rocks. I worried Alistair was still around, maybe parked nearby in his car, watching me. I was relieved when I spotted Leon in the distance, leaning against the lamppost, and in that moment I longed to tell him everything. But I was scared. What would he do? He could tell Frankie, and she would never speak to me again. She'd never forgive me for kissing her dad. Maybe Leon wouldn't believe me either. He might think that I wanted this, that I'd led Alistair on. And that's without even telling him about Jason. So many lies.

Leon rushed towards me as soon as he saw me, his face lighting up as though he hadn't seen me for weeks. 'How are you feeling?'

'Still a little bit peaky,' I said truthfully as I hugged him.

'Are you OK? You're shaking.'

'I'm fine,' I mumbled, my nose pressed into the shoulder of his leather jacket. It smelt faintly of cigarettes and dry ice from The Basement.

He kissed the top of my head and then pulled away. 'Come on, let's go back to mine, the house is empty for a change.' He grabbed my hand as we walked, him chattering all the way. I wanted to tell him about the Ealing job, but for some reason found I couldn't. He seemed so happy and after my encounter with Alistair I didn't want to upset the equilibrium. I craved normality. So I remained silent all the way back to his house.

When we got to Leon's we went straight up to his room. He put the Lightning Seeds on his hi-fi. A record, of course; Leon only bought vinyl. I listened, comforted by the sound of the needle's faint crackle, my head on his chest. He'd taken his jacket off and the soft cotton of his T-shirt felt soothing against my face. The late afternoon sun streamed in through his red and grey striped curtains. In that moment I felt safer than I had in a long time.

I manoeuvred myself so that I was leaning on one elbow looking down at Leon lying peacefully against the pillow. I smoothed his hair from his tanned face. Such lovely thick dark hair, I thought as I suppressed a sob. Leon reached up to touch my face tenderly.

'I got that job,' I said suddenly. 'They want me to start soon.' I grimaced to show how nervous I was feeling.

Leon's eyes widened in surprise. Then, to his credit, he whooped and sat up to hug me. 'That's great news, I knew you could do it.' Then his expression grew serious. 'How soon do you start?'

'September fifteenth.' My stomach dropped like I'd driven over a bump in the road.

He frowned, his eyes clouding over. 'I hope I'm not

sounding needy and intense, I'm pleased for you, babe, but . . . what does that mean for us?'

I hung my head. The best thing to do would be to finish it. I loved him but our relationship was built on a lie.

'Do you want to end things?' he said in alarm. 'Is that why you've been acting so distant?'

'No. I don't know. Leon . . . we've been together less than two months . . .'

He tore his gaze away from mine. 'But I love you,' he said quietly into his lap.

And I know it's ridiculous when we haven't known each other that long but I love him too. I couldn't allow my emotions to get in the way though. I needed a clean break. 'Leon . . . we hardly know each other.'

'Don't you love me?'

'It's not that – I do. But it's early days and there's so much . . . there's too much . . .' I wanted to tell him there was too much he didn't know about me.

'I've told you everything about me,' he said. 'I've never lied to you. I know you don't trust men because of your dad, but you can trust me, Soph.' He took both my hands in his, his blue eyes pleading. 'I'd never let you down. I promise.'

He sounded so heartfelt, so sincere, that my eyes filled with tears and I bit my lip in a bid to stop them overflowing. 'I know,' I said in a small voice. 'But I've let you down, Leon. I've let you down and I can't keep up the pretence any more. It's making me ill.'

I opened my mouth to tell him everything: about the night Jason died, about the afternoon in the hotel when I kissed Alistair, about his hounding me. I imagined the look of pain and anger on Leon's face, his hatred, his jealousy. I imagined him stalking off to have it out with Alistair, to maybe deck him. I imagined the police turning up and arresting him for assault and then arresting me for withholding information on the night Jason died and I closed my mouth and swallowed my words. How could I ever tell him? I'm in too deep.

'What do you mean, you've let me down?' His eyes flashed dangerously. 'Have you cheated on me, Sophie?'

'No . . . of course not . . .'

He didn't look convinced. Like I said, I've always been a crap liar.

'It's just . . . I can't commit to you right now. Not with everything that's going on. I'm going to be moving to London. You have to stay here to finish your apprenticeship. It's better to make a clean break.'

Hurt flashed across his face and just knowing I was doing that to him made my heart break. He squeezed my hands. 'Let's not make any hasty decisions. You don't need to leave for another three weeks. Let's see how things go. We could do a long-distance relationship for a while . . . when I've finished my apprenticeship I could move up. I –' His voice broke and he looked away, embarrassed. 'I don't want to lose you.'

I opened my mouth and then I shut it again. In that

moment I wanted to mould myself into him so that I could disappear completely.

We said no more about it as we lay on his bed, listening to the rest of the album. We clung to each other, my head on his chest, both knowing deep down that it couldn't last between us. Our days are numbered.

32
Frankie

The café swims and I have to grip onto the edge of the table, the coffee rising in my throat. *Leon* owns the apartment. Does this mean he's responsible for the fake baby crying? For the letters? He's obviously not living there. So what does he do? Go there when he wants to frighten me? When he wants to deliver his cowardly letters? And then he slinks off home to his brother so that I won't catch him red-handed? How juvenile of him. How pathetic. I told you, Soph. I told you he was bad news.

The other day in the car he was so hostile towards me, so cold. He hates me, I know that. But what I don't understand is why. What have I ever done to him to make him despise me so much? We slept together but it only happened that one time. Did you tell him about Jason? Does he blame us? It's obvious that now you're dead his rage is directed at me. Jason *has* to be the reason.

My fingers feel weak as I type Leon's name into Google. I'm not expecting anything to come up so I'm surprised when I see a small piece from a Bristol newspaper fill the screen. It's only a few paragraphs long with no photograph, but it talks about Leon selling shares in an IT business for a 'substantial six-figure sum' in 2004. A quick search on Zoopla confirms he bought the flat the same year. He must have been renting it out to tourists for the last twelve years. He told me he'd been working abroad so he hasn't been living there.

I sit staring at the screen in a daze, unsure of my next move. Should I confront Leon? Then I remember the way he reacted to me in the car on Sunday, his anger and hatred. I don't want to be on my own with him, he's obviously a psychopath. I tried to warn you about him but you didn't believe me. Oh, Sophie. Not that I blame you. Who would want to believe that a monster lurked beneath that sexy, moody exterior? And I was as taken in by him as you were – for a while, at least.

Not now. Now I see him in all his unattractive glory.

I grab my phone. The time flashes up: 09:37. Daniel should be at work by now and for a moment I consider not bothering him with this, I've already disturbed him enough. But how can I *not* tell him? This is huge. It's over – I can go home.

'Is everything OK?' Jenny is back, hovering by my shoulder, wearing a patient smile while craning her neck to take a look at the screen of my laptop. I pointedly shut the lid.

'Everything's great,' I say.

She frowns at the half-empty coffee cup at my elbow, little globules of fatty milk floating on the surface like pond scum. 'Didn't like the coffee? There's a Costa down the road,' she says, gathering up my cup and officiously wiping the ring of brown liquid from the white Formica table, leaving the faint scent of bleach. 'Nice to see you again, Frankie.' Then she bustles off behind the counter.

I take it as my cue to leave, although the place is still empty apart from the old man immersed in his newspaper.

The cold wind is biting and I pull my scarf further up my chin as I walk down the high street, stumbling and nearly breaking an ankle on the cobbled stones. These heels aren't going to last much longer at this rate. I huddle in the doorway of a shop selling cheap clothes, the pounding dance music an assault on my ears at this time of the morning. I ferret in my bag for my phone, my fingers already numb from the cold despite my leather gloves. A young woman breezes past pushing a buggy, a chubby-cheeked toddler in a pink hat snuggled beneath a fleece blanket. She gurgles at me and my heart pangs. I think of all the miscarriages, all those lost babies, and my eyes smart. I brush the tears away angrily. I haven't got time for regrets. I look away reluctantly from the little girl, pulling my gloves off with my teeth. The screen blurs and I blink away the tears and compose myself before calling Daniel.

'Yep,' he says, sounding distracted. I can hear the hub of noise in the background, the ringing of phones and the bark of voices. He's at work. How I long for work.

'Daniel,' I croak.

'Franks? Are you OK?' He sounds concerned.

'I'm sorry, I know you're at work. I'm sorry I keep disturbing you but I need to speak to you. It's urgent.'

'Where are you?'

I walk out of the shop and then turn to see what it's called. 'Fiz Fashions,' I say, reading the neon sign above my head. 'I'm standing outside. It's in the high street. Shall I meet you on the front?'

'Give me ten minutes,' he says.

'I'll be in my car. In the parking area opposite the Grand Pier.'

'We could meet in the Seagull?'

I consider this but the thought of seeing Helen, or bumping into Leon or Lorcan, is just too much. 'No . . . I'd prefer to wait for you in my car. But be quick. I'm . . . it's urgent. I think I know who killed Sophie.'

There is an audible pause on the line. Even the newsroom seems to go quiet, as though taking a collective breath. Eventually, 'Really? That's . . . I mean, how?'

'I'll explain everything. Just get here as soon as you can.' And then I put the phone down, thinking of Leon. Of you. And of leaving Oldcliffe for ever.

33
Sophie

Tuesday, 12 August 1997

It's late as I write this. Tonight I went to The Basement with Leon as it was student night – two beers for the price of one. I was feeling nervous about the prospect of facing Frankie now that I know I've got the London job.

The last time I saw her was Sunday. She'd popped over, before Leon, to see how I was and wanted to know when I'd be back working at the hotel. I told her I wasn't ever going back, making some excuse about the early mornings, but I could tell she was offended.

'But it was fun working together,' she'd pouted. 'I never see you any more.'

I told her we could go to the student night at The Basement together and that seemed to appease her.

The Basement tonight was crowded because of the two-for-one promotion. A group of jitters were head-banging in the corner to Nine Inch Nails. It was a different DJ tonight, someone called Tony (or Tone, as he preferred to be called, which isn't a very cool name for a DJ!), and he had a penchant for the heavier tunes.

A fog of dry ice hung above their greasy heads. It tickled my nostrils, making my eyes water.

'Are you OK?' Leon called over the music. We were standing at the bar. It was at least four people deep. At this rate we'd never get a drink.

I smiled at him but he eyed me with concern. We've both skirted around the issue of my new job, both refusing to acknowledge it despite it sitting heavily between us. So many things are wedged between us now – we are growing further and further apart.

Tone had changed the music to Rage Against the Machine and as I turned I saw Frankie emerging from the fug of dry ice like a singer in a pop video. She was wearing a short black shift dress and long boots.

'Soph!' she called, elbowing her way towards me. She almost got whipped in the eye by a man's greasy pony-tail as he threw back his head in the middle of the mosh pit. 'Watch it!' she snarled at him, although her words were lost in the music. 'Bloody jitters.' She enveloped me in a hug and then pulled away to survey me. 'How are you feeling? I was hoping you were going to change your mind about coming back to work. I miss you.'

'I got my old job back.'

'I don't understand why you want to work on that smelly fish stall again,' she said.

'I've already told you – I can't do early mornings.'

'I can't hear you!' she shouted over the music. She grabbed my arm, leading me away, and I threw a panicked glance over my shoulder at Leon, but he was too busy trying to jostle himself closer to the bar to notice.

I had no choice but to allow Frankie to lead me through the crowd and through the main double doors to the lobby, where the cloakroom, the exit and the ladies' loos are. It was quieter there, the throb of music dulled by the double fire doors. We stood near the exit, the warm summer air filtering through the doors. Frankie fumbled in her bag for her cigarettes. She calls herself a social smoker, only ever lighting up when we're out. I've never seen the attraction. I tried a cigarette once, behind the bike sheds in sixth form to impress Ian Harris. But the smoke got stuck in my throat and I'd coughed and spluttered and, not surprisingly, he never asked me to go with him to the bike sheds again!

'So,' she said through a flume of smoke. 'What's going on, Soph?'

I squirmed under the intense stare of those green eyes. 'What do you mean?'

'You.' She frowned. 'You've been avoiding me.'

'I saw you on Sunday.' I stared at my Gazelle trainers.

'For half an hour, and then you couldn't get rid of me quick enough. Something's going on. I'm not stupid.' She took another deep drag on her cigarette. 'And besides, if you're not avoiding me then why else would you go back to that slimy fish stall? My dad pays you twice what Stan does.'

'Hardly,' I muttered, still avoiding eye contact. I tried not to shudder at the thought of Alistair.

I looked up and met her eyes. They were hostile. She took another drag and then flicked the butt on the floor where it landed in a puddle of what looked like sticky beer but could easily have been urine. Her face softened. 'You used to tell me everything, Soph,' she said sadly. 'Things have changed. You've changed.'

I sighed, exasperated. What did she think was going to happen? That I would stand still for those three years, frozen in time while waiting to bump into her again? 'Frankie. We're not kids any more.'

'You were like the sister I never had.'

'I know . . . but . . .'

To my surprise her eyes filled with tears. I don't think I've seen her cry since 1986, when she fell off the roundabout and broke her collarbone.

'Oh, Frankie . . .' I rushed towards her and wrapped my arms around her. 'You'll always be my best friend.'

'I'm just being silly, I'm a bit pissed.' She sniffed against my shoulder and then pulled away, dabbing at her eyes. Her eyeliner had smudged and one of her false eyelashes was coming off at the corner. It looked like a furry caterpillar attached to her eyelid and the ridiculousness of it made me want to giggle.

Just then Leon came bounding through the double doors, bringing with him a burst of Green Day. He had a bottle of K cider in each hand. I prefer Diamond White but didn't have the heart to tell him after he'd spent all that time queuing. His face lit up when he saw me. 'There you are,' he said, handing me a bottle. 'Urgh, the music's crap.' Then he noticed Frankie and I saw him flinch slightly. 'Frankie. Didn't know you were coming tonight.'

'Me and Sophie were supposed to come together. But, of course, she ended up coming with you. Not that I blame her.' She flashed him a dazzling, toothy smile.

Since Leon admitted it had been Frankie – and not him – who had done the chasing I've not really seen them together. He'd called her a stalker. (Like father, like daughter!) If I'd had any doubts that Leon had been lying before, those doubts evaporated as I watched them together. As soon as Leon burst through those doors Frankie became coy, lowered her eyes (which looked a bit weird considering the dislodged eyelash), and twisted her thick hair around her finger. Leon's body seemed to close in on itself, like he was armouring himself against an imminent attack: hunched shoulders, arms folded, defiant and defensive. I was a fool to think that he secretly fancied Frankie. And it hit me as I watched her watching him: she was in love with him. She was acting around him exactly how she'd acted around Jason. I hadn't wanted to think about it too much before; maybe I was scared of probing too deeply, worried that Leon was the one lying. On the one hand I felt – still feel – angry at the lies Frankie told me on the night I first met Leon. But on the other hand I understand why she did it. She was in love with him herself and she didn't want him to go out with anyone else. I feel terrible for not realising how she felt.

In that moment I wanted to tell her that I was sorry. That I would never have gone out with him if I'd known. But I couldn't say anything in front of Leon. And I couldn't let her know that he'd told me the truth.

Frankie has always been so proud. She would be embarrassed if she thought I knew how she'd chased Leon and how he'd knocked her back.

'So,' began Leon and I could tell he was feeling uncomfortable. 'Has Sophie been telling you all about the big move?'

Frankie turned to me, her eyes wide. 'What big move?'

I wanted to hurl my bottle at his head. I knew I'd have to tell her some time, but just not yet. What if she told Alistair?

'Oh,' I tried to look nonchalant. 'I got that job in London.' I waved my hand as though it wasn't a big deal.

'Oh my God!' She jumped up and down in excitement. 'That's amazing news, Soph. Well done.' But there was something fake about her enthusiasm and I could tell that underneath all the exclaiming and hand-waving she was gutted that I was leaving. If it had been the other way around maybe I would have felt the same. 'Is it the publisher you were telling me about? The one in Ealing?' My heart skittered that she'd remembered. The less she knew about it the less Alistair knew about it too.

'Yes, but I'm going to be working at their central London offices.' The lie tripped easily off my tongue. After all, I've had a lot of practise. Leon frowned at me, his expression puzzled.

'I thought you said . . .' he began. But I cut him off before he could say anything else by rushing up to Frankie and hugging her again.

'I'll miss you,' I said. 'But when I'm settled you can come and visit.'

When Leon walked me home later that night he asked me why I'd lied.

'Because I don't want her to know too much about it,' I said. We had reached my house and were hovering by the garage.

A flash of disappointment crossed his face. 'But why? I thought she was your best friend.'

'She is, but . . . you know what she's like. As much as I love her I think we need some distance. Otherwise she'll be up every weekend! Anyway, I've said I'll go shopping with her next week.'

He looked down at his feet, stubbing the toe of his desert boot against the pavement. Neither of us had drunk that much but Leon seemed agitated.

'What is it?' I urged.

He looked up, his eyes sad. 'Do you want some distance from me too?'

'Of course not. You can come and visit. And maybe when you've finished your apprenticeship you could move to London too?' I wanted it so badly, despite the lies between us. In a perfect world we would head off to London together, make a life away from this place, away from Alistair and the ghost of Jason. Away from it all, to start again. But would the past just follow us? Could we ever truly escape?

The hope in his eyes made my heart ache with shame.

He gently pulled me into his arms and, as we

snogged, our bodies pressed up against each other so that we were as close as we could be with our clothes on. He had his hands on my bottom and one of my legs was wrapped around his when I heard the purr of a car engine further down the road. I didn't think much of it as I was so caught up in the moment, but as the car drove past it seemed to slow, causing me to open my eyes. I stiffened at the unmistakable outline of Alistair's black BMW. But before I could react, it sped off and rounded the corner out of sight.

34
Frankie

I sit in my Range Rover overlooking the Grand Pier. The sky has darkened and the wind's picked up. The grey clouds cluster together threateningly as though ganging up on me.

It's not even ten minutes before Daniel's car putters up alongside mine. I watch as he gets out, wrestling with his long coat against the wind. He knocks on my window and I unlock the door to let him in. He slides into the passenger seat, blowing on his hands and bringing with him the smell of the sea air. 'Shit, it's cold,' he says and I crank the heating up. 'So, what's going on, Franks? Why the mystery?'

So I tell him everything I've found out so far and watch as his eyes seem to grow rounder with every word I say.

'Leon owns the apartment?' he says, frowning. 'I never knew that.'

'And I never knew you owned mine.' I glare at him.

He shuffles, looking shamefaced. 'So you looked it up too?'

'Of course. Why didn't you tell me?'

'I don't know. I thought you might not want to stay there if you knew I owned it.'

I'm perplexed. 'Why ever not?'

'Too familiar perhaps, and the money thing. I couldn't afford to let you stay there rent-free, although I did do a reduced rate for you. But journalists don't earn much, you know, and I have rent to pay on the place I'm living in and . . .'

I hold up my hand. 'I don't give a toss about the money,' I snap. 'I just wish you'd been honest.'

He hangs his head, his dark fringe flopping into his eyes. 'I'm sorry,' he mutters.

I shake my head. Something doesn't make sense. 'Why would you choose to buy a flat overlooking the place where your sister disappeared? Isn't it a bit . . . ghoulish?'

His head shoots up. 'I've never lived there. I bought it a few years ago now. It came up on the market quite cheap as it needed renovating. I wasn't living in Oldcliffe then, but thought it might give me some extra income. So I rent it out during the holiday period.'

Who would have thought it, Soph? Your brother becoming responsible enough to think about a business opportunity.

'Did you know that Leon owned one in the same building?'

His eyes are earnest. 'I honestly had no idea. But it makes sense for similar reasons. To have a foothold here while he lives abroad.'

'Bit of a coincidence,' I can't help but mutter. He shoots me a look I can't read. Why do I get the sense there is something he's not telling me? Your brother was always so honest, so black and white. About his feelings, about everything. 'I think Leon's been writing the notes,' I blurt out. Hatred for Leon weaves its way into my heart, eating up any love that I might have had for him. 'He's obviously out to get me, Daniel. Do you know what I think?'

'Go on.'

'I think he hurt Sophie that night. Maybe it was an accident, maybe he did it on purpose. They finished that night, who knows why. Then I saw her in the toilets, she was crying . . .'

He frowns. 'What time was this?'

'I can't remember exactly. It's all in the original police statement I made. But I don't think I saw her again after midnight.'

'And Leon?'

'I didn't see him again, either.'

Daniel sighs. 'He's always said he left at eleven and Sophie was seen in the club after that . . .'

'But maybe he waited for her? They could have argued, then he pushed her into the sea.'

'He had an alibi.'

'What? His piss-head of a brother?'

'His sister-in-law, Steph. She said he was home by eleven thirty. Remember? He was up talking to her for ages, apparently pouring his heart out –'

I make an unattractive snorting sound, cutting

Daniel off. The silence in the car lasts a fraction too long to be comfortable and I wonder what he's thinking.

Eventually he sighs and runs his hands through his hair. 'Look, I don't like the bloke particularly. But do you think he would really have hurt her? I could see how much he loved her. And I saw how devastated he was when they finished. There was no reason why he would want to hurt her. And no witnesses, nothing. And remember, those kids from the beach said they saw a girl matching Soph's description walking along the promenade *alone*.'

'But you think someone *did* hurt her, otherwise you wouldn't have dragged me back here,' I say hotly.

Daniel is staring at me and the expression on his face isn't love, or even affection. It's disappointment.

'Frankie . . .' he begins, taking my hand. 'Oh, Frankie . . .' He turns my hand over in his as if contemplating saying something.

I frown. 'What's the matter?' I reach up and touch his face and say more softly, 'What is it, Dan?'

'It's been such a long time,' he says, his eyes fixed on mine. 'So many years. So many lies.'

What is he on about?

'What do you mean?'

He stares at me a little longer. The atmosphere in the car is thick. He's beginning to scare me.

'I just want it to be over,' he says, still holding my gaze. 'Don't you?'

And he's right. I do want it to be over, Soph. I want

to leave Oldcliffe. I want to get on with my life. I wish I could make a life with your brother, but somehow I don't think that will happen.

'Dan,' I say softly, my fingers caressing his cheek, 'it can be over. Now that we know it's Leon who owns the apartment it must be him sending the letters, he must know about Jason and –'

He moves away from me and I drop my hand in my lap as though it's been burnt. 'Why do you think it's Leon?' He looks out towards the choppy seas.

'I think Sophie admitted to him what happened with Jason. I think he killed her and now I think he's playing with me, biding his time before killing me too.'

'You think Leon wants to hurt you?'

'Why else is he doing this?' I cry, my voice rising. 'The recording that he set up in his apartment. I had seven miscarriages, Daniel. *Seven.* I can't have children. It's like he knows this . . . it's like he knows and is taunting me.' I can't prevent it. A tear snakes down my cheek.

Daniel shuffles towards me and puts an arm awkwardly around my shoulder. I notice his hip is jammed against the gearstick. 'Oh, Franks, I'm sorry.' We stay like this for a few minutes before he moves away from me, exclaiming that his arm's gone dead. 'And that bloody gearstick is cutting into my thigh.'

I can't help but giggle as he moves back to his seat, and it breaks the tension. Then, more seriously, he says, 'We should go to the police.'

The thought of involving the police frightens me,

Soph. I did love Leon once. And so did you. Could I really shop him to the police?

'We don't have any evidence,' I say.

'What about the computer? The notes?'

I frown. My eyes hurt. 'Well, yes. But . . . but is that enough? He's not threatened to hurt me. Yet. Will the police do anything? Will they believe me?'

'I don't know,' Daniel says, shaking his head. 'If something happened to you, Franks, I wouldn't be able to forgive myself.'

I fidget, worried about how he will react to my next words. 'I'm going home tonight, Dan. Back to London. I can't spend another night in that place. I know you own it and everything and no offence, but it freaks me out. Especially after last night.'

'I could stay with you . . . ?'

I was all set to go home but the thought of leaving Daniel behind, of not seeing him every day, makes me want to cry. I know he has a girlfriend but that doesn't stop me hoping that he might change his mind. That he might realise that I'm the one for him and not this Mia. And if I stayed in Oldcliffe and he spent the night, it might lead to something.

I swallow and try to regulate my breathing. 'What about Mia?'

A shadow passes across his face. 'She'll understand,' he says stiffly. 'To be honest, things with Mia . . .' He shakes his head as if trying to dislodge an unpleasant or disloyal thought. 'It doesn't matter. But I'm not going to leave you on your own tonight. And tomorrow we'll go to the police station and identify Sophie's remains. Just one more night, that's all I'm asking.'

'Thank you,' I say. I reach over and touch his hand, a thrill travelling up my arm.

A blush creeps up his neck, spreading to his face like a rash. 'Right,' he says, clearing his throat and moving his hand away. 'What are we going to do about Leon?'

35
Sophie

Tuesday, 19 August 1997

Alistair is still watching me. I can sense him. Sometimes, at work, I look up and through the throng of tourists on the promenade I'll spot him in the distance. Other times he'll actually be in the queue for cockles or cod and chips, leering at me over the heads of the other customers. The other day, when I was having an ice cream with Helen on the Grand Pier, he was there, sitting on one of the benches, pretending to read a newspaper.

'Oh look, there's Frankie's dad,' Helen said, stopping in her tracks, her hand on my arm to stop me. He'd looked up at us then, as if he knew we were talking about him, and treated us to a beaming smile. 'I have to say,' said Helen in a loud whisper, 'he's a bit of all right, ain't he? For a dad.'

'Come on,' I insisted, refusing to look at him and pulling her towards the exit. How I longed to tell her what a mentalist he is, how he won't take no for an answer, how he tries to kiss me, threaten me, unnerve me, stalk me. She wouldn't believe it. Who would? Appearances can be deceptive.

Alistair is creeping me out. I couldn't stop thinking about him as I walked around River Island with Frankie this afternoon. She insisted we catch the train rather than the bus to Bristol, moaning all the way to Temple Meads about the injustice that she still doesn't have her own car yet. 'My dad promised to buy one for my twenty-first but it still hasn't materialised,' she said, while I glanced out of the window and tried to avoid talking about my imminent move to London.

I hoped she wouldn't ask me anything about it. The less she knows the less chance Alistair has of finding out. But no such luck. In amongst the combat trousers, with 'Don't Look Back in Anger' blaring overhead, she broached the subject.

'So,' she said, while fingering the material on a particularly hideous pair of army-print trousers. 'What's happening about your job then? When do you start?'

I tried to look nonchalant and not as though I was counting down the days. 'September fifteenth.'

'That's less than a month. Surely you'll be making plans? You'll need to spend a day in London and find digs.' She shoved the army trousers back on the rail and moved to a row of corduroy miniskirts. 'We could go on Monday if you like? I've been thinking about it and wouldn't it be great if I moved up with you?' She flicked through the skirts but I could tell she wasn't really interested in them. 'Dad wants me to work for him and Mum, but I think it would be better if I could find a job in one of the big hotels in London . . .'

I needed to stop her before she ran away with herself. 'Frankie . . .'

She ignored me, pulling a maroon skirt off the rack. 'What am I going to learn at a little tin-pot business in the back of beyond?' she said, her nose virtually pressed up against the skirt's fabric. 'I've been thinking of moving away for a while . . . but it's no fun on your own, is it? Much better to do it with a friend. With you.'

'Frankie . . . listen . . .'

She replaced the skirt and spun around to face me, her eyes flashing. 'You're going to say no, aren't you? I can tell by your voice.'

'It's Leon. He wants to move up with me.'

'Leon?' She scowled. 'You're going to live together?'

A fresh wave of nausea engulfed me. It was as though I was weighed down by a heavy suit of armour. The thought of dealing with Leon, trying to appease Frankie, avoiding Alistair, was becoming too much. It made me want to hide away, to never leave the house again. 'I don't know yet, it's early days but we love each other.'

'Love?' The force of the word from her lips made me look up. Her face was unusually pale, her dark brows knitted together. 'I've told you, he's bad news.'

Anger burned in my stomach. 'He's not bad news.'

'He's obsessive and controlling.'

I longed to tell her that she had Leon confused with her own father, but I concentrated on keeping my voice level. 'He isn't, Frankie.'

'What about that night he punched his brother? Just

because he fancied you a bit. Who does that? He's jealous and possessive. Not to mention that he's Jason's cousin. What do you think he'll do if he finds out that you were there when Jason died? That it was your fault?'

'It wasn't my fault,' I cried, startling a woman brandishing a jacket nearby. I flashed her an apologetic smile and grabbed Frankie's arm, steering her towards an emptier part of the shop.

'It was your fault,' she hissed. 'It was both our faults. Your relationship is built on lies, Soph, and you know it.'

'That's why we need to move away,' I said as patiently as I could. I hated confrontation. 'We need to make a fresh start.'

Her eyes widened. 'And what about me? You're happy to leave me behind?'

I reminded her that we had been apart for three years already. That she didn't need me in order to move away from Oldcliffe. She'd had the guts to go to a boarding school on her own, where she knew nobody, and then on to university.

'But it wasn't the same without you,' she mumbled.

Our shopping trip was lacklustre after that as we floated in and out of Kookaï and Oasis empty-handed. In the end we decided to catch the earlier train home, Frankie sulking all the way.

'You know,' she said as we parted ways outside the Grand Pier, 'I was so excited when I bumped into you again, Soph. I thought it would be like old times. But something's changed. You've changed. First you quit the hotel so that we aren't working together any more, and then you get a new job in London and don't even tell me straight away. And now you want to move in with Leon even though you've only known him for two months, ignoring everything I've said about him.' Her voice was melancholy as she added, 'I don't feel like I know who you are any more.'

I wanted to open my mouth to protest. But what could I say when it was all true? I could never tell her the real reason I was pushing her away.

She glanced at me sadly, waiting for me to object. When I remained silent she turned and walked away.

36

Frankie

Daniel's jaw is set in determination as he raps his knuckles on Lorcan's back door. I would rather be anywhere but here at this moment. I press myself as far into the Leylandii hedge as I can, hoping it will swallow me up so that I don't have to face your ex-boyfriend's accusing blue eyes.

When there's no answer he bangs his fist on the glass so that it shakes in its fragile wooden frame.

'Maybe Leon's still in bed – it is only just gone ten,' I whisper hopefully. 'And he's not working at the moment.' The house has an air of emptiness about it; the curtains are all closed but it doesn't feel as though anybody is in. There are no raised voices, no sounds of activity coming from behind those thin walls.

The wind has picked up and the air is chilly, with a weak sun trying to break through the cluster of grey clouds. I wrap my coat further around my body and shiver.

'It doesn't look as though anybody's here,' he says unnecessarily. 'We'll have to come back. Although I'm not relishing the thought of a thump from Lorcan when we do.'

I stare at him in horror. 'You think he'd hit you?'

'Well, he warned us not to come back and yet here we are.' He grins, not looking the least bit concerned. 'People want to punch me all the time, Franks. Occupational hazard.' He laughs and I follow him down the garden path, the back of his coat billowing out in the wind.

He pulls the gate open and I almost bump into him as he stops suddenly in his tracks. Leon is standing on the driveway. He looks windswept and dishevelled in a black polo-neck and leather jacket, the beginnings of stubble on his tanned face. My stomach flips at the sight of him.

'Back again?' he says. 'What do you want now?'

I hide behind Daniel, even though I'm sure Leon can still see me.

The wind is picking up, I feel it pushing into my back like invisible hands trying to move me along the ground. Daniel has to shout to be heard above it as he explains to Leon what we've found. Leon doesn't answer but pushes past Daniel. I step back onto the overgrown grass, the damp seeping into the bottoms of my jeans, my heels sinking into the mud.

Leon stops on the path and assesses us coldly. He has an electric blue plastic bag hanging off his wrist and a newspaper rolled up under his arm. 'It's none of your business what I'm doing with my own apartment,' he says. 'But if you must know, I'm lending it to a friend. He's making a short film.'

'So the recording of the baby –?' Daniel begins.

'I don't know what you're talking about. Like I just said, a mate is using it at the moment.'

I frown. Something doesn't add up. 'But there are no clothes at the apartment, no personal things . . .'

'Had a good nose, did you? You shouldn't be in there anyway. It's trespassing.'

'Then don't leave the front door open.'

He glares at me but I don't look away. I won't let him intimidate me. How I hate him, Soph. And he hates me too, that much is obvious, which makes me think he must know about Jason. Why else would he dislike me so much? We used to get on OK, before he met you. We were friends, sort of. Until he ruined it all. And if he knows about Jason he could be lying about his so-called mate staying at the apartment. He could be using the place himself to write the notes, to unsettle me. What's his next move?

'Why are you staying here?' Daniel inclines his head towards the house. 'With your brother, when you've got your own apartment.'

'I rent it out. And like I just said, my mate's there at the moment.' A look I can't quite decipher passes between them.

Daniel steps back onto the grass and gently takes my arm. 'Come on, Franks. There's no point in this.'

Leon glances from me to Daniel and smirks.

'What?' snaps Daniel.

'Cosy. I remember you always had the hots for her, Danny Boy.'

'Fuck off.'

Leon emits a sharp, cruel laugh. 'I hope it's the last I'm going to see of you, Frankie,' he calls before sauntering off down the path towards the house.

I hope so too.

Daniel's car is all alone in the parking bay opposite the Grand Pier. I pull up next to it. Daniel is silent, brooding. He hasn't spoken a word to me on the short journey from Leon's house to here.

'Are you OK, Dan?' I put my hand out and touch his arm. I find that I keep doing that, Soph. Touching him. His cheek, his hand, his arm. Anywhere that I can get away with.

He shakes his head. 'I feel out of my depth, to be honest. I don't know what I thought I'd achieve by all of this. I'm not an investigative journalist, for crying out loud. I'm an editor on a small weekly newspaper.'

'Dan—'

'I know.' My hand is still on his arm and he covers it with his own. 'You need to leave tomorrow. I just want to know what really happened that night. She didn't just fall. She was killed. I have my suspicions about Leon but he'll never admit it. And there's no evidence.'

'What about the computer?'

He laughs but it sounds hollow. 'At best it proves that Leon's trying to spook you. But it still doesn't prove that he killed her.'

We sit in silence staring out to sea and the dark hump of Flat Holm Island in the distance. The wind is whipping up the sand on the beach and tossing it against the sea wall. A Coke can clatters along the promenade.

Daniel retrieves his hand from mine and turns up the collar of his coat with sudden purpose. 'I need to get back to work. I'm going to get the sack at this rate. I'll come over later.'

A frisson of excitement runs through me at the prospect. He bends towards me, his lips brushing my cheek, and I close my eyes and breathe him in; his musky scent mixed with the cold February air. And I think about how much I want him, like I've never wanted anyone else.

I watch as he rushes around to the driver's side of his Astra, his hair blowing in all directions, and I long to make it all better, Soph. I wish I could help him.

But I know that I can't.

37
Sophie

Tuesday, 26 August 1997

I sometimes wonder what I could have done differently to change the course of events that led to this. For the past two days, since it happened, I've been in my room going over and over it in my mind. Did it start with that kiss? If I'd never kissed him would he have become so obsessed, so weird? Or did it begin before then? Was he biding his time, waiting for me to grow up? Did we set the wheels in motion that night in 1992 when Frankie and I caused Jason to drown?

I can hardly bring myself to write this. I feel so many emotions. I feel broken, like a part of me has died, anger that I allowed this to happen, and shame. I'm so ashamed and I feel such an idiot. I knew it wasn't normal, what he was doing – how he followed me, harassed me – but I was a fool not to realise just what he's capable of.

I don't know what to do.

I've showered until my skin is raw but I still feel unclean, like a part of him is still inside me, even though I've doused myself. Every time I close my eyes I see his face leering above mine, his wet disgusting lips on my face, the feel of his rough hands on my body, and it's as though I'm on a boat and everything sways and I have to rush to the bathroom and puke until my stomach is empty.

On Sunday night Leon and I went to the pub. It wasn't late when he walked me home – just gone eleven. It was the type of summer evening I've always loved, the sky indigo blue, the smell of cut grass and pollen lingering on the pavements and in the warm air. We held hands and chatted, and in that moment I could believe that everything would be OK. That we could make it work in London, away from this place. We kissed goodbye outside my garage. I didn't want to hang about, just in case Alistair was watching us, so with the promise of calling him tomorrow I walked through the gate to my back garden. I remember the light was on in the upstairs window, my mum's bedroom, although the curtains were closed – she had the night off. Daniel was probably still out with his mates. I was deep in thought, my mind full of London, of Leon, of our new start, when I saw a figure hunched over the step outside the back door. I narrowed my eyes, trying to make out who it was, then he lifted his head and I froze. It was Alistair. He stood up when he saw me approaching. I couldn't believe his audacity.

'What the hell are you doing here?' I hissed. He stood there, his shoulders stooped, and even in the half-light I could detect the anguish in his eyes. I felt a flash of panic. 'What's going on?'

He ran his hand through his fair hair. 'I'm sorry to turn up here,' he said, his voice thick, and for a moment I wondered if he'd been crying.

'What's happened?' Was it Maria or Frankie? Were they hurt? Did they know?

He shook his head. 'I've been such a pillock, Sophie. The way I've been acting. Over you. I . . .' He gulped. 'I just wanted to say I'm sorry. I'm a pathetic middle-aged man having a mid-life crisis. That kiss . . . I allowed myself to think it was more.'

I glanced up at my mum's bedroom window. It was open. Could she hear us?

I lowered my voice. 'Alistair, let's just forget about it.' I went to walk past him when he grabbed my arm.

'Can we talk? Please, Soph.'

I brushed him off. 'Alistair, I'm tired. I need to get inside.'

He sighed and despite everything I felt a pang of sympathy for him in that moment. I so wanted to believe in him. I wanted to believe that things could return to normal, that he could go back to being my substitute dad, the man I'd looked up to, instead of the man he'd become: weak, pathetic, sad. So I allowed him to persuade me.

'Come and sit in my car,' he whispered. 'We can talk privately in there.' He pointed to my mum's window. 'We can't risk anyone hearing.'

I shrugged and followed him. What a naive idiot I am.

His car was parked down the street. I slid into the

passenger seat, the leather cold against my bare legs. He sat behind the wheel and rested his head against it. 'Alistair,' I began. 'Can't we put this behind us and move on?'

'Move on?' he muttered, his forehead still on the steering wheel. 'Do you mean with Leon?'

'I don't mean Leon. I just mean, can't we get on with our lives?'

He lifted his head and regarded me with red-rimmed eyes and for the first time I noticed the smell of alcohol on his breath.

'Have you been drinking?'

'A little. But I'm not drunk, Soph. I'm just upset. I know you don't want me but I think about you all the time. And I know it's wrong. You're my daughter's friend. I'm married but –'

'I'm sorry, Alistair. I'm sorry for kissing you, for allowing you to think there could be anything between us. But please . . . you have to let me go.'

He stared at me and for a terrible moment I thought he was going to burst into tears. Instead he turned the key in the ignition and, before I even had time to react, he'd put his foot down and sped out of the road. I fell back against the seat and quickly pulled the seatbelt around me. 'Alistair, don't be stupid! What are you doing?'

His jaw was set. I felt a stab of fear. He was probably over the limit – what was he planning to do? Drive into a brick wall and kill us both?

He headed through town, his foot pressed on the accelerator. My heart was in my mouth, my nose pressed to the glass, hoping to spot someone I knew, hoping to attract attention. But even if I did recognise anyone the car was going too fast for me to do anything. The town was deserted anyway, just a cluster of people clutching pint glasses hanging around outside the Seagull and a queue gathering by the chippy.

I tried to reason with him, tried to convince him to pull over, but it was as though he was in a trance. He continued out of town, along the coastal road then into woodland, the trees black and sinister in the darkness, their branches dense and overhanging so that they formed a tunnel. There were no lampposts, just a strip of cat's eyes winking in the distance. I felt sick.

'Alistair.' I tried to keep the fear out of my voice. 'Where are we going?'

He didn't answer, his jaw clenched, his eyes on the road. And then, without warning, he swerved the car off the road and into a car park, his BMW bouncing over the potholes. We were on the rough ground outside the abattoir, the place couples go to get off together in their cars. There was only one other vehicle: a white van burrowed in the corner, partly hidden by branches, the windows steamed up. Alistair parked as far away from it as possible, backing into a bush. Then he switched off the engine, the lights dying so that everything was black.

The only sound to be heard was Alistair's breathing. Excited. Quick.

'Alistair.' My voice sounded small in the darkness. 'We need to go home.'

He turned to me. 'I want you so badly I can't think straight,' he said. 'Please, Soph. If you just sleep with me once I promise to go away. I'll leave you alone. You can get on with your life, with Leon. Once I've had sex with you you'll be out of my system and we can both move on.'

I stared at him in shock. 'I can't sleep with you. What do you take me for, some kind of prostitute?'

He reached out and touched my hair. I backed away from his hand. 'Oh Soph, of course not. That's not what I'm saying. I know you fancy me but you're a nice girl. You don't want to be unfaithful to Leon. But I'll never tell anyone. I've got too much to lose.' He gave a sharp laugh. 'I'm married, for fuck's sake. Just one night. That's all I'm asking.' His voice was pleading, husky. 'Oh Soph,' he said again, and before I had a chance to react he was on top of me, pressing me back against the seat, his body pushing the air out of my lungs so that I could hardly breathe. I heard the sound of his zip being undone, his hand lifting up my skirt.

'Alistair, no!' I cried, but he pushed the seat back with his other hand so that I was lying flat and he was pressed against me.

'Sophie!' he said, his hand in my knickers, fingers probing me. I tried to scream but he clamped his other hand to my mouth. I couldn't move. His body was heavy on mine, I could hear the tear of fabric as he ripped my knickers off and then pulled his trousers down. He pushed himself into me with a grunt. Pain seared through me, splitting me in two. A tear rolled down the side of my face and into my ear. I closed my eyes so I didn't have to look at him and told myself it would be over soon. He thrust into me a few more times, his hand squeezing my mouth and jaw as he came with a groan, then he sagged against me. When I opened my eyes he was staring at me.

'Soph . . .' he began. The hand that had gripped my face now smoothed down my hair. 'Oh, Soph.'

'Get. Off. Me,' I hissed.

I pulled my dress down and turned my head away while he fumbled with his trousers. When he was safely back behind the wheel I pulled the lever on my seat so that it was upright again.

The windows were steamed up; to an outsider it would look as though we were an ordinary couple getting it on.

'I'm sorry,' he said, although he didn't sound it. He started the engine.

'I want to go home.' I refused to cry in front of him.

He was silent on the way back and didn't drive as erratically. Was it worth it? I wanted to ask him. Was I worth becoming a rapist for? But I didn't. I couldn't trust myself to speak, knowing I would cry. Out of the corner of my eye I saw my knickers, torn in two, at my feet. I bent over and picked them up, crumpling them into my hand. I placed my hands on my knees to stop them jiggling about.

'You know,' he said as he turned into my street. 'If you ever tell anyone I'll say it was consensual. You know that, right? It's my word against yours.'

'Don't you even feel a bit guilty?' I said as he pulled up outside my house, the engine still purring.

He stared at me, his eyes intense. 'I don't think you understand, do you? I always get what I want. And you won't admit it, because you like to believe that you're a nice girl, that you wouldn't cheat on that runt of a boyfriend. But you wanted it just as much as I did. And you'll be back. For more.'

'You make me sick,' I hissed, grabbing the door handle and almost falling onto the pavement.

But he just grinned, his face menacing in the interior light of the car. 'You tell yourself that, Soph, if it makes you feel better.'

I slammed the door and had barely stepped away from the car when he sped off, his wheels spinning against the warm tarmac.

I made it as far as the garden before I threw up in the dustbin.

38

Frankie

I can't face going back to the apartment yet, so I get out of the car and walk along the promenade. The wind tugs at my hair and gathers under the hem of my coat, trying to lift its edges. There is hardly anyone else about, which isn't surprising on a cold Tuesday afternoon in February. I sit on the sea wall, watching as the waves crash against the metal legs of the Grand Pier. Do you remember how we used to sit on this wall in the summer, Soph? We would sit for hours as teenagers eating pasties and chatting about boys. Things were never the same once you'd met Leon. If I'm honest, things were never the same after I left to go to that horrible boarding school.

I sit for a few minutes longer but the wind is so strong it's as though I've been slapped in the face, and my fingers and toes feel numb with the cold. I get up and head back to the car. When I'm safely ensconced in the driver's seat I ring Stuart and ask how things are ticking over in my absence. He tells me that one of the staff, Paul, has messed up another order.

'It was him last time,' he says, sounding frustrated. 'The mistakes are costing us time and money.'

I sigh. 'You have my permission to let him go,' I say. 'We can't afford any more of his mistakes.'

Stuart sounds pleased. 'Great. I'll have it sorted before you get back.'

'I'll be back tomorrow,' I say, pushing aside my feelings about leaving Daniel. I need to get out of this place. This town is my undoing. Then I call my mum to find out how Dad is, but there is no change from the slight improvement she told me about yesterday. I imagine Mum sitting by his bedside, clutching his hand and massaging his legs, the picture of the perfect, loving wife. Sometimes I wonder if she prefers him this way: vulnerable, malleable, unable to answer back. Unable to cheat on her or hurt her. I tell her what I told Stuart, that I'll be back tomorrow, but I can tell by her vagueness that I've already lost her. That her mind has returned to her wifely duties.

You could never understand my relationship with my mother, could you? You were always so close to yours. I admitted to you once on a sleepover how I felt about her. We were sharing a bed in your room; I preferred your house to mine. It was always so much cosier and not filled with strangers and their things. The hotel never felt like home and I was quite lonely, if I'm honest, stuck up in that attic bedroom while my parents' time was consumed by ensuring their guests were comfortable, that they had clean bedding, tidy rooms and a cooked breakfast and dinner. I would lie in bed at night listening to the faint chattering of my parents entertaining the guests, the shrill sound of laughter and the chink of wine glasses. Hotels, to me, have always been businesses, not homes, which is why I never stay in them now. It doesn't feel relaxing to me. It either feels like work or reminds me of walking on eggshells around other guests when I was a kid.

Your house had a mother's loving touch. My mum was perfunctory in the way she dealt with me. She cared about my welfare, she made sure I had clean clothes and food on the table. But she wasn't loving towards me. She didn't care about me, she never took time to get to know me. I now understand that she suffered post-natal depression, that she found it hard to bond with me. And it never mattered because I had Dad. He made up for my mum's coldness. But that night, as we snuggled under your duvet cover, I admitted that I felt Mum loved Dad much more than she loved me and that she was jealous of the attention he paid me.

You had sounded shocked as you'd whispered into the darkness, 'How can your mum be jealous that your dad loves you?'

'I don't know,' I'd mumbled, embarrassed. How could you understand when you had a mother whose love for her children was written all over her face every time she looked at you both? Then you told me about your dad, how you could barely remember him apart from the night when he had given your lovely mum a broken nose and the three of you had fled 'down South'. That was the only time we admitted this to each other. We never spoke of it again, but I've never forgotten it.

*

By the time I get back to the apartment it's nearly 3.30 p.m. Not long before Daniel comes over. I take a shower and change into my last clean pair of jeans and a figure-hugging jumper. I don't want to look like I've tried too hard.

I pour myself a glass of wine. I feel tense and on edge. Something is niggling away at my subconscious, something about Daniel and Leon. I perch on the old-fashioned school radiator, relishing the warmth that seeps through my jeans, and watch a white van trundle past as I try and organise my thoughts.

Daniel lied to me when he said this apartment was owned by his friend. Why didn't he tell me this place was his? I understand he might have felt a little embarrassed at having to ask me for money, but I would rather have given it to him than some faceless mate of his. I can't help but think it's an excuse, that he deliberately wanted to mislead me. But why? And the way he acted with Leon this afternoon – I can't put my finger on it, but it was odd.

I think back to the other day when we first went to see Leon. The way they had squared up to each other, how Leon had called Daniel 'Danny Boy'. He'd never called Daniel that back in 1997. It all seemed rather forced, as though they were actors in a play. And why has Daniel bought a place across the hall from his enemy, his nemesis?

I have a pain behind my eyes. The wine has already gone to my head. I've never been very good at holding my drink. A lightweight, you always called me. A cheap date.

I massage the space between my eyes, trying to knead the headache away. None of this adds up. The child crying, the letters. What does it all mean, Soph?

The letter box rattles, startling me. I put the glass down and hurry along the hallway, stooping to pick up a newspaper and then throwing open the door just in time to catch Jean on the stairs.

'Jean?'

She hesitates, her hand still on the banister, her eyes startled. 'Hi, Francesca, love.'

'Did you post this through my door?' I say, waving the newspaper unnecessarily high. I hurriedly glance at the door of the apartment opposite but it's firmly closed.

She nods. 'There were two in the hallway and I just assumed they were for us. It's only the local freebie but it might be worth a read.'

I frown at her. Why would she bother? She flashes me a maternal smile and then continues down the stairs, leaving me staring after her. Clutching the newspaper I return to my flat, puzzled. I throw it onto the coffee table where it unfurls and I gasp.

On the page staring up at me is a news story about my dad.

I grab the paper, noticing that the other pages have been folded back so that this is the first thing I'll see. I quickly turn to the front page. It is indeed a free paper but it's not from this town but somewhere near Bristol, and it's dated three weeks ago.

I run out of the apartment and go charging down the stairs in my bare feet. 'Jean!' I call, banging on her door.

She opens it up, her face set as if ready for a fight. 'Where did you get this from?'

She pulls her cardigan around her body. 'I told you. It came through the front door.'

'Why would a free Bristol newspaper come through the door? It's not even a recent copy.'

She shrugs, her eyes cold. 'How should I know?'

Is it her? Is she the one responsible for all the strange things that have happened since I arrived? 'Who are you?'

Her usually pleasant face contorts so that it looks as though a completely different person is standing before me. 'It doesn't matter who I am. But I know who you are. You're the daughter of a rapist.'

'How . . . how do you know?'

'Everybody knows.'

'He's innocent.'

'That's what they all say,' she spits. 'But I've known men like your father. They think they can get away with it. And now he's faking a stroke to try and get out of the trial. He's scum.'

It's as though she's hit me. 'You don't know anything about it.'

'Oh yes, I do. I knew there was something strange about you, all this looking over your shoulder, saying you were being followed. You looked like you were involved in something dodgy. Drugs, probably.' Her lips turn up into a sneer. 'Men turning up day and night. That girl on the stairs, creeping about. Lurking. It's not right.'

What is she talking about? What girl? Is she talking about you? 'Is that why you've been looking through my bin? Trying to find some dirt? Or a stash of drugs?'

'I didn't need to find any dirt. I heard all about it yesterday in the newsagent's. A lovely man couldn't wait to tell me that I had the daughter of a rapist sharing a building with me. He was the one who gave me the newspaper, if you must know. He could see how disgusted I was by it all.'

My blood runs cold. 'Who?'

'He didn't tell me his name. Tall, dark hair. About your age. Now leave me alone.' She glares at me and then slams the door in my face.

She could be describing Leon.

Or Daniel.

I climb the stairs to my flat, dejected, the newspaper still in my hand. I pour myself another glass of wine and slump onto the sofa.

Who would be malicious enough to give this to Jean to pass on to me?

The piece is short, not even five hundred words, yet it spills everything: my father, 'the one-time West Country hotel owner', charged with historic rape crimes and his severe stroke before the trial even began. All this time Daniel must have known. When he said he was sorry to hear about my dad I thought he meant his stroke. How naive of me. He's a journalist, for crying out loud, of course he was going to know about the charges hanging over my dad.

A young woman contacted police last year. She

remained anonymous. She made a statement saying my dad became obsessed with her, stalking her and raping her when she was twenty. It was less than a year after you went missing. Her testimony meant that others came forward of course. He admitted to having sex with these women but said it was consensual and my mum believed him. And I so want to believe him, Soph. But it's becoming harder to. Why would these women lie?

It's starting to get dark. The living room is freezing. The tip of my nose feels cold. I throw more logs on the fire, their crackling the only sound in the room. It's eerily quiet. No traffic noise, no roar of aeroplanes. I switch on a lamp and then go and stand by the bay window. Daniel said he would try and get away by three but there is no sign of him. The roads are empty, the clouds grey, bunched together as if in a frown.

The thought has been unfurling all day in my mind, ever since Daniel told me he owns this apartment – maybe even before then, when I saw the article he was reading on the Internet.

I no longer trust your brother.

A flicker of movement on the driveway outside catches my eye. I stand up and press my nose to the glass, expecting it to be Daniel. But it's not Daniel. It's you. You're standing by the wall, looking up at me. I know that it's you. I can tell by the point of your chin, by the inclination of your head, by the widow's peak in your fair hair. You're wearing an anorak with the hood pulled back and you're young, with smooth skin and clear eyes. My first thought is that you're not dead, that those remains found at Brean Sands aren't yours – except that can't be right because you don't look nearly forty. You look younger even than the day you went missing.

Ever since I've come back here I've felt your presence, Soph. I've felt you in the flat, on my walks, following me, beckoning me, and now I know why.

'Wait there!' I call, even though I'm sure you can't hear me. I grab my coat, pull on my boots and run as fast as I can, almost tripping down the stairs in my haste. I need to see you before you disappear again.

Because I finally understand why you're here. You're not going to leave me alone, are you? Until I've told the truth about that night.

39
Frankie

I can see you in the distance, the flash of your olive parka with the orange hood, like the one you had at school. You're just out of reach. Why aren't you waiting for me? I'm calling you but you're ignoring me. Sophie! I stumble as my ankle bends beneath me. Damn it, my heel has snapped. I lean over to pick up the sharp stiletto and shove it in the pocket of my coat. Then I run onwards, limping slightly now that my boots are uneven.

The wind has picked up and I'm sure I can hear Daniel calling me but I keep running after you. I can't let you go again.

I'm out of breath as I reach the lampposts at the entrance to the pier. Where are you? I look around me in bewilderment. You've vanished.

And then I see you. You've managed to get on the other side of the DO NOT ENTER sign so that you are standing on the pier. Part of me wants to tell you to be careful, that the boards are rotten and dangerous, until I remember that you are already dead. You're waiting for me and I know that you want me to follow. So I climb through the barriers, snagging my coat on the metal posts and scraping my arm but I don't care. I need to talk to you. I'm not scared any more. And then I'm standing facing you, the pier stretching out behind you, the pavilion a dark shape in the distance.

'Sophie . . . ?'

'Hello, Frankie,' you say softly, your words snatched by the wind. I feel like I'm in a dream, that this isn't really happening. Am I more drunk than I thought? Because I know that logically I can't be talking to a ghost.

'What do you want from me?'

'I think you know.' You don't sound like I remember you. For a minute this confuses me, throws me off track, and I have to reorganise my thoughts. I blink a few times but you're still standing there. Solid. Real.

'Frankie?' A voice startles me and I whip around to see Daniel standing behind me. He's also managed to get inside the barrier. 'You shouldn't be out here. It's dangerous.'

'You!' I cry, brushing the hair out of my eyes. 'You've been lying to me. About everything. Have you been sending the letters? What's going on, Daniel?'

He creeps towards me, his hand outstretched as though he's approaching a skittish horse. 'I can explain everything. Please, just come with me, it's dangerous . . .'

'I'm not going anywhere with you. I don't trust you any more. Something's going on. Did you give Jean that paper in the newsagent's . . . ?'

Then you step forward and for the first time I see that you're holding something in your hand. A pink striped notebook that's tatty with age. Your diary. I remember that diary, you took it everywhere, even when you had sleepovers at my house. You slept with it under your pillow.

Daniel turns to look at you and it hits me. He can see you too. I'm not imagining you.

'We know what you did,' you say. 'We have evidence, including this diary.' Your voice is different. And as you get closer I notice that your eyes aren't grey but blue. A vivid, piercing, navy blue. I know those eyes.

'Can you see her?' I shout to Daniel. 'Can you see Sophie?'

Daniel ignores me. 'Frankie . . . you have to listen to me. You don't have to pretend any more.'

'What do you mean?' I feel like I'm in a surreal dream.

'I know you killed Sophie. You killed my sister.'

'Don't be ridiculous!' I shout. 'How can it be me? What about the letters? They're from Leon. And the dog tags? He knew about Jason! He wanted to hurt me, he probably hurt Sophie. I've been trying to tell you since I got here . . . I've been trying to tell you . . .'

Daniel stares at me in disbelief and I run out of steam.

He's right, I don't have to pretend any more.

There are good and bad people in this world, Soph, and sometimes there are people like me. I don't think I'm bad. I've just done some bad things. You don't know how hard it's been, carrying your death on my shoulders for eighteen years. You don't know how much I wished I could take it back. It got easier to live with as time went by but I never stopped feeling guilty for what happened that night, Soph. I've always been good at compartmentalising. So I put what I did to you in a box and filed it in the back of my mind until that phone call unearthed it all.

That was why I was so reticent about coming back to Oldcliffe. Everyone knows you should never return to the scene of the crime. Yet how could I have let Daniel snoop around without me? I needed to stop him from finding out the truth by throwing him off the scent. Not that there ever really was much of a scent. Without a body there was no evidence. And I didn't think they would find much from a foot. I thought that when Daniel had seen your remains he would let you go. Of course, I hoped he'd suspect Leon but without any proof he'd never be able to do anything about it. Receiving those letters was a godsend because it gave me the opportunity to point the finger at Leon. All I needed to do was tell your brother what happened with Jason and bang: a motive. I cemented this further by posting myself the dog tags just in case there was any doubt in Daniel's mind that the letters weren't about Jason.

I'd wondered if the letters were really about you but I told myself nobody could possibly know what I'd done.

Except for Daniel.

'Have you known all along?' I ask him, unable to keep the surprise out of my voice.

He nods slowly.

'Why did you send the letters?'

'I didn't send them . . .'

'But then, who?' My head is pounding and I close my eyes, feeling disorientated. Can this all really be happening? I grab at my hair, pulling it hard from the roots.

I'm backed into a corner. There is nothing I can do. When I open my eyes Daniel is by my side, guiding my hand from my hair. 'Sophie came to you, didn't she, Frankie?' he asks gently. 'On that last night. She was upset so she left the club but you followed her, didn't you? And she told you what your father did to her, that she was pregnant. You accused her of lying, of having an affair with your dad. Why did you kill her, Frankie? To stop her from telling anyone?'

How can he know this, Soph?

The wind whistles around us. You're standing in front of me but you're not speaking, you're just staring at me with disgust. With hatred.

'Frankie!' Daniel's voice is insistent, urgent. He grabs hold of my upper arms and spins me around so that I'm facing him. There is desperation in his eyes. 'Please. If you feel anything for me at all put me out of my misery. We have evidence, we know it was you. But I want to hear it from your lips, Franks. I want to hear why you did it. Why you wanted to kill your best friend.'

I sob and sag against him. It's almost a relief to be able to tell someone. 'I'm sorry, Daniel. I never wanted to hurt you, but she took everything from me. She took Leon and then she took my dad. *My dad.* He loved me the best. My mum never gave a shit, I only ever had him. But even he preferred her to me in the end. Why did she have to take him, Dan?'

I feel him stiffen against me. 'Frankie. She didn't take him. He raped her.'

'She told me everything,' I cry. 'About the kiss in the bedroom, about how she'd led him on. She fancied him and she wanted him.'

'He raped her,' Daniel says again through gritted teeth. 'He terrorised her and stalked her and raped her. And he would have carried on doing it. When she was gone he did it to those other girls instead. He's a monster.'

'But he's my dad,' I wail. I didn't want to believe you at the time, Soph. You told me everything and I couldn't face the truth. When my dad was arrested six months ago it made me realise that you hadn't been lying, had you? My dad raped you. I'm so sorry for not believing you . . .

'And what about me,' says Daniel, his voice sad. 'I loved you. Wasn't I enough?'

'You didn't love me. You just fancied me . . .'

'No!' he shouts over the wind. 'I loved you. I loved the fact that you were funny, bright, independent, always up for a laugh. I loved that you had a vulnerable side to you too. I just didn't realise how insecure you really were.'

What a fool I've been.

You come towards me, your face pinched with anger. 'That's not all, is it? What about Jason?'

'Jason?'

'You wanted him too, didn't you? But you couldn't have him. So you pushed him into the sea.'

I forgot I'd told you all about that on the night you died.

'You said Jason was an accident, Franks,' Daniel urges. 'You said Sophie pushed him by mistake. During an argument. But that's not true, is it?'

'How do you know all this?' I cry.

'I want to hear you say it, Frankie. The police are on their way. They know everything – but I want to hear it from you.' His eyes are pleading.

'It was an accident,' I shout over the wind. 'Sophie had passed out. I tried it on with him, he turned me down. We argued. I didn't mean to push him. We were drunk. He lost his balance and fell . . .'

'Just like with Sophie?'

'It was an accident,' I repeat, breaking down. 'I was just a kid, Daniel . . . I didn't mean to hurt him.' It's true, Soph. I know you always wondered what really took place that night. You were so wasted you didn't really know what had happened. I was angry he had turned me down, I didn't know he was gay. But I didn't mean to kill him. I watched him splash about in the water. I could have saved him but I chose not to. Then I shook you awake and told you he'd fallen in.

I turn to Daniel. 'Were you just pretending, this whole time? To get me to confess? I thought you had feelings for me.'

He looks shamefaced. 'Because of our history I was willing to give you the benefit of the doubt. I know that accidents can happen. I hoped you'd explain yourself. Show remorse. I wanted you to confess.'

'Why?' I laugh bitterly. 'When you already know so much.'

His voice catches. 'Because I wanted to understand why you would do such a thing. Or are you just like your father?'

I stare at him in shock. Is that what he thinks? That I'm just like my dad? That night in The Basement, when I heard you being sick in the toilets, I knew you weren't drunk. Your pallor, your nausea. It didn't take a genius to work it out. You were pregnant. But before I could confront you about it you'd run off, out of the club. On the pier you broke down and told me everything, about the kiss, the stalking, the rape. Of course I didn't want to believe you, this was my father, the man I idolised, loved more than anyone in the world.

In the distance I think I hear the faint sound of a police siren.

Evidence. They have evidence of your death. I think of your Gazelle Adidas trainer that was left behind on the pier. I knew I should have chucked that in the sea after you, but I'd left it there. I never touched it though. I was careful about that. I knew about DNA, you see, even then.

'If you have evidence,' I say to Daniel, 'why would you want me to confess? Because I never will. Not to the authorities. I can't go to prison. I just can't . . .'

You step forward, looking smug. You flash your teeth at me. They are small and pointed. Not like yours at all. 'You already have,' you say and you reach into the deep pocket of your coat and retrieve a tape recorder. 'It's a Dictaphone. Everything you said is on this tape.'

'Mia . . .' Daniel's tone is a warning.

Mia? I stare at you. But it's not you, is it? Of course it's not. How could it ever have been? What was I thinking?

Those eyes, those teeth. That voice. It's not *you*.

'Who are you?' I snarl.

'My name's Mia,' she says. She has an Irish accent.

'Daniel's girlfriend?' I frown. But she's so young. Too young.

She shakes her head and laughs, her next words lost in the wind. The sky rumbles. Hard, angry rain bursts from the clouds. How dare she laugh at me, this young woman. How dare she stand here and throw accusations at me, turn Daniel against me. We could have been happy together but she's come along and fucked it all up.

Fury swells and builds, threatening to push itself out of my chest. I want to hurt her. I want to wipe that smug smile off her face. It's my turn to reach into my pocket. I pull out the broken piece of stiletto, faintly aware of Daniel's cries of horror, as though he's worked out what I'm about to do before it even crossed my mind.

'Mia, watch out!' There is fear in his voice. And love. Jealousy spurs me on and I charge towards her, sensing Daniel's presence behind me. I want her to cease to exist. The feeling is all-consuming, powerful. I want to wipe her out.

She darts past me, into Daniel's arms, and because of my uneven heels I stumble, falling to my knees with a thud. What was I thinking? I don't want to hurt her and I didn't mean to kill you. You have to believe me, Soph. I loved you. I'm sorry . . .

The creak of wood is barely discernible over the wind and rain. It takes a couple of seconds for the rotten planks to give way beneath me. I hear the wail of police sirens getting nearer. I don't try and save myself.

The last thing I see is their shocked, pale faces before I crash through the floor and into the angry, grey sea below.

40
Sophie

Tuesday, 9 September 1997

I 'died' on Saturday night.

It all began with a huge bust-up with Leon. I couldn't take lying to him any longer so I finished it. I'll always be haunted by his face, the crumple of his chin as he tried not to cry.

Frankie raced into the toilets after me and demanded to know what was going on. I locked myself in the cubicle and threw up. I couldn't face her or Leon, so when she went to get me some water I fled from The Basement as fast as I could, not stopping until I reached the entrance to the old pier, and then only because my side hurt with a stitch.

I leaned against the lamppost trying to catch my breath. I was trembling all over. A blister on my heel throbbed so much that I had to remove my trainer. I shoved it in the pocket of my tracksuit top and hobbled onto the pier.

'Sophie?'

Relief flooded through me when I saw Frankie standing behind me and not Alistair. It could so easily have been him. It made me realise how stupid I'd been to leave the club, how I'd put myself in danger.

'What are you doing here?'

I didn't want to talk to her. How could I even begin to find the words to explain all that's happened?

'Why are you going home? It's only eleven thirty. It's a Saturday night, for goodness' sake! We never leave the club this early.' She sounded out of breath. She must have had to sprint to catch up with me. I noticed she was wearing her long black platform boots, not easy to run in. They were the same boots she was wearing the night we met up again, when the summer had stretched out in front of us full of possibility. How had it all gone so horribly wrong?

My face was wet with tears. 'It's a long story.'

'You're pregnant, aren't you? I heard you throwing up in the ladies' loos. Something's going on, Soph, and I'm not leaving until you tell me what's wrong. I saw you having a huge bust-up with Leon. What happened? Did you tell him about the baby?' She walked towards me. 'Sophie!' She pulled my arm so that I was facing her. 'Are you listening to me?'

'Of course I didn't tell him about the baby!' I cried. 'What's one more lie? Anyway, why do you care?'

She frowned, hurt flashing in her eyes. 'Because I'm your best friend. We tell each other everything. But you never told me this. Why couldn't you tell me you were pregnant?'

'Because . . .' Tears were coming thick and fast now. I could hardly breathe, they were threatening to choke me. I took a deep breath. I had to tell her the truth. 'Because I thought it might be Alistair's. But it can't be. I know that now.'

Her expression darkened. 'Alistair's? What are you talking about?'

'Your dad!' I cried. 'Who do you think I'm talking about?'

Her voice was low, dangerous, as she said, 'You were fucking my dad?'

I stared at her, shock drying my tears. 'I wasn't "fucking" your dad. He *raped* me!'

All the colour drained from her face and I felt terrible. She staggered backwards as though I'd hit her. 'How could you? How could you lie like that? You're having an affair with my dad and now you're lying about it. You're such a little slut, Sophie Collier. You've taken Leon and now you've taken him.'

'Alistair raped me, Frankie. We didn't have sex. He forced himself on me, he –'

'Shut up!' She didn't shout but her voice was cold and there was a hardness to her that I'd never seen before. 'I don't want to hear your lies.' She stared at me, her eyes wild, just like her father's, her mouth downturned and trembling.

'Frankie . . . please.' A sob escaped my lips. I hated doing this to her. 'I wouldn't lie about something like this . . .'

She closed her eyes as though inwardly meditating, and started pulling at her hair. I watched her in alarm, wondering what she was going to do next, how she was going to react. Then she opened her eyes and walked towards me. 'This pier,' she said, coming closer to me, 'it's surely cursed, don't you think? Jason died here . . .'

I frowned. 'What's Jason got to do with this?'

'Oh, Sophie. You really are rather stupid, aren't you? And you like to think you're so intelligent. While you were passed out I shoved him into the sea. He was so off his face he didn't stand a chance. We'd had an argument, he turned me down. Nobody turns me down.'

'You killed Jason?' It was as though the breath had been knocked out of me. I remember passing out and Frankie shaking me awake, tears running down her face, telling me there had been an accident and Jason had fallen in. Never did I once suspect that she'd pushed him.

She started pacing, clearly agitated, as though trying to work out what to do. She was shaking her head, still pulling at her hair and talking quickly. 'I shouldn't have told you that . . . I shouldn't have said that. I'm just angry, what you said about my dad . . . and I didn't mean to kill Jason. It was a knee-jerk reaction. He turned me down, I was angry. We rowed and I pushed him. It was an accident . . .'

'Oh, Frankie!' I cried.

She wiped her tears with her sleeve. 'Why do you have to ruin everything?' she wailed. 'I loved Jason. I loved Leon. I loved my dad and you've taken them all!'

I stared at her, stunned. 'Is that really what you think?'

'Why you?' she sobbed. 'What's so special about you? What about me? Why does nobody love me?'

It made me realise, for all her beauty and show of confidence, how insecure she was. She looked so vulnerable, so lost. Part of me wanted to tell her to stop being so immature, but the other part of me wanted to hug her. I rushed towards her and she stopped pacing.

'Jason didn't love me. Not in that way. He was gay. And Leon . . . I never knew how you felt about Leon.'

Her face was pinched, mascara smudged around her eyes. We'd had fights but nothing quite like this. 'I didn't want to tell you,' she said. 'I do have some pride.'

'And Alistair . . . Frankie, you have to understand, he's become a stalker. He won't leave me alone . . .' And then I told her everything: the kiss in the bedroom, how he followed me, harassed me and then raped me in his car. I was so relieved that I was finally getting it off my chest that I didn't stop to think how I was affecting her. After I finished she looked like I'd physically punched her.

'My dad would never do those things,' she cried. 'Why are you lying?'

'I'm not lying. I'd never lie about something like this. You know I wouldn't. I'm sorry, Frankie.' I went towards her but she pushed me away so that I stumbled backwards.

'You're a filthy liar,' she yelled. 'Get away from me, Sophie. I hate you! I hate you!'

'Frankie, please listen . . .'

But she was in a state, rage on her face, tears spilling down her cheeks, refusing to listen. She shoved me again, harder this time, and then I noticed that she had her fingers closed around something; it could have been a rock, a stone, a piece of wood, I couldn't tell because, before I knew what was happening, she'd brought it down on my head, throwing me off balance so that I went toppling backwards, crashing through the barrier and into the sea.

As I fell I felt my trainer slip from the pocket of my top and fall with a thud onto the wooden planks of the pier.

I don't know what saved me. It could have been pure luck that when Frankie hit me it didn't knock me out, that the current that night wasn't too strong, that I managed to cling onto one of the metal legs of the pier. Or maybe it was Frankie's arrogance. She'd done it once, with Jason, so she thought it would be just as easy to dispose of me. But I wasn't drunk like Jason had been and I was a strong swimmer, so I hid silently behind one of the metal legs and watched as Frankie first checked the sea below, then paced up and down as if unsure what to do next. I was tempted to swim towards her, to tell her I was OK, but then she turned and ran. And suddenly I knew. She wasn't running for help. She was going to leave me here to drown, just like she did with Jason. How could I have got someone so wrong? I thought we were best friends, she had been like a sister to me.

From my position behind the leg of the pier I watched her rush back along the promenade towards The Basement as though nothing had happened, metaphorically wiping her hands. A job well done. I knew she'd slip back into the club and pretend she'd been there all along. What a good little actress she turned out to be.

Had the plan already begun to form in my mind? I'm not sure. But what cemented it for me was Daniel. As I swam back to the shore and clambered over the rocks, the water weighing my clothes down and making every step difficult, I saw Daniel walking home, a lone figure in black. He just happened, thank goodness, to look to his left and notice me, wet and bedraggled, picking my way over the rocks, the sharp edges cutting into my shoeless foot. He thought I'd fallen in and came rushing over, and I remember thinking, I wish I had drowned, then Alistair wouldn't be able to bother me any more.

I was shivering and crying, the sorry story spilling out of me as Daniel led me to the cove so that we were out of sight. He wanted to kill Alistair when I told him what he'd done. He stared at me open-mouthed when he learned that Frankie had pushed me, and that she'd done it before with Jason. He kept repeating over and over again how shocked he was that Frankie would do such a thing. He tried to persuade me to go to the police right there and then, but I was scared. It would only ever be her word against mine.

'You have to report Alistair. He raped you, for fuck's

sake, Sophie! And Frankie hit you and left you for dead . . .' He looked grey with shock. 'I can't believe this is happening.'

'They might never believe me,' I cried. 'And Frankie and Alistair will stick up for each other. Their word against mine.'

I was shaking so much I was worried I was going into shock. 'Here,' he said, shrugging off his coat and draping it around my shoulders. 'Put this on. Don't worry . . . We'll figure this out. I just wish you'd told me before.'

'What would you have been able to do?' I wailed. 'There was no way out, Dan. I felt like I was going mad.'

I touched my stomach, thinking of the baby that was already growing inside me. I was at least five weeks' pregnant – enough for it to show up on a pregnancy test anyhow, so surely the baby had to be Leon's? But until I had proof Alistair would always believe my baby was his.

'Let them think I'm dead,' I told Daniel desperately. 'Let Frankie believe she's killed me. It would mean I had an escape after all.' I could protect my baby.

Daniel didn't agree at first. He wanted to go to the police. He managed to get me home without anyone seeing us – although we thought we saw Jez at one point while we were at the entrance to the pier. He was on the other side of the road, but by the way he was staggering in a zigzag along the pavement, he was too wasted to realise who we were.

When my mum got back from work we told her

everything. She cried, she raged, she wanted to kill both the Howes. She tried to convince me to call the police but I refused to be put through the interrogation just to see Alistair get away with it. Everything would be dragged up in public, even what happened with Jason. And Frankie and Alistair would stick together. Like father like daughter. They would pin Jason on me too, say it was my fault, that I had been the one who had shoved him into the sea. I would go to prison.

I had no choice. Eventually Mum saw that too.

It was all so surprisingly easy. Mum stitched up the gash to my head. Daniel found a space on a ferry to Dublin in the early hours of the next morning. It was perfect because I didn't need a passport, so I'd leave no trace. The wages I had been saving were in a tin in my wardrobe, so I had enough cash. Then I would travel down the coast to stay with my aunt on her farm in a remote part of County Kerry.

When my mum and brother finally alerted the police to the fact that I'd never come home from the club, I was already in Ireland. I was already safe. I was already away from Alistair.

Tuesday, 12 June 2001

I've been 'dead' now for four years.

I had my baby in April 1998, a little girl called Mia, and I love her more than anything in the world – I never knew I could love so completely, so unconditionally. She has my blonde hair and Leon's startling eyes. As soon as she was born and I saw those bright blue eyes I knew she was Leon's daughter, she was the image of him.

Leon is my only regret. I wish he'd been able to meet his daughter, that I'd been able to save him from the pain of thinking that I'm dead, that I didn't love him. Because I loved him so much. And I hope one day he will realise just how much.

Some people might think I'm a coward, that I didn't stay and fight. But I was scared and I didn't want to continue to live in fear. I saw a way out and I took it. We ran before when we escaped my dad. I've spent most of my life running away.

If I'm truly honest with myself there's another reason why I stay away. It's not just about Alistair, it's about Frankie too. She was my best friend and I loved her like a sister. I can hardly think of a childhood memory where she's not in it. And I know I shouldn't make excuses for her, she left me for dead, but I believe she loved me too, in her own, warped way. She's unstable, she's made that obvious, and that terrifies me, but if I did go to the police – if they even believed me – then what? It would be prison for Frankie and I don't know if I could put her through that. I hate what she's done, that she's kept me away from Leon. But we were friends for a long time, nothing is ever black and white.

My aunt Sarah has been amazing; I help on her farm and have made a life for myself. Nobody has ever questioned who I am. Who I was. I'm just Sarah O'Donnell's niece. Eventually my mum moved away from Oldcliffe and came to live here too. We live a nice life, three women together. Our main aim is bringing up Mia. It's a quiet existence on Aunt Sarah's smallholding, and although it's not the life I envisioned for myself, I wouldn't change it. I do a bit of writing, I'm still an avid reader and I surround myself with books. But most importantly, Mia's safe. And so am I.

Tuesday, 21 May 2002

Today I had the fright of my life. The safe existence I've carved out for myself was so very nearly threatened.

I was in the stables when my mum came in, a haunted look on her face. 'Leon's here,' she'd hissed. Her hair was standing up on end, straw poking out of her jumper. He told her he'd been travelling and that he thought he'd look her up, wanted to see how she was. Daniel was currently living in London so Leon had no link to me or the past apart from my mum. It touched me that he cared how my mum was doing. Little did he know what he was walking into.

'What have you done with him?' I hissed.

'He's in the living room having a cup of tea!'

I almost wanted to laugh. It was too ludicrous. But the ever-present fear wound its way into my gut. If he can find us so easily then so can Alistair.

I discounted it at once. Leon isn't here for me; he just wants to find out how Mum is. Alistair has no need to come here, he thinks I'm dead. I knew that both Alistair and Frankie were too arrogant to think I'd survived that fall into the sea.

It was a risk, I suppose. He could have exposed us. And Mum's face, when I told her I wanted to see him, was frozen in panic. After all these years he deserved to know he had a daughter. For once I wanted to be honest with him. I owed him that much.

When I walked into the room he was sitting on the worn-looking sofa, cuddling one of Aunt Sarah's many dogs, a cup of tea growing cold on the side table. He always liked it lukewarm. He glanced up, expecting to see my mum, but when he realised it was me all the blood drained from his face. He looked like he'd seen a ghost – not surprising, really!

He had hardly changed; his hair was a bit longer, his face tanned from travelling, but there was something haunted about his eyes, a sadness that wasn't there before. Seeing him again took my breath away and all the feelings for him that I thought I'd buried rushed to the surface, dazzling me with their intensity.

He stared at me, his mouth falling open. 'Sophie?' He stood up, shaking his head, the dog springing from his lap. I could almost see the questions swirling around in his mind. Tears sprung to his eyes. Then his expression changed to one of fury. 'What the fuck is going on?'

I took his hand, indicating for him to sit back down on the sofa. 'I'm so sorry,' I said, blinking back tears. I couldn't cry. I needed to be coherent, to explain everything, no stone unturned. He deserved to know the truth at last.

'We all thought you were dead. Why would you do something like that? You put me through hell.' His eyes were hard, accusing.

I told him then about Alistair, about the kiss, about the stalking, the rape. 'I was terrified of him, Leon. He was never going to leave me alone.'

'So you faked your death?' His expression was incredulous. 'You should have come to me, Sophie. I would have fucking killed him.' He squeezed my hand and his eyes filled up as it dawned on him that he wasn't able to protect me. Nobody was. Leon's expression softened. 'You were going through all that . . . by yourself . . . I wish I could have done something. We could have gone to the police together.'

'I thought about it. But Alistair would just say it was consensual. What if nobody believed me? And not only that, he had a hold over me.'

'What sort of hold?'

I lowered my gaze, my hair falling into my face. 'I was there the night Jason died.'

His voice was gruff but he didn't let go of my hand. 'What happened?'

I took a deep breath before recalling the events of that night. 'Frankie made me believe that I'd been responsible for his death, but it was her, Leon. We didn't realise he was gay. She pushed him after he turned her down, he stumbled into the sea. She left him for dead. Like she did with me. I'm so sorry for not telling you before . . .' My voice caught in my throat.

His eyes widened in horror at this new piece of information. 'What do you mean, like she did with you?'

'She tried to kill me.' It still hurt to say it. Her betrayal would always cut deep. 'I told her about Alistair, she didn't believe me. Started accusing me of trying to steal him away from her. She's so messed up and I never realised it. We rowed, she struck me over the head, with a rock, I think. I fell backwards off the pier and she just walked off . . . she just left me there, hoping that I'd drowned. Like Jason.'

Leon looked sick with shock. 'Oh my God.' He took his hand from mine and ran it through his wild hair. 'I just can't get my head around any of this. I wish you'd told me. I would have helped you, Soph. I loved you. I've never stopped loving you.' He put his head in his hands and groaned and I knew what he was thinking. How could we have got Frankie so wrong? 'We have to go to the police. Frankie can't get away with it. It's her fault Jason's dead . . .'

I placed my hand tentatively on his shoulder. I knew it was a lot for him to take in. 'We can't. Listen, Leon. It was the chance I needed to get away. To start again. Away from Alistair. There was another reason too,' I gulped. No stone unturned. That's what I'd promised myself as soon as I saw him again. He needed to know everything. 'I was pregnant.'

His head whipped up, a mixture of hope and fear in his eyes. Hope that the baby was his, fear that it might be Alistair's. 'The baby was yours, Leon.' I took his hand gently in both of mine, hoping that he wouldn't bolt. That he would stay. 'We have a daughter.'

He cried as I told him all about her, our beautiful Mia; how she never went anywhere without her favourite teddy, that she sucked her thumb, that her favourite books were Charlie and Lola. 'She should be home any minute. Mum's picking her up from school.'

It was love at first sight for him when he saw his little girl. She looked small and vulnerable standing there, holding her grandmother's hand, with her blonde pigtails slightly wonky after a day at school, her teddy tucked under her arm, confusion in her eyes – eyes that were so like his. And I could see it written all over his face. I knew then that everything would be OK, that Leon would keep our secret.

We still have so much talking to do, so much ground to cover, trust to get back. But I hope, in time, that he can forgive me.

Epilogue
Sophie

Saturday, 12 March 2016

I'm writing this on the train, on the way to see Mia and Daniel. The soporific lull is relaxing, the countryside whizzing past in a blur of green and brown, the spring sun filtering through the trees. There are hardly any other passengers in my carriage; an older lady squirrelled away in the corner with her knitting and a teenage boy with headphones on, tapping his foot to the music, the beat of which I can just about hear. Leon reclines next to me, nose in a book, a reassuring presence because, despite myself, I feel the flutter of butterflies in my stomach at the thought of returning to my hometown. Daniel told me on the phone that Oldcliffe was different, and yet the same.

Yes, it's true, I'm returning to Oldcliffe after all these years. I never would have thought it possible. But everything has changed, thanks to my daughter and my brother. It's all over the newspapers, so I've been told; Daniel's been busy exposing Frankie. I don't blame him for that.

Leon and I had decided to go to Paris just after New

Year to stay with my friend Juliette and her husband, Olivier. (Leon had managed to arrange a fake passport under my writing pseudonym!) I'd met Juliette on a creative writing course ten years ago and we became good friends. It took me a while to trust her; after everything that happened with Frankie I never thought I'd have a close female friend again. Mia hadn't wanted to come with us, preferring to stay with Mum. She was in the last year of her A-levels so it made sense. Little did I know what my daughter was really planning on getting up to while I was gone!

It was the visit from the police that spooked me into fleeing to France in the first place. A few days after Christmas they called round asking to speak to my mum about Alistair Howe. Leon answered the door. I was on the landing and froze at the sound of his name, shocked that it could turn my stomach even after all these years. I lurked in the shadows, too afraid to come out, aware that I was supposed to be dead. But I could hear every word the policeman said, in his familiar West Country accent. It seemed that Alistair had been charged with raping three women between the years 1996 and 1999, that a new witness had come forward who he'd attacked the year before he raped me. Apparently she'd gone to the walk-in centre to get her lip stitched up and it was my mum who had treated her. They wanted Mum to give evidence against Alistair in court.

Fear enveloped me as I stood there. It threatened to crush me. All I could think about was running. Again.

When the policemen had gone I pleaded with Leon to take that trip to France. He'd wrapped his arms around me in response. 'Sophie McNamara,' he said into my hair, 'you don't have to be afraid of him any more. You have me.' We weren't legally married of course. It was impossible because I was supposed to be dead. But to all intents and purposes we were man and wife. And we let everybody think it.

'It's not just him that I'm worried about. If the police find out I'm alive you could get into trouble – so could my mum, and Daniel. I faked my death and you all helped me. Isn't that a crime?'

'Well . . .' He looked confused. 'Yes, I think so, but . . .'

'Please. Let's just go and stay with Jules and Ollie for a bit, they are always asking us over. We can let things die down, and then we can come back. Mia could do with a break too.'

Leon wasn't sure, he said he'd have to wangle it with work, but he eventually agreed.

At the end of January, Leon had to return to work and tried to convince me to come home with him, but Jules said I could stay on with them. And the truth was, I was scared. Scared that Alistair would go to court, that Mum would be called as a witness, that it would come out about what I did. And what about Frankie? I imagined the paparazzi at my aunt's farm; Alistair or Frankie would learn where we were living. I couldn't risk it. I thought the best thing for me would be to lie low for a while. Mia came out to visit a few times, on the Eurostar with Leon. She seemed thoughtful, morose. I asked her what was wrong but she wouldn't say. I began to worry that she was having boyfriend trouble, or worse. I wanted her to stay in France with us, but she refused. Then Daniel contacted me to say that Alistair Howe had had a stroke. He couldn't tell me how severe the stroke was, but knowing Alistair I was afraid he'd be back on his feet in no time. So I stayed on in France, just for one more week, I told myself, as the weeks turned into months.

It wasn't until a fortnight ago that I learned what had really been going on.

Leon, Mia and Daniel came over to France with the news of Frankie's death. They sat me down in Juliette and Olivier's shabby-chic kitchen and told me everything – about their plan, her confession, her fall through the boards of the old pier – while I stared, by turns shocked and impressed that they had pulled it off.

It had been Mia and Daniel's idea, they explained, to force Frankie's hand. Mia had found my diary shortly after Leon and I had flown to France. 'You were acting so weird,' she said, her eyes flashing, her jaw set as she defended her actions. 'I thought I was adopted or something. It was obvious you and Dad had this big secret.'

I felt like breaking down when she told me that she knew about the rape, about Alistair, and I wished, in that moment, that I'd thrown the 1997 diary away.

'It all made sense,' she said. 'Why you and Dad never got married for real, why you wrote under a fake name. Why you were always so reclusive, hardly trusting anyone.' She turned to Juliette as she said this, who sat there with her hands in her lap and no judgement on her face. Kind, loyal Juliette. 'You're Mum's only friend, Jules.' Mia swiped away tears with the back of her sleeve, embarrassed. 'I just wanted you to feel safe again.' Her voice caught in her throat and I leapt out of my chair to hug her.

Daniel took over the telling of the story. How a job had come up as editor at the newspaper in Oldcliffe, how a body of a young woman who had tragically jumped from the Severn Bridge eighteen months before was found floating in the sea. It had triggered an idea, he said, to make Frankie believe it was me. He knew she wouldn't believe my body would be intact after all those years, so he did some research and came up with the idea of the floating feet. He hoped it would mean Frankie wouldn't be able to resist coming back to Oldcliffe to see for herself. To make sure I really was dead. That she'd got away with it.

'We just wanted her to confess,' said Daniel. His face was pale and he had purple shadows under his eyes. I could tell the last few weeks hadn't been easy for him. He'd got justice for me but at what price? 'We knew we only had a matter of days in which to act. Leon found out about what we were planning and agreed to come back to Oldcliffe too, but that was mainly to keep an eye on Mia.' I was so thankful for that. The thought of my daughter running about my hometown in proximity to Frankie made me break out into a cold sweat. It still does.

'Dad said we could use his apartment to mess with

Frankie's head,' said Mia, grinning at me. 'I went to her place a few times, moved things around. Followed her, sent notes. That kind of thing. I made a recording of a baby crying; it was brilliant, Mum. It really freaked her out. She thought it was about herself though. She couldn't have kids, apparently. Seven miscarriages. If you believe her, that is.' She snorted, but a part of me was sorry to hear that. Mia would never understand, she didn't know Frankie, she will always see her as the villain who betrayed her best friend. She's so young, not yet eighteen, everything is more black and white for her. But not for me. And I suspect not for Daniel either. We all know how he used to feel about Frankie.

'She deserved it, Mum,' said Mia, catching my disapproving expression. 'You have life-altering injuries because of that night.' She meant the epilepsy, the migraines. She was trying to justify herself to me but I know my daughter and part of her would feel guilty for what happened to Frankie.

I've since heard that Alistair died from his stroke before he could be tried for six counts of rape, five counts of stalking, one count of assault and one count of kidnapping. After his death, a further three women have come forward with similar allegations.

Daniel gave the police the tape with Frankie's confession on it, told them everything. But as we didn't fake my death for financial gain we won't be charged.

It still amazes me that the three of them went to such lengths for me. I'm the lucky one. Frankie didn't destroy my life when she left me for dead, she destroyed her own.

Leon shuffles in his seat next to me, his long legs stretched out before him, the book he's reading almost on his nose. He wakes up with a start and a grunt before settling himself back down again. I look over at him fondly, at the man who has stuck by me through all of this. The love of my life. When he found me again, that day in 2002, and discovered I was alive, that he had a daughter, he never left. He forgave me. It wasn't easy at first, he had to keep his relationship with me a secret from his family, they couldn't know he had a daughter. He was never particularly close to any of them, which made it easier for us. And we'd both changed in those five years apart, but we fell in love again, our bond stronger than ever.

Frankie is still missing but the police don't think she would have survived the ice-cold February sea. I wonder how long it will be before her body washes up. If her body washes up. It's always there, in the back of my mind, that she might have survived. Like I did. I sometimes dream of her. In my dreams she's thrashing around in the murky waters, calling for me to save her, crying that she's sorry. I wonder if she really was sorry in the end, if she regretted her decision, if she would have done things differently if she'd had the chance. I know I would.

The train slowly pulls into the station. It's so familiar it makes me catch my breath: there's the kiosk that sold fizzy drinks and magazines, although it's painted green now and has a new sign; and the wooden bench where Frankie and I used to sit to wait for our train. I can almost see her perched there, in her retro 1960s dress and knee-high boots, pulling at a strand of hair.

And then I spot my daughter waiting on the platform, her arm linked through Daniel's, grinning and waving at the train, her bright blue eyes shining with excitement. I need to draw a line under all of this now. I need to concentrate on my future and not the past. Returning to Oldcliffe-on-Sea is just a temporary thing. A last goodbye. To the town, to Frankie.

After that the world is my oyster.

I no longer need to live in secret. I can stop running.

I'm finally free.

Acknowledgements

I am so grateful to Juliet Mushens, my amazing agent, for her unstinting support, help and advice, as well as finding me my editor, the brilliant Maxine Hitchcock, who I loved as soon as I met her. She and the rest of the team at Penguin have been invaluable in their encouragement, editorial advice, copy-editing, proofreading, cover design, marketing, publicity and everything else that it takes to bring a book to publication. I am in awe of all of you!

A huge thank you to my family and friends who have all been so kind and encouraging, who bought and read my first book, who recommended it to their book groups, and who passed it on to their family and friends. Your support means so much to me.

To everyone on Twitter or Facebook who came to say hello or told me how much they enjoyed my book. It was so lovely to hear from you.

To my beautiful children, Claudia and Isaac (who, again, won't be able to read this book for a long, long time!) and to my husband, Ty, who helped me brainstorm plot points when I was stuck, who read my first draft, who has taken such an interest in everything I write and who is always so encouraging. Thank you for all your support and your belief in me over the years (even when I found it hard to believe in myself!). This book is for you.

Acknowledgements

Reading Group Questions

1. Why was Frankie drawn to Sophie as a friend? Why was Sophie drawn to Frankie in return?

2. Why do you think Sophie feels so unable to tell anyone about her stalker? In what ways could she have acted differently?

3. The author uses the phrase 'like father, like daughter' in relation to Frankie and her father. How similar are these characters and in what ways? Frankie calls Sophie a liar when she reveals that Alistair has harmed her. How far will we go to protect our perceptions of the ones we love? Are we all in denial about our loved ones?

4. Do you think, on some level, Frankie believes her own story? Can you convince yourself to believe your own lies? How do you think the novel approaches the theme of memory?

5. Sophie's friend Helen insists that 'Friendship should be about give and take. It should be about equality' whereas Sophie thinks this is naïve.

Discuss power dynamics between friends throughout the novel and how they change.

6. What are Sophie's flaws? Is she purely a victim in this story?

7. Frankie addresses Sophie throughout the novel almost as if she is speaking to her. What do you think that the author was trying to portray by writing this way?

8. How does young Frankie from Oldcliffe compare to the Frankie we meet in the present day? What has caused her to develop in this way? If Frankie really believes such assertions as 'Nobody turns me down', what causes her to feel so entitled?

9. Do you believe that Frankie has real feelings towards Daniel? Discuss Daniel's relationships with the women in the novel.

10. What role does the atmosphere of the Oldcliffe setting play in the story?

11. 'I don't think I'm bad. I've just done some bad things'. Is Frankie 'bad'? What makes someone a 'bad' person?

12. What causes a friendship to turn to toxic envy? Are there barriers we should always uphold with our friends? Can people be too close?

13. What do you think happens after the novel ends? Does Frankie survive the fall and start a new life for herself, just like Sophie?

Read on for an extract from Claire Douglas's chilling new novel . . .

Publishing Summer 2017

@DougieClaire

ClaireDouglasAuthor

Prologue

He had such pretty eyes, they were his best feature. The colour of the ocean. Now they are as glassy and lifeless as a china doll's, staring up at the darkening sky, empty, unseeing. The rock falls from my open palm and rolls towards his body where it nestles softly against his thigh, as though apologising for the fatal wound it has caused.

Fear takes hold of me so that, for a few moments, I'm rooted to the spot and can do nothing but stare at the dent in his skull and the arc of blood that has sprayed from the back of his head, staining the grass red. Then I kneel down beside him, my knees sinking into the damp lawn. I'm careful not to touch him. I grab the rock that fell from my hand, pocketing it. I can leave no evidence.

I glance up furtively. The building is over two hundred feet away, the windows opaque, some with curtains hanging open, others with the blinds rolled up. Was anybody watching? I'm already starting to think like a criminal. Was I seen at the bottom of the garden among the weeds and overgrown grass?

Was I seen killing my husband?

Part One

One

The room is small and airless. It smells of bad breath and bitter coffee. I can feel sweat prickle my armpits, droplets running down my back and gathering at the base of my spine, seeping through the cotton of my blouse. I'm grateful for my short hair, a decision I'd made after Thailand eight years ago; I've never bothered to grow it again. At least the back of my neck feels cool. I sit at the table with my hands folded in my lap, trying to look demure. Trying to look innocent. Not that anybody is here with me. I'm totally alone. I wonder if they can see me. Are they scrutinising me for a reaction? Is there a camera hidden in this room? There is no two-way mirror, not like in those ITV crime dramas. I've never been in a police station before, but this room, this *smell*, is exactly what I would have imagined, if, of course, I'd ever imagined such a scenario. I can honestly say I never have. Why would I? I'd always assumed I'd got away with it.

Panic is swelling within me so that I have to make every effort to swallow it down, to not scream and beat my fists against the door. Is it even locked? I'm too scared to find out. I keep my eyes on that door. It's heavy and grey, I already feel as though I'm in prison. The only sound to be heard is the clock on the wall, ticking, time has slowed down. Waiting, all this waiting. Do they do it on purpose to try and make you crack?

They are going to ask me how it happened, how I got here. How can I tell them without implicating myself further? Without losing everything?

Of course, looking back, it all began with that holiday, that house swap. That's when everything started to go wrong. How could we have known as we trundled along in Jamie's car that day, with the roof down and the sunshine bouncing off the bonnet, that we were heading into a nightmare? Life can be like that, dramatically spliced in half; the before and the after. How I would have made more effort to appreciate, to *savour*, the before if I'd known about the after.

We had music on, I can't remember the tune, possibly something on Radio One because we liked to think we were still young, still down with the kids even though I was nearly thirty. Not that we could really hear it with the wind whistling past our ears. Ziggy, our Golden Retriever, was in the back seat, tongue lolling, a look of ecstasy on his face. It was only mid April and there was a chill in the air despite the blue skies, and I tugged the collar of my coat further up my neck so there was no exposed flesh. My left arm was in a sling so Jamie was driving, his face more alive, more vibrant, than I had seen it in months. As his hands grasped the steering wheel, his fair hair blowing about his forehead, I didn't have the heart to tell him to put the roof up. He needed that holiday even more than I did. I do remember running my fingers along my abdomen in the hope we might have conceived. We'd been married just under a year at that point, and had decided to try for a baby. I loved – love – kids. It's why I became a primary school teacher. I'm Head of English at an independent primary school in Bath. I'm still proud of the achievement, despite everything.

I felt the drag of car sickness as Jamie's Mini Cooper rounded bend after bend and I concentrated on breathing deeply, trying to push the nausea away, my nostrils desperately searching for the sea air that I had been promised but instead finding the pungent smell of rapeseed from the yellow fields. The skin on my arm itched beneath my cast.

Eventually, another bend and then a speck in the distance that grew bigger as we approached, breaking up the monotonous country roads; a tiny petrol station stood forlornly, like a lost child amongst the wild foliage.

'That must be the one,' I said, pointing at it in excitement, trying to remember the instructions that Philip Heywood had emailed to me the day before. It meant we were nearly at the house.

Jamie pulled in to the forecourt. 'Can you go and get the key then, Libs? I might as well fill her up as we're here. Then I'll take Ziggy over there so he can do his ablutions,' he indicated a patch of unruly grass next to the garage. I nodded, relieved to get out and stand on solid ground for a bit.

The guy behind the counter was barely out of his teenage years. He stared at me with a nonplussed expression on his acne-scarred face when I asked about the key to The Hideaway. 'I don't know nothing about a key,' he said while scratching a pimple on his neck. 'I'll get my manager. Name?'

'Pardon?'

He tutted, not bothering to hide his annoyance. 'What's your name?'

'Oh. It's Libby. Libby Elliot. I mean, Hall. I'm Libby Hall now. Mrs.' I could feel myself blushing, unused to using my married name; I'd continued using my maiden name for work.

He sloped off to the back of the shop, his long arms swinging like an ape's. Just as I was beginning to panic that this was some elaborate con and there was no key, or house by the sea, a buxom woman with a mop of dyed blonde hair came bustling over, the key dangling enticingly from her chubby fingers. I handed over my debit card for the petrol while the woman chatted away in a thick Cornish accent; *tourists, huh? You'll love the house. Beautiful views. Never been lucky enough to stay there myself of course.*

Jamie was impatiently tapping the steering wheel with his fingers when I got back to the car. Ziggy was stretched out along the back seat, taking advantage of the sunshine that beat down onto his golden coat. 'I thought it had all been a mistake,' he said, sounding relieved when I handed him the key. 'You know what they say. If it's too good to be true . . .'

As we headed down another narrow lane, thick hedgerows sprinkled with white blossom rearing up on either side of us, Jamie almost shouted, 'That must be it! There, on the other side of that T-junction!' His excitement accentuating his South London accent. I frowned, thinking he must be mistaken. The house he was referring to was huge; a detached, rectangular building with a round turret at the end, all Cotswold stone and glass. Trees and bushes in varying shades of green enveloped the house as if they were giving it a hug. Beyond the property I could see the stretch of clear blue sea sparkling in the distance.

'This can't be it,' I replied as Jamie veered off the road and onto the driveway, gravel crunching beneath the tires just as the nasal voice of the Sat Nav informed us we had reached our destination.

Jamie switched the engine off and I was thankful for the peace. We sat in silence for a few moments, surveying the house, the cheerful chirruping of birds and the faint growl of the sea the only sounds to be heard. I could smell the salt on the breeze, mixed with a trace of horse manure.

'It's quite remote,' I said, suddenly feeling a little overwhelmed. I grew up in the countryside – a little two-up-two-down in South Yorkshire – but I'd spent the best part of the last decade in a city. I was used to having neighbours.

'It's amazing,' said Jamie, his face alight. 'I can't quite believe we're going to be staying here. Good call, Libs.' He took a deep breath through his nose. 'Ah, smell that air. So fresh and clean. No pollution, no fumes.' Just cow shit instead, I wanted to say, but didn't. I sensed the tension of the last few months ebbing away from him, transforming him into the man I'd married and not the stressed person he'd become since he was made redundant and forced to set up on his own. The attack hadn't helped. He'd been so worried, wanting to kill the man responsible.

A squirrel scrambled up a nearby tree and Ziggy barked, a deep woof that shattered the silence, and he pulled against his restraint. Jamie laughed and leaned over the back seat to unbuckle him, clipping the lead onto his collar. 'Come on, boy, I know you're dying to explore.'

Jamie jumped out the car and ran around the front to open the passenger door for me. 'Very chivalrous of you,' I laughed, trying not to wince as I stepped from the car.

He frowned. 'Are you alright, Libs?'

'I just can't wait to get this cast off, that's all. It makes everything so bloody awkward.'

He stroked my cheek. 'Not much longer my little heroine.'

I thumped his arm playfully with my good hand. 'Stop taking the piss.'

He kissed the top of my head. 'I'm not taking the piss, you are a heroine,' he mumbled. 'Don't you forget it.' Then he bounded away from me, dragged by Ziggy, and I followed, reluctantly, half expecting an irate owner to come hurtling out of the house to tell us to get off his land. Noticing my hesitation, Jamie beckoned me to the door; slate grey aluminium, as clean and polished as the rest of the house. His eyes were bright as he looked up from the piece of paper he was consulting. 'It is the right place, look,' he said, to reassure himself as much as me. He prodded the paper with his finger and then indicated the stone sign with the words The Hideaway carved into it. 'Apt name. There isn't another house for miles. And it's not far from Lizard Point. I've always wanted to see the lighthouse.' He sounded like one of my six year olds.

I felt a stab of guilt that we'd swapped our poky two-bedroom flat in Bath, with the animal hairs and the dog food aroma, for this. I wondered what Philip Heywood and his wife were thinking? It wasn't even a Georgian flat, as one might expect in Bath, but late Victorian.

'Do you think it was okay to bring Ziggy? I never thought to ask.'

'Shit, Libs. Why didn't you check? I have no idea.'

'I didn't expect the house to be so big and posh that's why.' My fears were confirmed as soon as we stepped over the threshold. It definitely wasn't the sort of place to bring a dog. Everything was so white; the sofas, the rugs, the walls. Don't get me wrong, it was beautiful. It was straight out of a White Company catalogue. But I was worried we'd stain it somehow, with our messy ways – or, more likely, the dog's dirty paws.

I grabbed the lead from Jamie, too worried to let Ziggy go, unable to shake the feeling that we were trespassing, and wandered into the kitchen. It was huge and open plan with white gloss cabinets and marble worktops. Bi-fold doors led onto a wide garden that overlooked a beach below.

'Look at this, Jay,' I called, my head in the American-style fridge. I was practically salivating at all the food. 'There's enough here to feed a family of ten.'

Jamie ran up behind me and peered inside. 'Ooh they have paté, and look at all those beers!' He grinned at me. 'This is heaven!'

I frowned. 'Our fridge at home is practically empty,' I said, ashamed of the pint of milk and curled up ham that I'd left behind. I never even thought about stocking the fridge.

'Don't worry about it, they've got more important things on their mind. Come on, let's go and have a look around,' he said, grabbing my hand. 'And take Ziggy off the lead, he'll be fine.' We raced around the house like over excited teenagers, the dog at our heels. Solid oak floors, white walls, colourful abstract artwork, and in each room, large floor-to-ceiling windows with the most amazing views of the sea and the jagged beauty of Gerrans Bay. A huge black and white canvas of an attractive brunette in a white dress, strolling wistfully along a beach hand in hand with a little girl, dominated one of the walls in the living room. There were four large bedrooms, an open-plan family room, a study and a basement, although we didn't go down there on that first day. The house was much too big for the two of us. An uneasy feeling began growing in the pit of my stomach. I couldn't put my finger on it but something didn't feel right.

Even though the house was tidy there was evidence that a family lived there: expensive perfumes in the bathroom, clothes in the wardrobes (I couldn't help but take a peak: long summer dresses, flouncy blouses, strappy sandals, a man's linen suits), a pile of trainers in the boot room and a few board games in the smallest bedroom. There didn't seem to be enough stuff for it to be the Heywood's main home, it wasn't crammed to the rafters with junk like our flat was. I suspected it was just their holiday house.

The master bedroom was in the circular turret with curved floor-length windows. A four-poster bed dominated the room, all pale oak and floating muslin. I stood gazing out at the beach and the sea beyond. I couldn't see another soul.

I felt Jamie's presence next to me and he put an arm around my shoulder. 'It looks as though you can walk through the garden to the beach.' He sighed. 'God, Libs, what a stroke of luck.' I turned to face him, noting the bags under his eyes, his grey complexion, and pushed down my uneasiness, convincing myself the Cornish air would be good for him. And for me. I still had nightmares about that day at school, the intruder, his assault. It was lovely to get away. To forget for a while.

I glanced at Jamie; he still dressed like a student in his polo shirt, ripped jeans and trainers. 'We should have taken our shoes off,' I said, looking pointedly at his scruffy Converse. 'And we're going to have to keep Ziggy's paws clean. We should have bought those dog socks that we saw in the pet shop that time.' I giggled at the thought of Ziggy in the florescent green socks. He'd never forgive us.

Jamie laughed, loud and heartily. It echoed around the house. I hadn't heard that sound enough in the last few months and it made my heart soar.

I told myself to be happy, in that moment, that Jamie deserved this holiday, that we were lucky to spend a week in the Heywood's wonderful home. It was a place we could never have afforded to stay in otherwise.

I wish I'd trusted my instincts. I wish we had turned around and gone back to Bath. But it's easy to think that now, in hindsight. It's easy to think we should have made a run for it when on that first day we had no reason to feel unsafe. That came later.